MURDER AT WAKEHURST

Books by Alyssa Maxwell

Gilded Newport Mysteries
MURDER AT THE BREAKERS
MURDER AT MARBLE HOUSE
MURDER AT BEECHWOOD
MURDER AT ROUGH POINT
MURDER AT CHATEAU SUR MER
MURDER AT OCHRE COURT
MURDER AT CROSSWAYS
MURDER AT KINGSCOTE
MURDER AT WAKEHURST

Lady and Lady's Maid Mysteries
MURDER MOST MALICIOUS
A PINCH OF POISON
A DEVIOUS DEATH
A MURDEROUS MARRIAGE
A SILENT STABBING
A SINISTER SERVICE

Published by Kensington Publishing Corp.

MURDER AT WAKEHURST

ALYSSA MAXWELL

KENSINGTON
PUBLISHING CORP.

www.kensingtonbooks.com

KENSINGTON BOOKS are published by

Kensington Publishing Corp.
119 West 40th Street
New York, NY 10018

All Kensington titles, imprints, and distributed lines are available at special quantity discounts for bulk purchases for sales promotion, premiums, fund-raising, educational, or institutional use. Special book excerpts or customized printings can also be created to fit specific needs. For details, write or phone the office of the Kensington Special Sales Manager: Attn. Special Sales Department. Kensington Publishing Corp, 119 West 40th Street, New York, NY 10018. Phone: 1-800-221-2647.

Library of Congress Card Catalogue Number: 2021935302

The K logo is a trademark of Kensington Publishing Corp.

ISBN-13: 978-1-4967-2074-0
ISBN-10: 1-4967-2074-1
First Kensington Hardcover Edition: September 2021

ISBN-13: 978-1-4967-2080-1 (ebook)
ISBN-10: 1-4967-2080-6 (ebook)

10 9 8 7 6 5 4 3 2 1

Printed in the United States of America

To Allan and Norma, two ordinary Newporters who were extraordinary. Without you, my life would have been vastly different, and this series would never have been. You raised a wonderful son, and for that, I am forever grateful. We miss you both so much.

Chapter 1

September 14, 1899

The seemingly impossible had happened—and with so little fanfare, it might almost have gone unnoticed. Except that overnight, the world had changed and would never be the same.

And now here I stood, on a hillside that commanded broad views of Staten Island and the entrance of New York Harbor, feeling as bereft as the fallen leaves that rustled across the ground in doleful whispers. A chill penetrated my wool carriage dress and jacket, but I neither hugged my arms around me nor tugged my collar higher. Instead, I allowed the cold and damp to seep into my bones, a physical reminder of the current state of my soul. Dominating the view before me, the granite stones of the Vanderbilt Family mausoleum mirrored a cheerless sky—the clouds as gray as steel rails, their edges as black as coal-fed locomotives.

Cornelius Vanderbilt II lay dead—"Uncle Cornelius," as I'd always called him, even though, in fact, we had been cousins twice or thrice removed. How would this family ever go on without him?

Footsteps clattered as Aunt Alice, her grown children, and Uncle Cornelius's siblings and their families filed from the mausoleum. I turned away, unable to school my features to the stoic calm necessary for maintaining one's dignity. In fact, my facial muscles ached from the effort of holding them steady. Aunt Alice's eyes were red-rimmed, but not a tear had fallen since we had left the Fifth Avenue mansion that morning. Only Gladys, Cornelius and Alice's youngest child, had allowed her emotions their escape, but even she had wept only quietly during the funeral and, again here, during the interment.

"You all right, Em?" Brady Gale, my half brother, came up behind me and put an arm around my shoulders.

I shook my head and leaned against his shoulder, a few inches higher than my own. "No. Are you?"

"No." A gravelly sigh escaped him. The wind swept up leaves in a tiny whirlwind that hit a gravestone and scattered. "I know at first the old man only gave me a job because of you. That he probably would rather not have."

"That's not true. Uncle Cornelius—"

"It's all right. I know what I was. And I know how I've changed, because of you and because of him."

Yes—and no. Brady had once drunk too much, caroused too much, fought too much. In the end, though, it hadn't been me or Uncle Cornelius or any one person who had inspired him to alter his ways. It had been life and the frightening turn it had taken; it had been Brady himself who, when faced with a choice, had chosen correctly.

He went on after a grim laugh. "He's always had the utmost faith in you, Em, and gradually, ever so slowly, he extended that faith to me. I'll never forget that—" He broke off, swallowing hard and then clenching his teeth. His head bowed, his straight sandy-blond hair fell forward over his brow, despite his attempts to tame it with Macassar oil. I looked away, allowing him his moment of grief.

From across the landscaped clearing in front of the mausoleum, I caught my cousin Neily's eye. He stood alone beside some trees, looking as forlorn as those gray branches against the grayer sky. He'd observed the funeral at St. Bartholomew's Church in the City from the back row, and I knew he was waiting now until everyone else vacated the area to pay his last respects to his father.

The very same father who had disinherited him only a few years earlier. I had wondered if he would even come today, and would not have thought him unjustified in staying home. Neily's mustache and beard twitched as he returned my glance, revealing the bitter tug of his lips. He gave me half a shrug before dropping his gaze to the ground. He'd come alone, his wife and young son having remained in Newport. Grace, Neily's wife, had been the reason for the family rift, and Aunt Alice made no secret of her belief that Neily had caused his father's early death. The first paralytic stroke had occurred the day Neily had announced his engagement to his parents. The final one, only two days ago.

Like ashes scattering on a gust of wind, the black-clad assemblage broke apart to board the coaches for the short ride to the ferry, which would take us back to Manhattan. Brady and I rode with my cousin Gertrude and her husband, Harry Whitney. He held her hand. She rested her cheek against his shoulder. Grief hovered in Gertrude's eyes and tightened the lines of her mouth, but like her mother, she buried the full extent of her grief beneath a veil of dignity. We spoke little. I planned to linger only briefly in the City to say my goodbyes. The train ride home to Rhode Island loomed ahead of me. It was sure to be a bleak journey.

Yet, when we finally arrived at the Fifth Avenue mansion, Alfred, Cornelius's primary heir, took me aside in the central hall while the others filed into the drawing room.

"You'll stay another night, won't you, Emmaline?"

I shook my head as I pulled my gloves from my hands. "I

should be getting back. Besides, there are enough people here to console your mother. You don't need me."

"It isn't that—not *just* that—anyway." He offered me something approaching a smile. Younger than Neily, and younger than me for that matter, Alfred Vanderbilt was now the head of the family. He and Uncle William Vanderbilt would jointly hold the reins of the New York Central Railroad and dictate the company's major decisions. And yet, to me, he was still my little cousin Alfred.

I sensed in him a discomfort that bordered on embarrassment and couldn't fathom a reason for it. "Alfred, if something is wrong, please just come out with it. Nothing can be worse than today."

"It's nothing bad, actually. It's just so hard to speak of. So unreal and disquieting."

"Yes, I understand." I touched his wrist briefly. Alfred and I had never been as close as Neily and I, had never truly been confidants.

"It seems Father mentioned you in his will. Brady too. Our lawyer said so. The reading is tomorrow morning and I think you should stay and hear it."

"Oh." I couldn't have been more dumbfounded. While it didn't surprise me that Uncle Cornelius might have left me a token gift, I wouldn't have thought it significant enough to warrant me staying to hear the reading. My thoughts immediately went to Neily, who had been existing outside the family circle for the past four years. "What about your brother?"

Alfred knew which of his two brothers I meant. He shook his head. "I'll be surprised if Father left him anything at all. But don't worry, Emmaline, I won't let Neily suffer. I intend to—"

He broke off at the sound of his sister Gertrude's voice. "Alfred? Where are you? You're needed in the drawing room." She found us in the shadow of the Grand Staircase, a columned, circular structure carved from pure white Caen stone that dominated the Great Hall. She slipped her arm through her brother's. "Come. Mama is asking for you. You too, Emmaline. You know how you're often able to calm her when the rest of us can't." She chuckled lightly, without mirth. "You and Gladys. Her favorites."

"I'm hardly that," I said, and fell into step beside them.

That next morning, the family and I gathered in the library, a large room so heavily gilded, carved, and filled with sumptuous textures that I'd always found it difficult to concentrate amid such distraction. Today I barely saw the fortune's worth of treasures as we settled in. Brady and I sat together on one of the sofas, the furniture having been rearranged so that the seating all faced the rosewood and inlaid ivory desk. The man who occupied the desk chair, Uncle Cornelius's lawyer, stared silently back at us from within the pockets of sallow flesh that surrounded his eyes.

We were waiting . . .

"Sorry I'm late." Neily spoke in a murmur to no one in particular and shrugged himself into a high-backed chair with a lion's head carved into the apex of the frame. Gertrude frowned and looked away. Alfred, Gladys, and youngest brother, Reggie, appeared relieved. Alice Vanderbilt gave no reaction, as if Neily didn't exist; as if no one, or perhaps merely a ghost, occupied that lion's-head chair.

The lawyer cleared his throat and began. Names, figures, and properties touched my ears but made little impression. I could think only of Uncle Cornelius, of his life cut short so cruelly, and of how this family would continue without him. Then I heard my name spoken. "To Emmaline Cross, whom I consider my niece and has often been like a daughter to me, I leave the sum of ten thousand dollars and an additional ten thousand in New York Central stock."

My mouth fell open. The blood rushed in my ears. The

lawyer continued, but I remained fixed on what I'd heard, or *thought* I'd heard. Surely, it must be a mistake. Oh, next to the Vanderbilt millions, such a sum might seem trifling, but to me . . .

My heart pounded against my stays. What would I do with so much money? I couldn't begin to fathom it. I almost didn't wish to. One would think I would be overjoyed at such a boon. But thus far, my life had had a routine, a method, an established order of the way things were done. Suddenly all of my meticulous arranging and scheduling and thrifty budgeting fell in jumbled heaps around me.

Before I could contemplate any further, for good or ill, the sound of Brady's name brought me tumbling headlong out of my thoughts. Uncle Cornelius left him a sum nearly as generous as mine. Brady smiled even as his eyes shone with moisture, and it made me gladder than I could express that Uncle Cornelius had embraced my half brother, who was related to me through our mother, and not a Vanderbilt at all, as part of the family.

"To Cornelius Vanderbilt the third . . ."

Neily sat up straighter, while his siblings suddenly found the floor at their feet terribly interesting. His mother, on the other hand, continued staring straight ahead, as if once again her eldest living son did not exist.

". . . I leave the sum of one half of one million dollars and a further million in trust . . ."

A vast sum, staggering from my point of view, and my first thought was thank goodness his father hadn't cut him off entirely. But one glance at Neily's tight-lipped expression, the ruddy color that flooded his face, dissuaded me of that conclusion.

To him, the amount could only be perceived as a slight. His siblings would each receive many millions. Alfred received the bulk of the fortune—an astonishing 70 million, plus most of the shares in the New York Central Railroad, along with countless other assets. Neily would receive none of that. He could live on what his father left him, certainly. Or so an ordinary individual might think. No, it wasn't so much the money, or the lack of it, but the sentiment behind Cornelius's bequest to his eldest son; the insult that now, in order to maintain the lifestyle he and Grace were accustomed to, they would have to continue living off her dowry, essentially making Neily a "kept" man. Despite his having attained a master's degree in engineering at Yale, and proven himself to be a brilliant innovator, he could never earn the kind of money needed to run several estates and travel back and forth to Europe each Season.

Uncle Cornelius had had the last word, a reprimand from the grave to which there could be no response.

That afternoon, I boarded the northbound train considerably wealthier than I had ever dreamed of being. From now on, I would have significantly fewer financial worries, as well as the ability to increase my charitable contributions. My altered circumstances made the trek north a bit less desolate, though I could not say I felt anything approaching cheerfulness. But the children of St. Nicholas Orphanage, to whom I regularly gave what I could, would certainly benefit from Uncle Cornelius's largesse. So would Nanny, my housekeeper, and Katie, my maid-of-all-work. Far from being mere servants in my household, they were family, kindred spirits, and beloved figures in my life. And from now on, they would no longer have to go without. None of us would. The house could be repaired when needed, fading furniture replaced, our larder kept full.

Despite what might be considered my good fortune, I spent the next few days enveloped in a deep sense of gloom. All the money in the world could not make up for so great a loss, neither to the country nor to myself. However much members of the Four Hundred might be criticized for their extravagant lifestyles and lack of empathy toward the lower classes, I knew my uncle Cornelius had not been such a man. Quite the contrary. If anything, he had been criticized by his own peers for his lack of vices. He'd shown no interest in yachting or horse racing, extravagant late-night parties, excessive spending—with the exceptions of his homes in New York and Newport, where no expense had been spared—or any of those overindulgences for which the Four Hundred were infamous. It had even been a rare day that found him on the golf course or the tennis court. Rather, when not working diligently to expand the family business concerns, he had dedicated himself, along with Alice, to philanthropic projects to the benefit of many.

Each night, in my restless dreams, as well as waking moments, I kept picturing him as I'd seen him last: serene, composed, his face surrounded by the satin lining of his coffin. His had been a well-favored countenance, some might even have said handsome, but there had been nothing there to suggest greatness—at least, no more so than the average individual. Yet, no one had ever doubted that greatness. How could such a formidable man, who could command a room with little more than a soft word—even in illness—be so suddenly and irrevocably gone?

Meanwhile, I went through the motions of daily life.

"You're not eating enough," Nanny pointed out to me on the third morning I'd been home. She gestured toward my plate of half-eaten toast and congealed eggs. "It won't help anyone for you to starve yourself. It won't bring your uncle back."

I glanced up from the newspaper I'd been pretending to read, the black print smudging my fingertips but failing to leave any impression on my brain. "I'm not starving myself. Don't be melodramatic."

Nanny shrugged, but a silvery eyebrow rose above her half-moon spectacles in that way she had of chastising me without speaking a word. For an instant, she appeared to me years younger—the nanny who had essentially raised me, while my parents entertained their artist friends at our modest home on Easton's Point. It had been Nanny who had bandaged my skinned knees and elbows, taught me my letters before I'd gone to school, listened to my childish secrets, and coaxed me to finish whatever had been put on my plate each day. I had known Mary O'Neal all my life, and when I'd inherited my current home, Gull Manor, from my great-aunt Sadie, I could think of no one else I'd rather have there with me as my housekeeper and my friend.

But she often knew me better than I knew myself, and at times I found that irritating. "Fine." I picked up my toast and took another bite. The bread tasted like dust, the blueberry jam like paste.

"Katie," Nanny called into the kitchen, "please bring Miss Emma another plate of eggs. She let the first ones go cold."

"Never mind, Katie," I countermanded. "Nanny, I'm fine. Just not hungry. I promise I'll eat a good lunch."

"Hmph."

The ringing of our telephone saved me from further debate, and I hurried out of the morning room and to the front of the house. There, however, I stopped in my tracks while the jangling continued, for in the alcove beneath my staircase lurked another reminder of Uncle Cornelius's kindness. When his summer cottage, The Breakers, had been built on Bellevue Avenue, he'd had electricity and telephones installed. At the same time, he had insisted on installing one of those latter devices here at Gull Manor. I had protested. It had seemed so extravagant, but he had adamantly insisted.

"You're all alone out there on Ocean Avenue, Emmaline," he'd said in that firm way of his. "You and that housekeeper of yours, two defenseless women living on the edge of the ocean far from town. Anything could happen. Do you think I'd ever forgive myself if a simple telephone call might have saved you?"

There had, of course, been no arguing with that.

I hurried the last few feet along the corridor and snatched the ear trumpet from its cradle. "Emma Cross here."

"Emma, it's Grace."

My heart lurched. Why would Neily's wife be calling me, especially first thing in the morning? I happened to know she rarely rose before ten o'clock. And like most members of the Four Hundred, New York's highest society, Grace Wilson Vanderbilt disdained using telephones, considering them intrusive and vulgar. Typically, she had her social secretary, butler, or housekeeper make her telephone calls for her.

"Grace, has something happened? Are you and Neily all right? Little Corneil? Where are you?"

"Emma, calm down. We're in Newport, at Beaulieu. And we're fine. I'm terribly sorry to worry you, but I've a favor to ask. An important one."

"Goodness, Grace. I'll admit you did give me a fright." I leaned against the wall while my racing heart gradually slowed. "What can I do for you?"

"It's Neily." I heard a combination of distress and resignation in her voice.

"I thought you said nothing is wrong."

"Nothing is . . . yet. But there's a party at Wakehurst tomorrow night and Neily is insisting on going."

"Now, while he's in mourning?"

"That's what I said. No matter the situation between his parents and us, he just lost his father and has no business socializing. He's being so stubborn about it. He insists he lost his father years ago, and therefore has nothing more to mourn now. But you and I both know it's not as simple as that, or he wouldn't have gone to the funeral. I'm afraid he'll drink too much, something will set him off, and he'll end up doing or saying something regrettable."

"Oh, Grace, has he been drinking?" I knew all too well how some men resorted to alcohol in times of strife.

"No more than usual," Grace assured me, but went on to add, "not yet, anyway. But I'm afraid being out among people might encourage him to overindulge. He's not in a good state of mind. He's angry, and whether he wishes to admit it or not, he's also grieving."

Angry—yes. As for grieving . . . Grace was right in that however much Neily might deny it, he had lost a parent. He must not only be mourning his father's loss, but also regretting the lost opportunity to ever make amends.

"I'll talk to him, Grace. I'll try to make him see the folly of attending this party."

"Talk to him? No, that's not what I'm asking. He won't listen. His mind is made up."

"Then . . . what do you wish me to do?"

"Come with us, Emma. Please. At least if you're there, you can prevent him from doing something foolish. If he gets in a state and I try to restrain him, he'll consider it nagging. Coming from you, he'll see the sense in it."

"Grace, I don't know . . ." The mere thought of attending a function among the Four Hundred exhausted me. In fact, it seemed callous and selfish of James Van Alen to hold a party at Wakehurst at this, of all times. True, the event would have been planned weeks ago, and true again, the remaining members of the Four Hundred would be leaving Newport shortly in favor of their winter homes, so that a postponement wouldn't have been practical. Had it been me, however, I would have canceled and sent my regrets to the invitees, many of whom had prospered as a result of their acquaintance with Cornelius Vanderbilt.

"Emma, please. I'm frightened for Neily's sake."

"I do have to work the next morning, you realize."

"Pooh. You work for your beau, and he'll forgive you an hour's tardiness this one time. Please do this for me."

Her quiet pleas broke through my reservations, and I let out a sigh. "All right, I'll come."

"Thank you, Emma. I'll send over an outfit for you to wear. It's a Renaissance theme."

I very nearly groaned out loud. "A fancy-dress ball?"

"No, not exactly. He wishes us to wear clothing that is reminiscent of the period. Inspired by it, but not what one would call a costume, because as he said when I inquired, that would be inelegant. Van Alen's calling it an Elizabethan Fete. You know how he is about all things English. The invitation came on parchment, handwritten in old-style script, in metered rhyme, no less. Would you like me to read it to you?"

"No, thank you," I quickly replied. I hoped I wouldn't feel pressured to dance, and perhaps I could keep an eye on Neily while remaining along the edges of the festivities. My heart certainly wouldn't be in it, but Neily and Grace were dear to me, and perhaps Neily would be persuaded to leave early. With that thought to bolster me, I said my good-byes, hung up, and went about my day. But a sense of misgiving never quite left me.

Chapter 2

Despite Grace's assurances that it would not be a fancy-dress occasion, I admit I had feared what she would send for me to wear to James Van Alen's fete. Would my neck be imprisoned in a stiff, scratchy ruff that would leave my skin irritated for days to come? Would the weight of the skirts drag at my every step? Or perhaps a steel farthingale would deny me the relief of sitting for even a moment.

I needn't have worried. She sent a simple forest-green silk gown with an overskirt parted in the front to show off the beautiful details of a lighter green damask beneath. Over it went a rose velvet jacket, beribboned and beaded, which flattered my proportions, while the tight sleeves, which puffed at the shoulders and elbows, made me feel like a princess of yore.

Nanny put up my hair with my enameled combs and added tiny rhinestones, which she had attached to hairpins, for extra sparkle. I'd have to go without my diamond teardrop earrings, which had been a gift from my parents. I had decided earlier this summer that someone else needed them more than I did and had gladly parted with them. I only hoped that they had proven useful in helping a young woman begin a new life. Before I left the house, Nanny tied a black ribbon around my upper arm, in memory of Uncle Cornelius.

Wakehurst sat across from Ochre Court on the landward side of the road, a short walk from The Breakers. A stately house of limestone blocks, peaked gables topped by spires, and leaded, diamond-paned windows, it had been designed after Wakehurst Place in Sussex, England. Like my uncle Frederick Vanderbilt, James Van Alen had wished his home to emulate the estates of England's landed nobility. The house had been designed by Dudley Newton, a Newport architect who had also fashioned Mr. and Mrs. Fish's Crossways, but with markedly different results. Their house could be called neo-Colonial and was purely American in design.

Neily helped Grace and me down from their victoria carriage. He wore his typical evening attire, but in place of the usual white satin vest and cravat, tonight he sported burgundy silk damask, with garnet shirt studs. Grace looked positively regal in matching burgundy velvet and an array of diamond and ruby jewelry.

The candles glowing in Wakehurst's windows issued a warm welcome to arriving guests. A melody, played on harp, lyre, and mandolin, drifted from the gardens, along with a muted hum of voices. Etiquette brought us into the house first, where we were greeted by a pair of footmen liveried in doublets and hose. The vestibule opened onto a vast corridor, the Long Gallery, which sprawled the length of the house. Directly opposite the front door, the Jacobean staircase sheltered a fireplace and seating arrangement that conveyed a cozy greeting to all who entered.

The footmen guided us, and several other newly arrived guests, along the priceless Persian rugs lining the Long Gallery. Doorways at the far end led into the dining room and the library, both of which had been disassembled from European palaces and reconstructed here. A pair of mastiffs—shockingly large, but placid and amiable—had trotted out from one of the rooms behind us, perhaps awakened from a nap by our arrival. They followed us when the footmen led us through the dining room and outside onto a veranda covered by a gaily-striped awning. From there, we descended a set of stone steps to the garden, stretching from the side rather than the rear of the house. Box hedges, sculpted trees, flowerbeds teeming with autumn flowers, and pathways lined in brick formed the perfect symmetry of a sixteenth-century formal garden.

We might have stepped back in time. The fantastical scenes devised by the Four Hundred to impress each other never failed to amaze me, and this fete proved no exception. Tiny lanterns, like fairy lights, had been strung liberally through the beech and elm trees, while torches flickered over the flowerbeds. The string ensemble we had heard from the front drive sat together beneath a bright blue pavilion, while guests strolled the walkways with etched silver goblets in hand. Holding court over it all, the manor house rose up like a fortress against the night sky, pinioning the clouds with its peaks and spires.

A small army of footmen in doublets circulated among the guests. By the aromas scenting the air, I surmised the folded pastries contained a variety of game fowl. There were skewers of veal and venison and tender cuts of beef; shrimp and oysters, stuffed olive leaves, and a host more to tempt the pallet. Though small tables were scattered throughout, there would be no sit-down dinner. James Van Alen intended to keep his guests busy tonight.

On the east border of the garden, a stage had been set up, and on it several actors, male and female, were reciting lines

I recognized from Shakespeare. To complete the scene, a fellow in a jester's costume, complete with parti-colored hose, fool's scepter, and bells, tumbled and twirled down the walkways. His stocky, muscular body moved with a grace I would not have thought possible as he called out good-natured insults to passersby, making them laugh. The dogs took an interest in him, probably because of the bells, sniffed him thoroughly, and ran off in a new direction.

For the others, it might have seemed like a page out of a fairy tale, but for me, the effort of getting through the night loomed like an endless ordeal. I resolved to simply put one foot in front of the other and perform the task Grace had set for me: watching out for Neily.

As the three of us circulated, I recognized among the guests several members of the Astor and Berwind families; Mr. and Mrs. Fish; John Morgan and his wife, Fanny; George Jay Gould and his wife, Edith; and a good number of others of the Four Hundred despite the lateness of the Season. Their jewels, satins, and brocades glittered in the torchlight. There were, however, no other Vanderbilts present, as they were in mourning. I felt a stab of guilt, and suddenly regretted wearing anything but black.

"Jimmy Van Alen's outdone himself this time," Grace said with a sardonic chuckle, which made me believe that, like me, she would have preferred to stay home.

"They don't call him the American Prince of Wales for nothing. By Jove, I think it's splendid." Neily gazed around like a child at Christmas. Did anyone but Grace and I perceive the forced nature of his wonderment? He snatched two silver goblets from the tray of a passing footman and held one out to me. "Emmaline?"

"No, thank you. Grace may have it. I don't think I'll have anything stronger than lemonade tonight."

"You disappoint me, Emmaline." He pressed the goblet

into my hand. The metal imbued warmth into my palm and the scents of cloves and cinnamon rose on wisps of steam. "I demand you have fun tonight," Neily said with uncharacteristic vigor. "Besides, wine won't agree with Grace. Not just now."

"Why ever not?" A possible answer occurred to me before I'd finished asking the question. I whirled on Grace, experiencing a genuine burst of happiness for the first time in days. "Grace, are you. . . ?"

She nodded, beaming. "Yes, but only just, so no telling anyone."

Despite her command for discretion, I couldn't help throwing my free arm around her. "I'm so happy for you both, and for little Corneil. Does he know yet? I don't suppose he could possibly understand, but he'll be a darling big brother, I'm sure of it."

Cheers and applause drew our attention to the strip of lawn on the west side of the garden. Neily walked a couple of paces in that direction. "What could that be about?"

A number of guests had gathered there, and now, as they shifted, I saw an archery course with four targets set up parallel to the garden. "It looks like an archery competition," I said, and Grace cast me a significant look. I understood. She thought the competition would be a good way to keep her husband occupied and out of trouble. I agreed. It would also be an efficient means of prying the wine goblet out of his hand, at least temporarily. "Come, Neily. Let's join them."

He bounded on the balls of his feet. "Let's, indeed."

Before we took many steps, however, a shadow fell before us and a figure blocked our path. "Zounds, I did wonder if you'd come, good sir."

James Van Alen, Wakehurst's owner and our host this evening, let go several more exclamations conveying his zeal at finding Neily in attendance. A man of about fifty, he wore a thick mustache, but was otherwise clean shaven, with neat dark hair that had only begun to gray and recede at the temples. His enthusiasm for sports kept him fit, while his passion for living kept him youthful, so that he seemed nearer in age to Neily, only in his twenties, than Neily's father, who had turned fifty-five on his last birthday. Once married to Emily Astor, he'd been widowed for nearly twenty years and exhibited no signs of wishing to remarry. I had no doubt being considered one of the Four Hundred's most eligible bachelors also kept him young.

His slightly glassy eyes and high color suggested he had been imbibing liberally tonight, but his use of Elizabethan phrasing surprised us not in the least. He used such language frequently as a matter of course, whether he'd been drinking or not, earning him a reputation of being an eccentric.

"Van Alen." Neily gave the man's hand a hearty shake. "And why, pray tell, should I have stayed away?"

"Forsooth, you should not have, my young friend." The reply left little doubt as to Mr. Van Alen's sentiments concerning the feud between Neily and his parents. Had any uncertainties remained, he dispelled them by first assessing Grace through his monocle, and then raising her hand to his lips. "My dear Mrs. Vanderbilt, who 'doth teach the torches to burn bright,'" he quoted from *Romeo and Juliet* while still bending over her hand. "'It seems she hangs upon the cheek of night, like a rich jewel in an Ethiope's ear.'"

Grace blushed prettily and laughed. "What a scoundrel you are, Jimmy."

He shared her laughter and turned to me. "Mistress Cross, Newport's lovely young scribe. I do hope you'll take careful note of everything I've done to make this evening memorable."

"She's here as a guest, Jimmy, not a reporter." Grace slipped her arm through mine as if to challenge him to refute her claim. I braced for him to remember he had not included my name on his guest list. Instead, he smiled politely and shifted his attention back to Neily and Grace.

I took the opportunity to slip away, hoping to exchange my goblet of wine for something rather less robust. I made sure to keep Neily and Grace in my sights, as I intended to return to them as soon as Mr. Van Alen moved on to other guests.

"Miss Cross, I certainly didn't expect to find you here tonight." The familiar, youthful face of Ethan Merriman made me smile in earnest. Ethan worked for the same newspaper I did, the *Newport Messenger*. He had, in fact, more or less followed in my footsteps as a society reporter. But whereas I had chafed at being relegated to a traditionally female role within the profession of journalism, Ethan enjoyed it wholeheartedly. I noticed his gaze drop to the black ribbon encircling my arm.

"Trust me," I said with a rueful flick of my eyebrows, "I hadn't expected to be here, either. Nor do I particularly wish to be. I only came at the request of my cousin's wife."

"I saw you enter with Mr. and Mrs. Vanderbilt." With a grin, he held up his pencil and writing tablet. "I made a note of it, with descriptive comments on your attire. You look positively royal, Miss Cross."

"Borrowed from Mrs. Vanderbilt," I assured him. "You know, Ethan, now that I'm no longer the *Messenger*'s editor-in-chief, we needn't stand on formality. You may call me Emma."

Only a few weeks ago, I'd given up the position I'd taken on as a favor to a dear friend, and which had seemed a great triumph for me when I'd accepted. How many women could boast of commanding a team of reporters, typesetters, printers, and newsboys—even at a small publication such as the *Messenger*? But a year into the job, I'd realized not only was

I wrong for it, but it was wrong for me. My passion lay in reporting, not administrating, and the *Messenger*'s owner, Derrick Andrews, and I had come to an amicable agreement. He had summarily fired me as editor-in-chief, and promptly rehired me as the *Messenger*'s chief news reporter. What a vast relief it had been.

Ethan eyed me dubiously as these thoughts passed through my mind, his own mind obviously working over what I had said. "I don't think I could, Miss Cross. Wouldn't feel right."

"Whatever you prefer, then, Ethan. Is Mr. Andrews back from Providence yet?"

"He's expected tomorrow."

The prospect cheered me. Derrick had been gone just over two weeks, since before I'd gotten word about Uncle Cornelius. There wouldn't have been much he could do if he had been here, except perhaps accompany me to New York. But that might have been a signal to the family I wasn't yet ready to give.

I let Ethan get on with his work, as unlike me, he *hadn't* come to the fete as a guest, but as an employee of the *Messenger*. Despite members of the Four Hundred often complaining about how the press hounded them and invaded their privacy, at times like tonight's party they invited in the society columnists with instructions to record as many details as possible. How else would those not here be able to admire the untold riches on display?

After exchanging my wine for a frothy punch, I hurried to rejoin Neily and Grace. I met them where the four geometric segments of the garden converged at a marble statue at the center. With Grace on one arm, Neily offered me his other. "Planning to have a go at the archery?"

"Of course I am," I replied without hesitation. "I might not be much of a horsewoman, but I can hit a target. Most of the time," I added with a laugh. "Grace, how about you?"

"No, I'll be a spectator, thank you."

We joined the small crowd at the west edge of the garden and watched the current group of four send their arrows hissing through the air to hit the targets with solid thumps. I was gratified to see that no one missed; in fact, one competitor hit a bull's-eye nearly dead center and a cheer went up.

Holding her bow gracefully out to one side, Miss Imogene Schuyler curtsied to her admiring audience. A tall beauty, Miss Schuyler hailed from a Dutch family who had first touched our shores more than two hundred years ago. They had made their fortune in New York real estate, putting them on par with the Astors and the Stuyvesants. Her blond hair, piled high and dressed with jewels, framed flawless features and dramatically pale skin, while her silk gown poured like liquid silver from her shoulders to the tips of her beaded shoes, accenting her torso and hips along the way.

She had outshot even the men, but none of them seemed to mind. Rather, they added their congratulations and assurances that Miss Schuyler would win tonight's competition.

"Hmph," Grace whispered in my ear, "we'll see about that. Imogene Schuyler is a spoiled brat and doesn't need any further encouragement to believe herself superior to everyone else."

I bit back a grin. Did I hear a touch of jealousy in Grace's tone? When she had still been a single young woman, the beautiful Grace Wilson, with her stunning auburn hair and green eyes, had been the toast of many a social season. Even now, as Neily's wife, she remained a much-admired woman. She had no reason to envy young Imogene Schuyler, but perhaps being in the family way made her feel vulnerable.

Relinquishing her bow to the next competitor, Miss Schuyler went to the side of a young woman dressed simply in nut-brown silk, wearing little jewelry, and bearing a stoic expression. So plain was she in her appearance, my first thought was that Miss Schuyler had brought her maid with her. They spoke some words to each other, shared a quiet smile, as if they knew something that eluded everyone else, and turned their attention back to the archery. If they were friends, they were an odd pairing.

"Do what you can to outshoot her, Emma, not to mention outshine her," Grace said, relieving me of my goblet of punch and giving me a nudge.

"I'll do my best." I turned to my cousin. "Neily, shall we?"

He put in our names, and after another several rounds, our turn came. There were two sets of lines on which competitors were to stand, one for women and, several feet farther back, one for men. A little murmur went up when I paced to the latter and stood beside Neily. He winked at me. I winked back. Archery had been a favorite pastime at The Breakers when we were children. Of course, not the Italian palazzo that stood on the property now, but the original turreted, wood-framed house that burned down in 1892. During the summers when the family had been in residence, I had often been invited to visit my cousins. Archery, croquet, cricket, and badminton were but a few of the activities we had enjoyed together.

Maude Wetmore, home from a recent trip abroad, stood on the other side of Neily, but closer to the target. Jerome Harrington, a young scion of a banking family, stood at Maude's other side. We were each supplied with a leather brassard to protect our forearms.

My competitive instincts took over as I placed my feet solidly on the ground, left foot forward. After nocking my arrow, I raised my bow and checked the rotation of my elbow to ensure my arm extended straight out with my bow perfectly vertical. I scrutinized my finger placement on the bowstring as well. Tuning out the voices and movements of our audience, I focused on the target, steadily drew back until my hand came just below and to the right of my chin, held my breath, and, without further ado, released my arrow. It sang through the air straight and strong, with almost no arch. I smiled a fraction of a second before it hit the bull's-eye with a solid and satisfying *thunk*.

"Well played, Emmaline." Neily's arrow had struck a bull's-eye as well, but mine had hit closer to dead center. Our two companions also shot well, with Miss Wetmore's arrow hitting smack on the bull's-eye's outer line and Mr. Harrington's landing just outside of it.

As I accepted Neily's compliment with a confident grin, a woman's voice called out, "But we shall see if she can do it again, shan't we?"

Although I didn't immediately recognize the voice, the cross expression that realigned Grace's features inspired me to follow the path of her gaze. Imogene Schuyler stared back at me, the unspoken challenge on her features clearly meant to unnerve me. It was then I remembered that Miss Schuyler had become engaged to Jerome Harrington only last month, a perfect merger of real estate and banking. She must have hoped for a dual win at archery for herself and her fiancé. Her friend appeared to hold similar sentiments, as she arched an eyebrow at me from behind a pair of oval spectacles.

Neily and I traded glances. He smoothed a hand down his mustache and beard and showed me a confident grin—confidence that extended to me as well as to him. I accepted the next arrow and repeated my technique exactly. Once again, my shot soared true, coming to rest well inside the bull's-eye's boundary. A third shot proved there had been no luck involved in the first two.

My efforts were met with a hearty round of applause, although another quick glance in Miss Schuyler's direction confirmed my suspicion that she had not joined in. Her lips were pinched, her eyes narrowed. How odd, I thought, her caring so much about winning a silly competition among friends. And besides, there were still others yet to compete. It was quite possible I'd be unseated.

Still, a sense of accomplishment warmed the air around me, until a wave of guilt came crashing down. What was I doing joining in on the evening's merriment? I had come only to help Grace keep an eye on Neily, not to enjoy myself. Thoughts of poor Uncle Cornelius, not to mention Aunt Alice and the rest of the family, doused whatever pleasure I had derived from proving my skills with a bow. I hoped someone *would* do better than I had.

Neily had moved off with a group of his peers, while Grace had been surrounded by several of her female friends. I went to her, and when the circle failed to open for me, I patiently waited for a lull in the conversation before whispering in her ear, "Grace, Neily seems fine tonight. I think I'll go."

She whirled to face me. "Emma, you can't. The night is still young. I won't have a moment's peace if you're not here." For good measure, her fingertips strayed to the front of her dress, just below her waistline, in a reminder no one else but me would notice. I wanted to cry foul play, that it was unfair of her to use her secret pregnancy to persuade me to stay. But I did no such thing, and for that matter, neither did I leave.

Grace linked her arm through mine and drew me into the circle of her friends. Among them, only young May Goelet had the good grace to greet me and offer condolences for Uncle Cornelius. Then she congratulated me on my good showing at archery. The rest smiled tightly and changed the subject. It was nothing new for me. As a Vanderbilt cousin, I sometimes mingled with high society, but I had never pene-

pressed his disapproval loudly and publicly. Upon hearing of it, James Van Alen challenged his soon-to-be father-in-law to a duel—pistols at dawn! Luckily, both men had backed down, and Mr. Van Alen married Emily Astor with no further ado.

I let go of my fears that the sword fighters would come to harm, but the sound of their clashing grated on my nerves and prompted me to retreat farther from the center of activity. I found myself near a tall hedge bordering the south end of the garden, deserted at the moment. Or so I thought. No sooner had I arrived in my quiet corner than angry words hissed back and forth on the other side. Several archways were carved at intervals in the thick foliage to allow access to the lawn on the other side. I stopped well before the first arch, poised to listen.

"You most certainly *were* flirting with that woman," a female voice accused. "Stop denying it. Don't you dare insult my intelligence."

"I don't know what you're talking about," countered a youthful male voice. "She's an actress, for heaven's sake, and not even a very good one. Do you seriously think I'd flirt with a creature like that? Or, if I did, that it could possibly mean anything?"

Who were they? Their voices might be young, but I heard nothing of innocence in their mutual animosity.

This was wrong of me, I acknowledged with a pang of guilt. I began to move away.

The woman spoke again, her voice sizzling with contempt. "I will not be made a fool of."

"Then you'd better grow yourself a stiff upper lip, hadn't you? Men will have their fun. It's got nothing to do with you."

A feminine gasp penetrated the tightly packed leaves. "It has everything to do with me, if I'm to be your wife."

"*If?* Thinking of backing out?" A low vibration in his

voice implied a subtle threat that raised the hackles at my nape and my concerns for the woman's welfare. "You do and you'll lose your reputation for all time. You know how it works. No matter the reason for breaking our engagement, you'll be damaged goods from now on. People will talk. They'll whisper behind their hands about you and that friend of yours."

"Do not make me loathe you."

"It is your privilege to do so." My mouth dropped open at his nonchalant arrogance.

There was a pause, so strained I could feel the tension through the hedge. He made the word *friend* sound tawdry. Why?

"Now you see here," the woman said evenly. I could practically see her standing taller, piercing him with an unblinking, unapologetic glare. "I am the one bringing the money into our marriage. If you wish to enjoy any of it, you had better toe the line."

"Threaten me, will you?" He let go a laugh. "Or else what, my dear?"

"Or else I shall tell my father what you've been up to, that's what." A sharp *thwack* accompanied those words, followed immediately by a grunt.

I heard footsteps and the swishing of hems through the grass on the other side of the hedge. Quickly I moved away, toward the stage, but not before I heard one last parting shot from him, no doubt aimed at her retreating back. "Go ahead, Imogene. It was your father who insisted on the marriage in the first place."

At that moment, Imogene Schuyler swept into the garden proper, her head high, her curls proudly glinting with jewels, her gown flowing like quicksilver, and her eyes utterly dry. Even beneath the fairly lights, she resembled no pixie about to grant a wish, but rather an imp intent on destroying any-

thing that crossed its path. I cringed at the thought of her realizing I had been listening, but she breezed by me without a
glance in my direction. Even when the colorful image of the
jester bounced into her path, executing a perfect backward
somersault with a chime of his bells, she merely circumvented
him without missing a step, leaving him to gaze after her
with one hand on his hip.

Only once did her head turn, when she passed the stage.
Watching her from behind, I couldn't guess at whom she
glanced, but I did see who returned it: an actress dressed as
Titania from *A Midsummer Night's Dream.* She and an actor
playing Oberon had replaced the earlier Petruchio and Kate.
The woman had striking eyes, tilted and heavily lashed, and
silvery blond hair, although quite possibly she wore a wig.
Imogene quickly looked away, but Titania's gaze followed
her across the garden.

One more person moved into Miss Schuyler's path and attempted to halt her progress: a bearded gentleman with thick
silver hair and a slope to his nose so like Imogene's he could
only be her father. Judge Clayton Schuyler had stepped
away from a circle of acquaintances and beckoned to her.
"Imogene, come here, please."

Strictly speaking, the Schuylers were not members of the
Four Hundred, though the distinction was an academic one,
at best. They were a Philadelphia Main Line family, meaning
they were among that city's oldest and wealthiest residents,
their estates situated in the beautiful countryside along the
Pennsylvania Railroad's Main Line, which connected one
end of the state to the other.

Perhaps Judge Schuyler wished to introduce her to his acquaintances; perhaps he objected to his daughter walking
unescorted through the fete. When she failed to stop, he attempted to snatch her hand, but she sidestepped him and
hurried away. I wondered where her mother was. Then I

spotted her friend, standing alone by the center statue, watching Imogene traipse toward the house.

Moments later, I heard a cough from behind the hedge and Jerome Harrington came skulking through an archway. His palm cradled his cheek and a careless flop of hair obscured one eye. When he lowered his hand, I saw the welt where his fiancée had struck him.

So did most everyone else in the general vicinity, for suddenly dazzling light flooded the south end of the garden, as well as the other side of the hedge, as previously unseen electric bulbs burst to life. Jerome Harrington raked the hair back from his face and stood blinking in the glare, the ruddy handprint on his cheek blazing for all to see.

Chapter 3

Mr. Harrington shoved his hands in his trouser pockets and strode off through the garden. Like Imogene, he pretended not to see the stares that followed him as he shouldered his way through the crush. He kept going until he disappeared onto the veranda. He had distracted me from watching Imogene and I lost track of which way she had gone. I hoped she hadn't also retreated to the house. If they met again inside, who knew which of Mr. Van Alen's treasures might go flying in fits of temper?

So then, matters were not well with Jerome Harrington and Imogene Schuyler, for all they had initially seemed the perfect young couple. In fact, Ethan had termed them thus in his society column earlier this summer, when the engagement had been announced. Two well-established, wealthy families—both their fathers respected and powerful, their mothers grandes dames of impeccable taste. Jerome and Imogene made an exceedingly attractive couple: He with his youthful version of his father's distinguished looks; his hair light brown and streaked with gold, his eyes amber, and his features smooth and congenial. And she, a blue-eyed golden-haired beauty; tall, lithe, graceful; her nose possessed of the perfect aristocratic tilt. And yet . . .

Imogene believed she held the upper hand—the wealth. I wondered how many people knew of the Harringtons' financial difficulties. Or were they merely Jerome's difficulties? Had he, like Neily, had a falling-out with his family? If so, they had kept it a tightly held secret. Either way, my guess was that not a soul, other than Imogene and her parents—perhaps—knew the truth. *Surely*, they knew, and I wondered why Judge Schuyler had insisted on the marriage regardless.

Interesting. One might almost believe the reason to be an indiscretion on Imogene's part, but, no, not with a wedding announced more than a month ago and planned for next month. If Imogene was with child, the wedding would have been scheduled immediately, and she would not have attended tonight's fete.

I glanced back at Titania on the stage. She appeared once more absorbed in her role, but her temporary lapse as she'd gazed after Imogene Schuyler lent credence to the latter woman's charge that Jerome had been flirting with one of the actresses.

A shift in the garden scattered my thoughts. James Van Alen advanced across the main walkway, clapping his hands and calling for attention. The actors on the stage fell silent, though it took Neily another couple of lines before he noticed their silence and closed his mouth. Guests gathered around Mr. Van Alen, who led them as a procession to the hedge and through the arches to the other side. His tremendous dogs followed, trotting and dodging in and out of people's way. Grace hurried toward me, her striking auburn hair fiery in the electric glare, her jewels ablaze.

"Emma, do come!" Her cheeks glowed with excitement.

"Do you know what's about to happen? Where's Neily?" She glanced around and spotted him before I replied. "Neily, come here. You'll never guess what Jimmy has planned for us. Neily!" Her husband didn't look over, and no wonder, for at least a dozen yards separated him from us and he could not have heard her over the commotion. A frown creased Grace's brow. "What is he up to?"

Neily had turned away from the stage and stood now in profile to us. He faced a man I didn't recognize, standing practically toe-to-toe with him. A wariness came over me, for even at that distance, I detected tension between them. The man's attire caught my notice for not quite meeting the standards of a gentleman of the Four Hundred. It would not have been noticeable previously, but now beneath the electric lights, I saw that while the quality of his evening attire appeared up to snuff, something about the way the trousers and tailcoat fit him did not. The trousers hit at the ankle with a crease, while the tailcoat strained at the shoulders, almost as if the garments had been made for another man, someone an inch or so taller, but with a bit less girth around the waist and shoulders.

He was older than Neily by perhaps a decade, placing him in his midthirties. His top hat sat balanced atop a head of dark brown hair cut short and slicked severely back, and by the uneven line of his nose, I guessed it had seen a break or two in its day. No beard or mustache helped balance out the misshapenness.

A man this rough around the edges had probably worked his way up the social ladder, perhaps even from its lowest rungs, and had not yet learned all the rules. His wealth, however, would buy him a certain amount of tolerance, which would explain his presence here tonight.

Whatever he and Neily were saying to each other, it wasn't cordial; their expressions and body language revealed that

much. Had this individual bumped into Neily? Or the other
way around? I knew it didn't take much to set off a man in
his cups, and that tempers could easily flare. When Neily
fisted his hands and craned his neck toward his adversary, I
hurried in their direction.

"Neily, I believe your wife needs you," I said when I
reached them. Neither man turned to regard me. I tried again,
this time wrapping a hand around Neily's upper arm and
speaking more insistently. "Neily, Grace has been asking
for you."

Once more, he seemed not to hear me. But with a jingling
of bells, an ally appeared at my side. "'Thou sodden-witted
lords! Thou hast no more brains than I have in mine elbow!'
Come, then, good fellows, forget thy quarrel and attend the
joust!" The court jester shook his scepter in their faces, ringing its bells to rouse them from their standoff. Then, with a
quick nod to me, he scampered away, likely fearing a box to
his ears from either man.

Neily blinked and turned his face to me. "What did you
say? Is Grace all right? She isn't ill, is she?"

"No, she's fine. She's right over there." I pointed to where
Grace stood watching us, the frown still etched between her
red-gold eyebrows. "Surely, you don't wish to keep her
waiting."

"Go on," the other man said in a deep growl of a voice.
"See to your woman."

I gasped. Here, among these people, referring to Grace
Wilson Vanderbilt as "your woman" constituted as much of
an insult as if he had used a profane term to describe her.
Neily stiffened, his hands clenching again. Truly fearing a
brawl, I resorted to tugging, and finally managed to ease him
away. Once we'd gone a few steps, the rigid anger drained
from his limbs. I burned to ask who that man was, but didn't
dare risk renewing Neily's ire, out of fear he might decide

to turn back and confront his foe. Still, I continued to wonder about him, about his ill-fitting clothes and his less-than-impeccable manners. Undoubtedly, he hailed from new money and had not yet learned the ins and outs of high society. Unless he proved a quick study, he'd soon find himself shut out by the Four Hundred, even the more tolerant ones.

What had he and Neily argued about? Perhaps, after all, it had been a simple matter of short tempers and excessive wine. As we traversed the garden, Neily's stride became loose, slightly wobbly. Grace took possession of his arm when I delivered him to her, and she mouthed "Thank you" in my direction. I walked at Neily's other side as the three of us moved along with the guests surging toward the hedge. Grace and Neily went through, but I lingered in one of the archways, astonished by what I saw.

If I'd considered Mr. Van Alen's mastiffs uncommonly large for their species, the two horses that came into view astounded me with their height and breadth, each one standing some eighteen hands high. Like opposing chess pieces, one gleamed ebony, while the other glowed ivory beneath the electric lights. More astonishing still, on the back of each horse, in a saddle with a low cantle and a high square pommel, sat an honest-to-goodness knight. They were wearing armor, I might add, beneath bright, flowing surcoats, one crimson and the other azure. Each knight held a lance a good ten feet long.

Had I passed through the arch earlier, I would have seen the posts that had been erected down the length of the lawn, connected by lengths of green ribbon, except for at the center, where an opening allowed the guests to walk through. Wooden stands had been erected on the far side, the seats upholstered in gold. Amid giggles, cries of delight, and bellowing anticipation, Mr. Van Alen's guests took their seats in the stands.

I, however, did not. After waving to Ethan, who was making his way with the others to find a seat, I turned and reentered the garden. A joust—I had no wish to gaze upon such a spectacle. Yes, perhaps every precaution would be taken. Perhaps, like the swordplay, this would be an exhibition with no real force. And, yes, I had attended countless polo matches that put horses and riders in some amount of danger. But polo ponies underwent years of training; running toward each other at top speed, while the men on their backs aimed their mallets at each other, was not part of the game.

As a form of entertainment, this seemed unnecessarily perilous.

More than anything, I wished to leave the fete. I had served my purpose in keeping Neily from falling to fisticuffs with that other man. His carriage stood somewhere on the drive, or along Ochre Point Avenue. A footman would find it for me, and the driver would certainly oblige me by taking me home.

Behind me came the sound of hooves galloping across turf. I tensed, waiting for the crash of wood against armor. It didn't come, and the crowd expressed its disappointment with jeers and a collective groan. Like the Roman populace at the Colosseum, they had quickly developed a craving for blood, it seemed. Perhaps not literally in this case, but surely a few of them shared my concern for life and limb.

Once more, the galloping hoofbeats drummed against the lawn, this time followed by a crescendo and the delighted cheers of the spectators. I kept walking, only to become aware of another sound: the barking of dogs. Continuous, insistent barking. While their distress over the spectacle on the other side of the hedge wouldn't have surprised me, the ruckus didn't seem to be coming from that direction. They must have run off again to a different part of the grounds. I thought to dismiss it, as I had dismissed the joust, for I could do little about either. Yet . . . something about the strained quality of those barks stopped me cold. I'd heard that kind of barking before, neither playful nor defensive, but urgent and distraught.

My own dog, Patch, had vocalized just such sentiments on several occasions, and dismissing his efforts to gain my attention had always proven a mistake. This was no attention-seeking scheme on the part of these dogs, either. Changing direction, I now headed toward the rear of the sprawling house. As I left the glare of the electric lanterns, the shadows fell heavily around me. Before me loomed a ghostly grove of young elms surrounded by stands of hydrangeas and rhodo-dendrons, all reduced to shades of charcoal. The barking be-came louder here, and then I heard the sort of growling that dogs make when they close their teeth around something and attempt to pull and tug.

As I progressed, I came to the kitchen windows at ground level, the light from inside spilling across the grass and cast-ing long shadows from the foliage. I circled a stand of hy-drangeas—and pulled up short.

A man lay on his side on the ground. His top hat had tum-bled a couple of feet away. A pungent odor drew my atten-tion to a smoldering cigar inches from his unmoving hand. The dogs had sunk their teeth in the back of his coat and were attempting to drag him, perhaps to bring him where he might be helped. I called to them, and as if startled, they loosened their jaws and sprang toward me. One yipped, a higher-pitched sound than I would have expected from so large an animal. The other whined deep in his throat. With-out needing to bend, I placed a hand on the back of each furry neck. For another several seconds, I stared down at the prone figure, as if by the force of my will alone I could change whatever ill fortune had occurred here.

For you see, I had dealt with death numerous times in the

past, and my thoughts leaped immediately to foul play. But with a jolt, I remembered Uncle Cornelius, also gone, but not by the hand of another. That jolt sent me the necessary few steps closer to the man in hopes he could still be helped. I sank to my knees, placed a hand on a motionless shoulder, and gave a shake. "Sir? Sir, are you all right?"

That little shake sent him rolling toward me, onto his back. The bearded face, the lion's mane of silver hair, the nose with its aristocratic tilt, in a masculine version of his daughter's, were all familiar to me. A small cluster of scarlet feathers quivered slightly above him, like a tiny bird hovering in the air. And then I perceived the arrow protruding from Judge Clayton Schuyler's chest, and the blood saturating his evening coat.

With the image of Clayton Schuyler, prone and bloodied, flashing in my mind, I made my way to the main garden, a dog collar gripped in each hand. I couldn't simply leave the mastiffs to continue barking at the body and attract others to the scene. I handed them off to the first footman I came upon, told him to take them inside, and ignored his quizzical looks.

The glare of the garden lights dazzled my eyes as I half blindly retraced my path to the joust. My heart throbbing in my temples, the blood rushing in my ears, I stumbled into flowerbeds and shrubbery. Thorns tore at my hems, but I kept going in a desperate hurry to reach Mr. Van Alen. Suddenly the hedge towered over me and I stumbled through the nearest archway.

A shout went up—then a chorus of shouts.

I stood at the edge of the jousting course. The mounted knights had already begun their stampede toward each other, fast closing in on me. Their hooves pounded like bass drums in my brain and yet I found myself unable to move. Did they see me? Perhaps not, with their visors down. I couldn't think fast enough, couldn't move in obedience to the orders being shouted at me from across the course, where the stands loomed some ten rows high.

Hands clamped my shoulders from behind. I was jerked roughly backward and I stumbled. My legs tangled with another pair and then we both went down, hitting the ground in a painful knot of limbs. I felt the jarring impact, but heard nothing, saw nothing, for several dizzying seconds. Then, slowly, I realized the horses now stood at opposite ends of the course, panting and stomping, but unharmed. There had been no impact; the riders must have seen me at the last instant, and through their training, they were able to avert the attack and pass each other—and me—harmlessly.

Beneath my rumpled skirts, I saw a man's trousers, and then his arms, which had gone around my waist as we fell. I tried to find purchase to lift myself off my savior, but to no avail. My bones were like water. Then a hand reached down from in front of me.

"Emmaline, are you all right?" Neily sounded stone-cold sober and filled with concern. He crouched to my level. His fingers closed around mine and gently he drew me, not up to my feet, but forward, until I sat on the grass beside him. The person who had saved me from certain death was able to negotiate a more upright position as well.

"Are you all right, Miss Cross?"

I turned, astounded to discover my guardian angel had been none other than Jerome Harrington. "Yes, I . . . Mr. Harrington, are *you* all right? I'm so sorry, I didn't mean to be so foolish. It's just that . . ."

Just that a man lay dead on the other side of the property, and no one here yet knew, and someone must be told, only not like this, not so bluntly. Many of the spectators had abandoned the stands and gawked down at the man and woman sitting in so undignified a manner on the ground.

Isn't that Emmaline Cross? Is she drunk, to wander so

carelessly into the path of a joust? Ruined the evening for the rest of us, she did . . .

"Emma! Oh, Emma." Grace pushed her way through the others and sank beside me in a pool of burgundy velvet. Her arms went around me and she pressed her cheek to mine. "What happened? Why would you ever do such a foolhardy thing?"

Yet, I heard no real admonishment in her voice, only the kind of fear that comes after the fact, when one counts one's blessings and is grateful that what might have been had not, in fact, come to pass. Without relinquishing her hold on me, she pulled away to regard me. Her eyes narrowed in their scrutiny, and then understanding flashed. "Emma, what is it? You *aren't* foolhardy. Something has happened." She spoke in a whisper only Neily could hear, and perhaps Mr. Harrington, who had remained seated on the ground close by, his legs outstretched, his hands propped on the ground behind him.

I nodded beneath a wave of gratitude. Leave it to Grace to read me correctly.

"Neily," she said, "help me get Emmaline up." Between the two of them, I came shakily to my feet. The first face I saw was Mr. Van Alen's. He looked . . . annoyed.

"I'm glad to see you're unharmed, Miss Cross. Now, would you care to explain yourself?" His Elizabethan jargon had disappeared. My near accident had truly left him shaken.

"Yes, I would, Mr. Van Alen." Like Grace, I also spoke in whispers. "But not here. Somewhere private."

His mustache twitched. "Very well." He inquired after Jerome Harrington's condition, and then, putting on a brave face, he called out in his habitual way, "Prithee, carry on, one and all. 'Tis naught to fret about. 'All's well that ends well.'"

His assurance brought on a collective release of breath. Many of those who had left their seats turned back to resume them. Others drifted back through the arches into the garden, in search of refreshments. That made up my mind for me. Already I had begun to think more clearly. I couldn't simply lead James Van Alen to where Judge Schuyler lay, or others might follow out of curiosity. That could cause a panic.

"Miss Cross, Miss Cross." The next face that filled my vision was Ethan's. He looked distraught, close to tears. Before he could get out another word, I offered reassurances.

"A close call, Ethan, nothing more. I'm fine." I reached out, clasped his hand, and drew him closer. Lowering my voice again, I said, "I hope you've been observant and took good notes tonight. We may particularly need your insights tomorrow."

He nodded vaguely, his mystification clear. However, he asked no questions and allowed me to be led away by Neily and Grace, the pair of them supporting me. Together we made our way, with Mr. Van Alen, to the house. I didn't realize Mr. Harrington had also come along until we'd climbed the veranda steps and entered the library. Of all the downstairs rooms in Wakehurst, the library alone lacked the dark paneling so prevalent elsewhere. The pearly white walls made the room a brighter, less solemn environment, albeit carvings and moldings embellished nearly every surface.

Apparently, seeing how I could now balance on my own two feet, Grace and Neily released me. I was about to choose a seat—dare I sit on the settee purported to have once belonged to Napoleon?—when Van Alen held up a hand. "Not here, where others might come in from the garden. If you wish privacy, follow me." He spared significant glances for Neily and Grace, but when I didn't protest their presence, he gestured for all of us to follow him.

The dogs came loping out of a room along the corridor and followed along, oblivious now to anything being amiss.

Mr. Van Alen brought us across the house to his private den in the north wing, where I discovered more dark-wood paneling. Paintings hung in abundance, while a sextet of swords arced above the fireplace. Sweet-smelling tobacco permeated the air. The furnishings were leather, large and inviting. I could resist no longer and virtually dropped into a saddle-brown armchair, probably Mr. Van Alen's favorite. I didn't care. The dogs found their way into a corner and stretched out on the Aubusson rug.

Meanwhile, Grace perched on the arm of my chair, while Neily took a seat on the sofa opposite. I could hear Jerome Harrington hovering behind me, but I didn't turn. If he wished to linger, so be it. I had questions for him, anyway.

Mr. Van Alen turned up the gas jets on the sconces, brightening the room. Wakehurst had not been electrified like The Breakers or Ochre Court. The electric lighting outside had been installed specifically for the joust. Otherwise, Mr. Van Alen preferred gas and candlelight, more in keeping with a Tudor manor house. Taking a seat beside Neily, he leaned a little forward and clasped his hands. "Now, then, Miss Cross, you have something to tell me?"

Once again, he used straightforward language. I drew a breath. "There is no good way to say this. There has been a death. One of your guests."

Even as Grace gasped and Neily swore under his breath, there came a sudden shuffling from behind me. "My God, who?"

This time, I did turn around to gaze at Jerome Harrington. "Your father-in-law-to-be, Mr. Harrington."

"Cl-Clayton Schuyler?" Mr. Van Alen stammered. I turned back around to see his color rise, his eyes fill with horror. "How? Where?"

"In the garden behind the house. He's been shot through the chest with an arrow."

* * *

After my terrible news, Mr. Van Alen jumped to his feet. "The authorities must be sent for."

He asked us to wait where we were and strode from the room. I assumed he had agreed to install a telephone somewhere in the house, probably in his butler's pantry. The dogs, apparently, decided the order didn't apply to them, for they sprang to their feet and padded after their master.

When he didn't return in several minutes, Jerome Harrington circled my chair and slumped onto the sofa beside Neily. "Why the devil has he been gone so long?"

Neily patted Mr. Harrington's shoulder. "I would imagine he went to find Imogene and her mother. And perhaps to post a pair of footmen near the body."

Mr. Harrington shook his head in a gesture of disbelief. "Good God."

Still perched beside me, Grace placed a hand on my shoulder as well. "Can I have one of the footmen bring you something? Tea? Something stronger?"

"Forget the footmen." Neily sprang to his feet and went to the liquor cabinet in the corner. "Van Alen keeps his finest brandy in here. Emma?" He didn't ask Mr. Harrington. He had already chosen two crystal snifters from the half dozen ranged in a circle around the decanter.

Grace cleared her throat. "Neily, haven't you had enough tonight?"

"No, my dear, I don't think I have. Not as of several minutes ago." He swore quietly, a mild oath, but with the force of a full exhalation behind it.

Grace said nothing more. Neily took a healthy swig of his brandy before crossing the room to hand the other one to Mr. Harrington. Then he studied me a moment before returning to the cart to pour a third. He pressed the snifter into my hand. "Drink it. Don't argue."

I hadn't been about to. The cut crystal bowl stabbed against my palm. I distributed the weight into both hands and raised the snifter to my lips. The brandy stung my nose, and when I sipped, it burned all the way down. Some of the numbness left me, allowing a few coherent thoughts to circle round the chaos.

I regarded Jerome Harrington across the expanse of carpet. With a sconce behind him, his youthful features remained mostly in shadow. He'd drunk half his brandy already, and now the glass hung suspended from his two hands as if forgotten. A detail came back to me, not only about the argument I'd overheard between him and Imogene Schuyler, but something else significant as well.

But first things first. "Mr. Harrington." I paused, waiting until he raised his gaze to me. His eyes were heavy-lidded, not quite focused. One might have thought he had found the body, he seemed so dazed. "Mr. Harrington, I want to thank you for what you did out there."

"'Out there'?" The words appeared to startle him.

"Yes, at the jousting course. I might have been killed. I wasn't thinking straight, or I would never have wandered so carelessly into the path of those horses."

"Oh yes. That. You're quite welcome, Miss Cross." I wondered what else he thought I meant. The argument, or something more?

"Such a fortuitous thing that you were coming from the direction of the house just then," I added, "and that you weren't already seated in the stands."

"Come to think if it, Harrington," Neily said, unwittingly taking over for me, "where *had* you been?"

Where, indeed?

But we were not yet to be enlightened. Mr. Van Alen's dogs streamed through the open doorway, and a moment later, he ushered in Imogene Schuyler and her mother, Delphine. Neily and Jerome Harrington came to their feet, and Mr. Van Alen gestured for the two women to be seated. Then, ever so gently, he told them what he had learned from me.

When he finished, a thick silence fell, but only briefly. Imogene alarmed us all by leaping to her feet, cradling her face with her hands, and letting out a scream. Sobbing wildly, she sank to her knees. For a long moment, the rest of us simply watched her, uncertain what to do. Even her mother sat frozen, staring down at her, unblinking. It was Grace who finally slid from her perch on the arm of my chair and crouched beside the inconsolable Imogene. So violently did her shoulders heave, tresses of her blond hair spilled from her meticulous coif. In the face of her distress, my throat tightened almost to closing and my chest ached with grief for her.

And yet . . . when Grace managed to lower Imogene's perfectly manicured hands from her face and began to raise her to her feet . . .

Could I be mistaken? Had she wiped the tears away on her palms? I detected no traces of moisture on her hands or her cheeks. I glanced up in confusion at her mother. Delphine Schuyler's eyes were stone-cold dry as well.

Chapter 4

For the next quarter of an hour while we waited in near silence for the police to arrive, I went over every detail of the scene I had stumbled upon behind the house. Evidently, Judge Schuyler had left the main garden to smoke a cigar, not an uncommon occurrence, since ladies often objected to the odor. He might also have been ruminating over his daughter, who had refused to join him when he called to her. I remembered the footmen had removed the archery equipment to the veranda. I hadn't seen exactly where they had stowed it, but one could safely assume they had tucked it out of sight somewhere, to be put away after the fete. Had the killer stolen a rare opportunity to arm himself or herself with bow and arrow, lean over the rail, and take aim? With the distraction of the joust about to begin, no one in the main garden would have noticed.

My gaze kept drifting to Imogene Schuyler and her mother. Despite Imogene continually raising a lace-edged handkerchief to her eyes, neither she nor her mother shed a single tear, or my name wasn't Emma Cross. Jerome Harrington made no move to comfort his fiancée, nor did she seek him out. Rather, they sat practically at opposite ends of the room, Mr. Harrington having moved to an upholstered bench in front of one of the windows.

Sitting across from me on the settee, Mrs. Schuyler sat very still, very upright, her hand entwined with Imogene's, until finally, her gaze shifted to me. "You found him," she said in a light Southern cadence, her voice deep and husky, like the lower notes on a clarinet.

"Yes."

"What were you doing there, beyond the main garden, all alone in the dark?"

Mrs. Schuyler's question startled me, and also drew Imogene from her dark musings. Her eyes narrowed as they focused on me, and her head tilted in speculation. "Yes, why were you there?"

From their tones, it seemed they were accusing me. I repeated a detail they had already been told. "I heard the dogs barking, carrying on."

"There were plenty of reasons for the dogs to be barking." Delphine Schuyler tipped up her head to view me down her narrow nose. Her gaze held steely calculation and a cold, almost cruel, light. "The joust, the activity of so many guests. Why should you have taken any notice? And why weren't you finding a seat in the stands?"

At that moment, Imogene blinked rapidly and turned her face away from me. Had her mother's question about taking a seat in the stands triggered the response? It made me wonder if Imogene had already reached the stands, or, if like Jerome Harrington, she had been elsewhere on the grounds at the time.

Grace, meanwhile, had returned to sit on the arm of my chair, her hand on my shoulder. That hand tightened possessively. "Miss Cross didn't wish to witness the joust."

"I didn't care for such a spectacle," I explained. "I didn't wish to see anyone hurt. Especially the horses."

"Such care you take for horses and dogs, Miss Cross." Miss Schuyler gave a soft sniff.

"See here." Neily came to his feet. "What are you insinuating? That my cousin had something to do with—"

"Neily." Grace held up a hand, a gesture for him to silence himself before he said too much. "Miss Cross has a tender heart when it comes to animals. There is nothing wrong or unusual about that."

"My own dog," I said, "has upon occasion warned me of danger with barking very like what I heard from those two tonight." I gestured toward Mr. Van Alen's mastiffs, which continued dozing in the corner. "I know the difference between casual or excited barking and barks of distress. That's what drew me into that part of the property. By the sound of it, I sensed something was terribly wrong."

The Schuyler women's expressions were fraught with suspicion and contempt. The mother raised an imperious eyebrow at me. "Do you wish to know what I think?"

I said nothing, just held her gaze. She apparently took that as approbation.

"I think you followed my husband into that area of the garden for a tryst. I think—"

Whatever else Mrs. Schuyler might have accused me of, Grace's protests cut her off. "Miss Cross would never! I assure you, Delphine, you are quite wrong. Why, I've never known anyone more honorable than Miss Cross."

Mrs. Schuyler's only reaction was to purse her lips.

"He'd gone out to smoke," I said, picturing the half-smoked cigar still burning in the grass near the judge's body. I told them what I had seen.

Both Schuyler women shook their heads in disbelief. With an arch look, the mother said, "He carried no cigars with him. His doctor warned him off smoking months ago. It aggravates his dyspepsia."

She had effectively called me a liar, something I would not allow. "Then somebody gave him one. The police will easily be able to tell if the cigar had been his or not." Indeed, I thought, there would be traces on his fingers, his lips, the odor of tobacco on his clothing and in his mouth. Mrs. Schuyler continued to glare her accusations at me, obviously unconvinced.

"I believe Mrs. Schuyler and Miss Imogene could do with something fortifying while we wait for the police. I know I could. Anyone else?" Mr. Van Alen came to his feet and went to the liquor cabinet. Neily and I said we'd gladly accept refills. Grace abstained, as she had earlier.

"I'll help. I need something to do." Jerome Harrington followed him and returned with a snifter in each hand. Imogene accepted a glass of sherry from him without a word, without so much as an upward flick of her gaze. Mrs. Schuyler merely nodded as she took hers.

Grace attempted to make conversation. "I suppose the guests have all been sent home, Jimmy?"

Mr. Van Alen, concentrating on filling a crystal cordial glass, nodded. "I had my butler inform everyone there'd been an accident and pass on my regrets for an abrupt end to the evening."

"Good thinking." Grace drew a breath to say something more, but I spoke first.

"Do you have a detailed guest list, Mr. Van Alen?"

"Of course." He handed the decanter to Jerome Harrington, who carried it across the room to me and refilled my snifter before moving on to Neily. "But what difference . . . ? Oh yes. The police will want to know who was here tonight. What villain could have done this?" He let out a pensive sigh. "'Thou detestable maw, thou womb of death . . .' 'Cowards die many times before their deaths; the valiant never taste of death but once.'"

Shakespeare. An admonishment formed on my tongue; this was no time for the fanciful quoting of long-dead playwrights. But perhaps he found comfort in it. I glanced at the clock on the mantel. Jesse Whyte, my friend on the police force, should arrive any moment. What a relief it would be to have him here to take charge with his levelheaded efficiency. If Mrs. and Miss Schuyler were to raise their intimations again, Jesse would not give them a serious thought.

Yet, their implied accusations had rattled me, leaving me with a defensive and vulnerable sensation I didn't particularly relish. A sense of relief washed over me when the sounds of activity drifted down the corridor. Moments later the butler announced a new arrival.

"Sir, Detective Gifford Myers to see you."

"Thank you, Henslow, send him in."

What? A frown immediately tightened my features, and quite without realizing it, I pushed to my feet. "Where is Jesse? Detective Whyte, I mean."

Of course, neither Mr. Van Alen nor his butler had an answer for me. A man about Jesse's age, somewhere in his thirties, strode into the room. He wore a dark suit of clothes of middling quality beneath an open overcoat, which showed slight fraying at the hem and cuffs. Coming to a halt, he took stock of each of us. A forefinger rose to smooth one curling end of his mustache, though it needed no smoothing. "Which one of you ladies is Miss Emmaline Cross?"

I resisted the urge to raise my hand, schoolroom style. "I am."

He came around to the front of my chair. "I'd like to start with you, then."

I couldn't help shaking my head, not in protest, but in puzzlement. "But where is Detective Whyte?"

"He's not assigned to this case. I am."

"I've never seen you before." I couldn't accept this startling change in police department procedure without satisfying my curiosity first. Jesse Whyte had been Newport's main homicide investigator for years now. What could have happened to alter that? A sudden fear closed around me. Had something happened to him?

"I'm new. Transferred from Tiverton only yesterday." His perfect triangle of a beard bobbed up and down as he spoke, the point appearing to threaten the knot of his cravat with each word. Yes, a fanciful impression on my part, but his unexpected appearance—and the lack of Jesse—had thrown me into a state of befuddlement.

He dug into a coat pocket and withdrew a tablet and pencil. His next question, however, was addressed to Mr. Van Alen. "Is there a room I can use for my interrogations?"

The word *interrogations* planted a tiny seed of dread. And not only in me. The others winced, too.

Van Alen coughed and cleared his throat. "Why don't you stay here. Everyone else, please come with me. We'll retire to the dining room and I'll have my servants bring in some food." To the detective, he added, "I'll post a footman outside the door. You may let him know whom you'd like to . . . interview . . . next."

As the others stood to leave, Grace held her place beside me. "Detective, I'd like to remain with Miss Cross, if that's all right."

He looked her up and down once. "And you are?"

She gave him her most imperious tone. "Mrs. Cornelius Vanderbilt. Cornelius the third," she added, as if clarifying were of great importance.

He jotted her name on a page in his tablet. "And you saw . . . what?"

Neily answered for her. "My wife and I didn't see anything. We had taken our seats to watch the joust when my cousin came to alert Mr. Van Alen about . . . about Judge Schuyler's death."

"I see." Detective Myers made another notation. "If neither of you saw anything, your presence here is unnecessary. You may both go home."

"We're not going anywhere." Grace sounded affronted. "And as I said, I'd like to stay with Emma while you question her. As her friend. For moral support."

The man's brow knitted into a scowl. "Is there some reason Miss Cross especially needs moral support?"

Neily and Grace replied at the same time, each blurting out an angry protest.

"I don't know what you're getting at, but—"

"Of course she needs moral support." Grace huffed in indignation before continuing to say, "She discovered a man murdered in these gardens not an hour ago."

"Yes, well, I'm sorry. But I must question the witness alone."

At least he didn't say *suspect.* I turned to Grace and gave her hand a squeeze. "It's all right. I'll answer the detective's questions and see you in a few minutes." I looked up at Neily. "I'll be fine, I promise."

Detective Myers studied his notes in silence for several moments, until I once more became aware of the ticking of the mantel clock. He frowned. "Let's go over this again, Miss Cross."

I suppressed a groan, but just barely. I had lost count of the number of times I'd recounted how I came to find Judge Schuyler's body. I had explained about the dogs, the lights from the house, the cigar, even going so far as to suggest that perhaps someone had given Judge Schuyler that cigar to entice him into the seclusion behind the house. "Nothing is going to change."

"Perhaps not," he replied absently. "What did you do prior to deciding you didn't wish to watch the joust?"

"I . . ." I had been eavesdropping, actually, but I didn't wish to tell him that. "I circulated through the gardens. Like everyone else."

"Did anything in particular catch your notice?"

I paused again, remembering how the argument between Imogene Schuyler and Jerome Harrington had most definitely caught my notice. I should simply have told Detective Myers about it, yet some impulse prevented me from doing so. I didn't know why, for surely Imogene Schuyler wouldn't spare *me* when it came time for her to be questioned. Or her mother, for that matter. Did I truly believe the young woman could have shot an arrow into her father's chest? No. Despite how angry she might have been over her arranged marriage with Jerome Harrington, resorting to murder seemed more than unlikely.

Although she had proven herself to be an excellent shot.

"Miss Cross, answer the question, please."

"Oh yes. Um . . . the Shakespearean stage caught my interest, for one."

"Anything else?"

"The archery competition." The moment I mentioned it, I wished I hadn't.

His eyebrow went up. "Archery. Did you participate?" At my nod, he continued, "And did you do well at it?"

"Well enough. But so did many other guests."

"Such modesty, Miss Cross. When I arrived earlier, I heard you won the ladies' competition."

I shrugged. "Did I? I hadn't been told." I felt the temptation to point out how well Miss Schuyler had performed, but I held my tongue. Instead, I wondered how he had come by his information. "I wouldn't have thought you'd had time to question anyone when you first arrived. Or that there had been any guests left. Hadn't they all gone home?"

"Most, but not all. So you participated in the archery." His dismissive tone indicated he would give me no further hints as to whom he had spoken to. "Anything else?"

"I enjoyed a cup of mulled wine, walked with my cousins—"

"Mr. and Mrs. Vanderbilt?"

"Yes."

His frown reappeared, even tighter. "Tell me, isn't the entire Vanderbilt family in mourning? Didn't the patriarch die only days ago?"

"Yes, that's true, but—"

"Aren't you yourself in mourning, Miss Cross?" He gestured with his pencil at the black armband I had all but forgotten I wore. "I have it on good authority you're a favorite of the family, albeit a distant cousin."

He had apparently done a thorough job of researching his subject. "Yes, I am. But Mrs. Vanderbilt asked me to accompany them tonight."

"Odd. Why would that be, Miss Cross? Forgive me, but I'm guessing this isn't your usual social circle."

A sigh made it all the way to my lips before I bit it back. "Mrs. Vanderbilt didn't wish to be here tonight, but her husband insisted. Things being what they are, with his father's death still so recent, Mrs. Vanderbilt feared he might do or say something regrettable. So she asked me to come along. You see, Mr. Vanderbilt and I have been close since we were children. Mrs. Vanderbilt believed my presence would influence her husband in a positive way."

"I see." He drew out that second word, leaving me to wonder what exactly he did see, what conclusions he had drawn. "Are you aware of the tensions that existed between Cornelius Vanderbilt the elder and Judge Schuyler?"

"What? What tensions?"

"Of the business sort. Apparently, the judge made a ruling

recently that favored union workers over a corporate alliance that included the New York Central, along with several other companies."

"Were these railroad workers?"

"One would assume."

"I had no idea. My uncle rarely shared the details of his business affairs with me. Why would he?"

The detective made a notation. "So, then, your cousin has been behaving in a way that raised his wife's concerns."

"I didn't exactly say that."

"You implied it." His gaze pinned me to the back of the chair. "Could he have been upset with the judge?"

"I don't think so."

"Why don't you?"

Because although Neily still worked for the New York Central, he took no part in the running of the company and hadn't since his parents had disowned him for marrying Grace. But it wasn't my place to explain any of that. I shook my head, unwilling to put words in my cousin's mouth. If he wished to tell Detective Myers about his difficult relationship with his father, he could do so. "You'll have to ask Mr. Vanderbilt about that. Besides, he was surrounded by friends and acquaintances the entire night. I never once saw him go off on his own."

"Supplying your cousin with an alibi, Miss Cross?"

"Merely stating a fact, Mr. Myers."

"Hmph." The quirk of his mouth told me my answer hadn't impressed him. "Does your cousin smoke cigars?"

I spoke from between gritted teeth. "Not to my knowledge."

"All right, Miss Cross, that will be all for now."

I remained sitting. "Did anyone count the bows?"

"I'm sorry?"

"The bows. The footmen brought them up to the veranda.

One can assume the murderer took one from there. The arrow that killed the judge looked like some of the ones used in the tournament. Was there a bow missing?"

Detective Myers pinched his lips together and gave me a disparaging look. I didn't think he would reply, but he said, "Apparently, the bows are all accounted for."

I took in that information. "Then . . . it's highly likely the shot was made from the veranda, and the bow replaced with the others immediately afterward."

"No, you don't, Miss Cross. You will not involve yourself in my investigation." He sighed dramatically. "I see you can't help yourself, but for your own sake, you had better learn some self-control."

A retort leaped to my tongue, but I knew better than to voice it. He wished me to go, but I hesitated again. "Will you answer one more question for me?"

"Probably not." But with a shrug, he relented. "If I am at liberty to do so."

"Why isn't Jesse Whyte on this case? He's been handling homicides in Newport for years now."

Detective Myers smiled, but not in a friendly manner. "You have yourself to thank for that, Miss Cross. You see, the police are tired of your meddling."

"I've assisted in solving numerous cases."

"Have you? Some on the force believe those cases would have been solved sooner without your interference."

"Jesse doesn't believe that."

"Hence he has been reassigned." He waggled a finger at the door. "On your way out, tell the footman I'd like to question your cousin next. Mr. Vanderbilt. Alone."

"You said Neily and Grace could go home." In my sudden discomfiture, I used their given names.

"I've changed my mind."

*   *   *

If I had believed those of us in the dining room would be able to speak freely, I was proven wrong. A uniformed officer had accompanied Detective Myers to Wakehurst, and it wasn't my old friend, Scotty Binsford, but a man with whom I had little rapport. Not that he was to blame for that; unlike Scotty and myself, he had lived in Newport only a few years.

His presence effectively halted any flow of conversation there might have been, and judging from the gazes we darted at one another, discussion would have been abundant. The brooding silenced weighed as heavily around us as the dark, carved woods and hand-tooled leather panels on the walls.

Neily returned from the study, looking pale and drained, and wouldn't quite meet my eye. The same could be said for Grace, when her turn came; except that unlike her husband, she cast me a remorseful gaze before taking a seat at the table. That look sent a chill through me. What had it meant? What had she said?

Detective Myers called for Imogene and Delphine Schuyler together. How I longed to follow them and press my ear to the study door during their interview. I was quite certain that their time with the detective *would* be an interview, rather than an interrogation. They were the bereaved wife and daughter, essentially victims of the crime. But I couldn't banish the image of their dry eyes from my mind. Nor my question of where Imogene had gone after her argument with Jerome Harrington.

About two hours later, on the way home with Neily and Grace, I remembered something else that had happened, that had been eclipsed by Judge Schuyler's murder. Their luxurious, high-sprung victoria carriage negotiated Bellevue Avenue, and even the more pitted and twisting Ocean Avenue, with a minimum of discomfort. The three of us sat side by side, each of us brooding silently. Grace hadn't mentioned her time with Detective Myers, and I hadn't yet discovered the reason for her remorseful glance at me. I'd give her time, perhaps call on her tomorrow.

I glanced around her at my cousin and regarded his profile in the moonlight. "Neily, who was that man you argued with before everything happened?"

He didn't turn to regard me. "What man? I don't remember."

"Don't you? You were by the stage, reciting the lines along with the actors, when Mr. Van Alen announced the joust. You turned to follow the crowd but were detained by a rather large, sturdily built man."

Grace watched him closely, saying nothing.

Neily fidgeted with his cuff link. "I couldn't say. We must have bumped into each other."

"I thought so at first, but it looked more serious than that, Neily. You were clenching your fists. I went to separate you because I feared you'd come to blows."

"We didn't, did we?" He tossed a defiant gaze at me, reminding me of the boy he had once been, challenging his siblings.

"No, you didn't," I conceded. "He seemed rude to me, and his clothes didn't quite fit him properly, did they?"

"Really, Emmaline, the things you notice." Neily sank lower on the velvet seat.

"I'm only saying he didn't seem to belong among Mr. Van Alen's guests."

"Did you mention him to the detective, Emma?" Grace asked.

"No. I'd forgotten all about him until just now."

"It doesn't matter," Neily said. "He was no one. No one at all."

Chapter 5

After I arrived home, Nanny made no secret about what she thought of Detective Gifford Myers. "The man's an idiot. How dare he treat a respected member of the community, such as yourself, like a common criminal?"

"I suppose he was only doing his job." We sat outside the kitchen door—Nanny, Katie, and I—enjoying the cool breezes rolling in off the ocean. Nanny had heard me come in and padded her way downstairs to ask how the evening had been. Katie had still been up, writing a letter to her family in Ireland. Nanny had brewed a pot of strong tea and Katie had carried the tray outside, to the long wooden bench under the moonlight.

"It sounds to me like he's tryin' to make a name for himself, being new to Newport and all." Katie lifted the teapot and questioned Nanny and me with a look. I shook my head, as I was still nursing my first cup.

Nanny held hers out for Katie to refill. "Yes, making a name for himself as an idiot. And replacing Jesse? Absurd. Why, you and he make a fine team. You've proven that, and then some, over the years."

A little gleam entered her eye. There had been a time when Nanny had hoped Jesse and I might make another sort of team, one that involved setting up a household together as man and wife and raising a small army of children. There had been moments when I might have agreed with her, but for the wrong reasons. At any rate, I believed both Jesse and I had made the right decisions concerning our futures, and we would always remain close friends.

"I think that's part of the problem," I said, responding to her last comment. "It doesn't sound as if the department appreciated my helping Jesse with cases."

"Then they're a department of idiots."

"Nanny, please." I chuckled—I couldn't help it. Once she made up her mind about someone, she rarely changed her opinion. "I do regret that Jesse's career might be suffering because of me."

Nanny and Katie both nodded their agreement, and we were all quiet for several moments while we sipped our tea and watched the ragtag clouds whipping across the moon.

Katie was the first to break the silence. "Then he made no arrest, this Detective Myers."

"Apparently not. He let everyone go home." I drew in a salt-laden breath of air. I told them about the argument between Miss Schuyler and Mr. Harrington. "The murder could have occurred anytime after I saw the judge beckon to his daughter, until I found him during the joust. Which makes the whereabouts of the pair during that time highly significant."

"I'll wager it happened as the joust began, right before you found him. The joust provided the perfect distraction, after all. He couldn't have been dead long." Nanny reached up with her free hand to tuck a stray wisp of silver hair back beneath her kerchief.

"That does make the most sense," I agreed.

"Poor Judge Schuyler." Even by moonlight, Katie's eyes were a bright cornflower blue as she leaned around Nanny to regard me. "It's not many a swell that champions workers. Could it have been another of his class, someone angry about the judge's ruling?"

I thought of Detective Myers's insinuations concerning Uncle Cornelius and, more important, Neily. The thought of the police making that kind of connection unnerved me, especially when I knew Neily would never have committed murder on his father's behalf. But that didn't mean some other member of the Four Hundred hadn't taken revenge against Clayton Schuyler, someone who had lost a good deal of money due to the ruling.

"I don't suppose the judge hailed from a working family and made his own way up?" Katie sounded a little dreamy, as if she very much wished to believe this version of the story.

I shook my head. "The Schuylers are an old Dutch family from New York, even though this branch moved to Philadelphia and Judge Schuyler served in the Pennsylvania judicial system. Their wealth goes back generations, and they're heavily invested in real estate, railroads, and steel."

"That makes it all the more unusual that he sided with those union workers." Katie gave her head a quick shake, stirring her spiraling red curls, which she had let down for the night. "And so much sadder that he's gone. We need more men like him. So few swells spare a thought for anyone but themselves and their purses." This last she said with more than casual disapproval. Katie had once worked at The Breakers for my relatives, Cornelius and Alice. She ducked her head. "I'm sorry, Miss Emma, I'm speakin' out of turn again."

"Nonsense," I said. "You may always speak your mind here without fear of reprisals."

"What kind of workers were they?" Nanny asked.

"If the judge's ruling affected the New York Central, they had to be railroad workers of some sort," I replied, wishing I had more information. Though most industries experienced strikes on a fairly regular basis, I could remember no articles about this particular matter from the Associated Press, no reports bearing Judge Schuyler's name.

Nanny lifted her ear to the breeze, and I became aware of a knocking that had been going on these many minutes. "It's that shutter again," she said with a sigh.

"I'll try to fix it in the morning." And then I remembered that, thanks to Uncle Cornelius's generosity, I wouldn't have to. Katie had spoken true in one sense. People like the Vanderbilts could be callous and indifferent one day, and generous to a fault the next, if the cause appealed to them. I had long been one of those causes. "Come to think of it, I'll hire a handyman to come out and tighten all the shutters and see to anything else that needs fixing."

I fell to brooding about the events at Wakehurst. Something kept nagging at me. "That man who argued with Neily . . ."

"What man?" Nanny's question startled me out of my reverie.

"Haven't I mentioned him?"

"No, you haven't. You named everyone the detective questioned. Who did Neily argue with?"

"That's the problem. I don't know, and Neily wouldn't tell me."

" 'Wouldn't,' or *couldn't*, Miss Emma?" Katie again leaned around Nanny to see me.

"I'm not sure. Neily was fairly deep in his cups, and at the time, I thought perhaps one of them bumped into the other and it escalated from there. You know how young gentlemen can be." I considered. "Except that the other man had at least a decade on Neily, so he was no hot-tempered young buck. And then there was the matter of his clothing." I described my impressions of his attire.

Nanny had been about to start on her third cup of tea, but held it aloft without sipping. "Either he's such new money, he hasn't had time to find a good tailor, or he didn't belong there. Did you ask Mr. Van Alen?"

I shook my head. "Regretfully, no. I'd forgotten all about him until the ride home in the carriage. It had seemed no large matter, except . . ."

"Except what, my lamb?"

"Neily looked so angry, I hurried over to them to prevent a fight."

"That doesn't sound like your cousin," Nanny said with conviction, and even Katie nodded. Her ordeal at The Breakers, which had led to her dismissal, had been appalling, but Neily had played no part in it. She had never had a negative thing to say about him.

"No, it doesn't. Even drunk. Of course, he's distraught over his father's death, for all he won't admit it. That can make anyone act out of character." I sighed. "But this . . . I don't know."

"I do," said Nanny quietly. "You need to find out who this man is, and why he attended the fete tonight. He could be the answer, Emma. Or part of it."

"What about Miss Schuyler?" Katie faced straight ahead, toward the ocean lapping at the edges of the property. Moonlight played on the foamy eddies and on the droplets dancing over the rocks. "It sounds as though she had the strongest reason to want to be free of her father, not to mention having a sharp eye with a bow and arrow."

"You said both Jerome Harrington and Imogene Schuyler set off toward the house after their argument," Nanny reminded me. "Does Detective Myers know anything about Miss Schuyler's objections to the marriage?"

"I don't know," I replied. "I didn't hear him question

Miss Schuyler or Jerome Harrington, so I don't know how much they admitted to him."

"Well," she said, "perhaps someone should make certain he knows."

The next morning, I rose early and dressed in somber colors with my black armband in place. Drab I might have appeared, but my attire felt far more appropriate to my mood than my finery of last night. I would not miss the ensemble once I returned it to Grace.

After a light breakfast, I made my way into town. My carriage, a simple two-wheeled gig that required only one horse, needed repairs. Some were minor, such as tears in the leather seat and canvas roof, and some more extensive: the seat spring was rusting and the long wooden reaches were splintering. The threat of an accident had been weighing heavily on my mind, but thanks to Uncle Cornelius's generosity, I could have these matters addressed right away.

After stopping at Stevenson's Livery on Thames Street and arranging a schedule of repairs, I left my horse and buggy there and walked across town to Marlborough Street. I carried an umbrella, as the weather was misty with a fairly dependable promise of rain, at least a sprinkle or two. The leaves were beginning to change, their deep colors enlivening the weather-beaten storefronts and warehouses along Thames Street. The scents of decaying foliage mingled with fishy brine from the bay to tickle my nose until I sneezed several times. This, in turn, prompted several passersby to give me a wider berth.

On Marlborough Street, I hesitated, staring up at the front of a brick building that looked more like someone's large Federal-style home than a police station. Gifford Myers wouldn't be happy to see me, but I hadn't come to make anyone happy. I had come to tell the man what I had witnessed the night before. I should have told him everything then, but fear of incriminating someone mistakenly had prompted me to hold my tongue. That had been wrong. As he himself had insisted, this murder was a police matter. Well, then, the police needed every shred of information available. Only then could they sort through the facts and reach a logical conclusion. With my resolve firmly in place, I mounted the steps and went inside.

My friend Scotty Binsford happened to be manning the front desk, which renewed my hopes that I would be permitted to speak with Detective Myers. Behind Scotty, in the main station room, uniformed officers and plainclothesmen bustled back and forth. I heard voices, the ringing of telephones, and the *clackety-clack* of typewriters. Scotty's sheepish expression, however, dampened my hopes immediately.

I pretended I hadn't noticed. "Good morning, Scotty. How are you?"

"Fine, Emma, just fine." Scotty was a large young man about my age, broad of chest, who had me raising my chin to look up at him, even though he occupied a stool. This made him a rather formidable police officer, at least in appearance, as long as the criminals weren't privy to his gentle nature. Not that that prevented him from carrying out his duty. "I should be asking you, after what happened last night. I'm surprised to see you in town this early."

"I'm here because of last night."

His mouth turned downward. "I was afraid you'd say that."

"Why is that?"

"Because I have instructions to take a statement if you showed up today and send you on your way."

A huff escaped my lips. "Do you, now? From whom? No, let me guess. Is it Detective Myers?"

Poor Scotty, his cheeks flamed. "I'm sorry, Emma. If it were up to me . . ."

I placed a hand on the counter between us. "I know that,

Scotty. I certainly don't blame you for following orders. But this is ridiculous. I have information that might be important to solving Judge Schuyler's murder."

"Which is why I'm supposed to take your statement." He dragged a clipboard onto the counter. He placed a jar of ink and a pen beside it. "If you'd like to write down anything you think is important, I'll see that Detective Myers gets it."

I scowled at the writing equipment before looking back up at Scotty. When I spoke, it was in an undertone. "Tell me, what do you think of Gifford Myers?"

Scotty's blush rose once more. He glanced over his shoulder, through the doorway into the main room. Turning back, he whispered, "I think it's unfair they took Jesse off homicide."

It surprised me to hear him use Jesse's given name, rather than refer to him as Detective Whyte. It showed me Scotty was speaking as a fellow Newporter, and what's more, he was talking as a neighbor, someone who had grown up on the Point. It was a neighborhood where people stuck together. I gave him a firm nod. "As do I, Scotty."

"I could let you see *him*, you know. Detective Whyte, I mean."

I nodded more vigorously. "Yes, please."

"Wait here." Scotty slipped into the main room as I stood at the counter and fumed about Gifford Myers's refusal to see me. How dare he assume I could have nothing useful to offer, and how dare he refuse to see *any* member of the public.

Scotty returned a minute later, with Jesse following. He looked grim, and I could see reflected in his hazel eyes a flicker of the same anger coursing through my veins. He bade me good morning and came around the counter.

"Walk with me, Emma." Rather brusquely, he led the way to the street door and held it open for me. On the sidewalk, he offered me his arm, and with his free hand slapped his derby over his auburn hair. We walked to the corner in silence. I could sense Jesse's tension, as well as feel it in the bend of his elbow.

"Jesse, what's going on? Why has this new man, this Gifford Myers, replaced you? Is it permanent?"

"I don't know, truth be told," he said with a shake of his head. "Could be. I guess it depends on his performance." At Meeting Street, we turned toward Washington Square.

"Jesse, won't you tell me what's going on? Judging by what Detective Myers said last night, I'm afraid I'm to blame for this change."

He breathed in deeply and let it out with a sigh. "Here's the problem. The state has gotten wind of how often you've helped with cases, and now Police Chief Rogers's job is at stake."

"But that doesn't make sense. The cases were solved. I should think that's a good thing."

"You would think so. But the chief has been accused of allowing a . . ." He flicked a glance at me and shrugged. "In their words, allowing a 'mere woman' to do his department's job. So he's replaced me as Newport's main homicide detective with a man who will refuse to work with you."

I brought us to an abrupt halt, forcing other pedestrians to sidestep us. "Oh, Jesse, that's not fair."

"No, it isn't," he agreed. "But it's the way things are."

"I'm so sorry. If I'd guessed something like this might happen . . ."

He shook his head. "Don't be sorry, Emma. The department is losing an invaluable resource."

"It most certainly is, but I'm sure in time they'll come to their senses and realize no one is better at the job than you."

"I meant *you*," he said with a pensive smile, and we started walking again. We crossed Washington Square and turned up Touro Street.

I held the brim of my hat against the breeze. "Do you know if he has any leads yet?"

"He's going over the guest list now, especially those who participated in the archery. He figures the killer is something of a marksman." Jesse gave a nod. "He would have to be, to have shot a man from the veranda in the dark."

"Don't forget, the judge wore a white shirt, white cravat, and white silk vest. All of that would have caught the light from the windows and made him stand out from his surroundings."

"Even so."

"Yes, even so," I conceded. When Touro Synagogue came into view ahead of us, we swerved right onto Spring Street. "He specifically asked me about my participation in the archery contest," I said uneasily.

"He's an idiot," Jesse grumbled.

I let go a laugh. "Nanny would agree. Where are we going?"

"Max Oberlin's Gentlemen's Outfitters."

"Why there? Have you ordered a new suit of clothes?" It would certainly surprise me if he had, the shop being more expensive than a man on a detective's salary could typically afford.

"No, there's been a robbery. I've been given the case." I heard the disdain in his voice, the contempt. Normally, a pair of uniformed men would be sent to investigate a robbery at a clothing shop, not a seasoned detective. Waves of remorse crashed over me as I acknowledged the extent of the damage I had done to Jesse's career.

Max Oberlin met us at the door to his shop and locked it behind us after letting us in. I expected to see the interior in disarray, with clothing spilling off the shelves and strewn across the floor. Instead, we were greeted by neat stacks and artfully dressed mannequins. Except for one, which stood denuded of its attire.

Mr. Oberlin offered Jesse his broad hand to shake, and then met my gaze on an equal level, as we were of similar height. Jesse explained my presence by identifying me as a reporter for the *Messenger*. Mr. Oberlin nodded and bade me good morning; we knew each other vaguely.

Jesse scanned the shop. "You were broken into, Mr. Oberlin?"

"I was, yes." He pronounced *was* as *vas*, with a light German accent. He waddled slightly as he crossed the shop to the unclothed mannequin. "One of my most expensive ensembles is gone."

Jesse remained silent a moment, his eyebrows gathering. "That's it? That's all that's missing?"

Mr. Oberlin nodded and patted the side of his grizzled hair in place. "As I said, it is very expensive. Evening clothes made from my finest fabrics. For a Mr. Arnold Jenson. I was displaying it before his final fitting. Now I have no suit and no payment to look forward to."

Jesse lowered his head and touched his fingertips to his brow. I could all but see him withering with dismay that he should be saddled with such a minor case. I, on the other hand, snatched eagerly at Mr. Oberlin's news, for a reason of my own.

"Can you describe the clothing?" This earned me a quizzical look from Jesse, but he allowed Mr. Oberlin to reply.

"Of course I can," he said with all the dignity of a skilled tailor. "Black trousers with satin braiding down the outer seam. Black tailcoat, well fitted for a trim waist, broader in the shoulders, black satin lapels. Silk vest in dove gray. White silk cravat. Tailored white shirt. Nothing flashy, simply the height of elegance."

I thought back on the details of the evening clothes worn

by the man Neily had argued with. The fit—less than perfect—had caught my notice much more than the fabrics or trim, but as I pictured him in my mind, I felt sure this could be Max Oberlin's missing ensemble.

"A top hat as well?" I asked.

"Yes, also a top hat." He gestured to a shelf of them; there was an empty space where a hat should have been.

"When was the approximate time of the break-in?" Jesse slipped his tablet and pencil from his inner coat pocket.

"I cannot say. I close at precisely six o'clock every evening. This had to have occurred sometime between when I left the shop at six-thirty yesterday evening and this morning, when I reopened an hour ago."

"Do you live upstairs?" Jesse made a notation.

"I do. But I heard nothing. Nothing at all."

"Were you home all evening?"

"I was. Oh, except for when I went out to purchase some bockwurst and bread for my supper. But it couldn't have happened then. I wasn't gone long enough, and I would have noticed something amiss when I returned. No, it must have happened after I went up to my rooms."

Jesse made another note. "Had you noticed any suspicious characters hanging around the area earlier yesterday?"

The man shrugged. "Who has time to be looking out windows?"

Jesse conceded his point with another nod. "Fair enough. Any unusual customers lately?"

"No one I can think of."

"Detective Whyte," I said, "perhaps you might interview this Mr. Jenson."

This clearly puzzled Mr. Oberlin, as well as troubled him. "You think my customer came and stole the clothing so he wouldn't have to pay for it?"

"No, no," I hastened to assure him. "Nothing like that."

"Then what?" Jesse's bafflement seemed to equal Mr. Oberlin's.

"I might have seen this stolen ensemble last night, at Wakehurst." I didn't wish to explain any more than that—at least, not yet. I gave Jesse a significant look, hoping he would understand and trust me.

He turned back to Mr. Oberlin. "I'll be interviewing the neighbors to see if anyone saw anything." Jesse looked around the shop. "Where did the individual break in?"

"This way." Mr. Oberlin led the way into the back, past his dressing rooms, cutting and sewing rooms, and a storeroom. A narrow hallway led to a rear door. "Here. The lock has been broken."

Jesse crouched to examine the latch. The wood had been splintered; slivers along with a few screws lay scattered on the floor. Jesse opened the door and looked out, no doubt taking note of which neighbors to follow up with. "Looks like he used a crowbar to force the lock open. Odd you didn't hear anything. Let's hope someone else did."

He spent the next several minutes asking further questions, making notations, and surveying the store and its contents to make sure nothing else was taken.

"What about cash from your register?" he asked.

"I never leave cash in the register overnight," the man said as if offended by the very idea.

"And you have how many employees?"

"Two, besides the woman who does some of my plain stitching. Shirts, cravats, that kind of thing. But she works from home. My two assistants leave with me each night."

"And where are they now?"

"I sent them home, told them to come back later this morning. No need to be paying them to watch you do your work, Detective."

I felt sure they hadn't thanked him for that. Even a couple

hours' wages could make a difference in how well a family ate in any given week. But I schooled my features not to reveal my sentiments.

We soon bade Mr. Oberlin good day, with Jesse promising to keep him informed. To humor me, he had Mr. Oberlin give him Arnold Jenson's address. I waited until we had walked several doors down before turning to Jesse. "We've got to see my cousin Neily. And then visit this Mr. Jenson."

"Are you going to tell me why?"

I explained as we made our way back to the station.

Chapter 6

Jesse and I agreed that Arnold Jenson could wait. My main reasoning behind wishing to meet him was to compare him with my memory of the individual whom Neily had argued with at the fete. We climbed into a police carriage and rode out to Beaulieu, the Italianate villa built forty years earlier, which Neily and Grace leased each summer. Situated on Bellevue Avenue between Beechwood and Marble House, Beaulieu presented an older style of grandeur than the other cottages inhabited by the Vanderbilts in Newport. Two identical wings flanked a central tower beneath a steep mansard roof, and a charming veranda surrounded the house on three sides. That Neily loved this house said something significant about him: he valued comfort over impressing his neighbors, and didn't care to entertain on quite as lavish a scale as many others of the Four Hundred.

Which was not to say Neily and Grace didn't entertain in an impressive style, nor that Beaulieu wasn't a masterpiece of midcentury stateliness.

We were admitted into the Grand Foyer, an extensive hall

tiled in black-and-white marble, onto which the five main rooms of the first floor opened. Directly ahead, to the rear of the house, lay my favorite: an octagonal parlor that over-looked the veranda and, beyond, the gardens and the sea. But it was not to this room the butler led us. A gentle click of wood upon ivory, followed by a muffled thump, rendered the butler's assistance unnecessary. I had already guessed Neily to be in the billiard room, and no wonder. I knew it to be a habit of the Vanderbilt men to retreat to their billiard tables when they were troubled.

Nonetheless, the butler announced us while we waited. I half wondered if Neily would guess the nature of our visit and try to put us off. If he hadn't wished to confide in me last night, why would he today? But within a moment, he appeared and even summoned a smile, though I detected a wariness in his dark eyes.

"Emmaline, what a treat. I'm sorry to tell you Grace isn't here at the moment. She's taken Corneil over to Shady Lawn to see her parents." He gave my cheek a quick peck. Up close, I saw his features were tired and colorless, making him appear older than his twenty-six years.

"That's all right, we've come to see you. Neily, you know Detective Whyte."

That circumspect gleam in his eyes increased as he nodded to Jesse and, to his credit, offered his hand to shake. "Come, we'll retire to the drawing room. Have you eaten?"

"Please, nothing for us," I said as we followed him.

"I thought that other detective—Myers?—was handling Judge Schuyler's murder."

"He is," Jesse said. "This is actually about another matter."

"'Another matter'?" Neily gestured for us to precede him into the drawing room, where the gilded trim on the paneled walls reminded me of the ballroom of its neighbor, Beech-wood. The room lay in shadow, the heavy curtains along the east wall having been drawn against the morning sunlight. The butler trailed us into the room.

"Shall I open the draperies, sir?"

"No, thank you. I prefer it dark."

Jesse and I traded puzzled glances. The billiard room had been flooded with light. It seemed only in our company did Neily prefer shadows. To hide what?

"What can I do for you, then?" he asked, and I heard the reluctance in his tone.

"There's been a robbery in town," Jesse said, leaning forward in his chair. "At Max Oberlin's Gentlemen's Outfitters."

Neily frowned. "I know the place, but I can't say I've ever purchased anything there. My clothes are gotten mostly in New York. I don't see how I could possibly help you."

"You may yet be able to," I said. "You see, I believe a suit of evening clothes stolen from the shop turned up at Wakehurst last night, worn by an uninvited guest."

Neily shrugged. "It wouldn't be the first time someone intruded on a party, especially one held out of doors."

"That man you argued with . . ." I trailed off when Neily surged to his feet. He paced in front of us, his hands clasped behind his back.

"I told you, Emmaline, he was no one. I was . . . you know . . . a bit swizzled by then, wasn't I? Not my finest moment, I'll admit."

"We're not here to cast judgment." I came to my feet as well, prompting Jesse to do the same.

"We'd merely like to know his identity," Jesse said.

"I'm sorry, I have no idea who he is. Never saw him before in my life."

"What did he say that made you so angry?" I persisted.

Neily shook his head, his mouth a slash of irritation. "I

don't recall. I'm sorry, but I have nothing more to say on the matter."

I was certain he remembered much more than he was admitting, but he left me no choice but to drop the matter. "Can I ask you about something else?"

"I'd really rather you didn't." Nonetheless, he held out his hand to allow me to continue.

"Last night, Detective Myers mentioned a conflict existing between Judge Schuyler and the New York Central. And that the judge ruled in favor of union workers. Do you know anything about that?"

"Emmaline, you know I'm not part of that end of the business any longer. I'm a mechanical engineer. You'll have to speak with Alfred or Uncle William if you wish to know more about the matter."

"All right, then, Neily. I suppose I'm finished annoying you for one day. But if you should recall anything . . ."

"Yes, yes," he said, nodding, but I heard his continued annoyance, his impatience to have us gone. "I'll let you know immediately. Detective Whyte, I'm sorry I couldn't be of more help to you."

Couldn't, or wouldn't, I thought.

"I understand, Mr. Vanderbilt." Jesse studied Neily's expression as he spoke, leading me to suspect he didn't believe Neily, either. "My deepest condolences on the passing of your father."

"Yes, thank you." Neily shook Jesse's hand again and walked us through the Grand Hall to the front door. "Emmaline, I'll tell Grace you were here. She'll be sorry to have missed you. But you'll come another time, won't you?"

"Of course, Neily." I took his hand and deposited a kiss on his cheek, his beard tickling my nose. He spoke as if this had been a social call, so eager was he to dismiss our questions, and ourselves.

Once back in the police carriage, I turned to Jesse. "Well?"

"He's hiding something, all right. What I can't figure out is why. Who could this mystery antagonist be, and is your cousin trying to protect him, or avoid being implicated himself?"

"Implication in what, though?" I mused aloud as apprehension gathered in the pit of my stomach.

Jesse took up the reins and gave them a light flap above the horse's back. The carriage rocked into motion. "That may be for Gifford Myers to discover."

"Will it?" I adjusted my straw sun hat, unpinning and pinning it back in place to meet the changing angle of the sun. "We'll see about that."

Our second stop brought us just off Bellevue Avenue, to the home of Arnold Jenson. Situated on Berkeley Avenue, the house was a dignified Federal manse nestled in sculpted evergreens, Japanese maples, and towering elms. A housekeeper admitted us and had us wait in a parlor furnished in burled walnut and brocades that complemented the floral wallpaper. I sat on the deep-seated tufted sofa, while Jesse remained standing near the fireplace.

Mr. Jenson's appearance in the doorway startled me, as for an instant I believed him to be the very man I had seen with Neily the previous night. His height, the breadth of his shoulders, the tapering of his torso . . . yet I immediately perceived the difference, the refinement lacking in the other man, the confidence rather than defiance. This man's attire fit him as it had been meant to, as though it had been designed for him, as it assuredly had been. Besides, where the other man's nose had obviously suffered a break or two, this man, I felt certain, had never been at the receiving end of a punch.

What I also learned was that if the man from Wakehurst

wore *this* man's clothing, he would, indeed, strain the fabric ever so slightly.

"I am Arnold Jenson." He extended his hand to Jesse first. "What may I do for you?" Jesse explained our purpose, and the solicitous light faded from Mr. Jenson's pale blue eyes. "That suit is for my daughter's wedding next month. I do hope Mr. Oberlin can make another, unless we're so lucky as to have the original turn up. Any hope of that?"

"I can't say," Jesse admitted, "but we have a couple of questions." Though our original intention had been only to compare Mr. Jenson to the man from last night, we had realized ahead of time the necessity of making our visit appear to be legitimate police business.

"Wait." Mr. Jenson held up a hand and appeared to scrutinize me. "Forgive me, but why are you here, Miss . . . ?"

"Cross."

"Hmm. Emmaline Cross, the Vanderbilt cousin."

I nodded.

"Surely, you're not a police officer," he said with a dubious look and a mirthless chuckle.

"No, I'm a reporter for the *Newport Messenger.*"

Concern replaced his doubt. "I'd prefer not to have my name in the newspapers, thank you, Miss Cross."

"It needn't be. I'm merely gathering some facts for a basic story of local interest. How long have you done business with Mr. Oberlin?"

"Ever since we've been in Newport. About two years now, on and off."

Jesse took over the questioning. "Never had a problem at the shop before?"

"Never. Oberlin delivers quality goods and does so on time." He shook his head and exhaled as though a weight sat on his shoulders. "This is most inconvenient, I'll have you know. I don't see how he'll have a new set of clothes ready for me in two weeks, when we leave for New York. Not with the quality of the first set. And to think, I would have had a final fitting this afternoon, and by tomorrow morning, the suit would have been delivered. I suppose I'll just have to find something in the City."

"Mr. Jenson," I ventured, hoping Jesse wouldn't object to what I was about to say, "I might have seen your clothing last night, at the fete at Wakehurst."

"Wakehurst? How the blazes would my evening clothes have gotten to Wakehurst?"

Jesse shot me a glare from beneath his brows, but I remained focused on Mr. Jenson. "On another man, perhaps our thief."

Mr. Jenson gave an indignant sniff. "It was certainly our thief, if he wore my clothes." He left off, his mouth falling open. "Hold up a moment. I remember . . . several days ago, when I went to Oberlin's for a fitting, I was standing on the platform in front of the mirrors in the fitting room. Oberlin left me for a moment, and since I stood fully dressed, he left the curtain gaping. A fellow entered the shop, looked around. Seemed frightfully interested in evening clothes. I noticed him checking the pricing board behind the counter. And then he saw me."

Jesse and I exchanged startled glances. Jesse asked, "Did he speak to you?"

"He only wished me a good afternoon. But I noticed him sizing me up, or rather my attire, as I supposed at the time. I thought nothing of it, other than that the fellow wished to form an opinion of Oberlin's talents. Say, do you think this same bounder came back and stole my evening clothes?"

"It's possible." Jesse took out his tablet and pencil. "Can you tell us what he looked like?"

"Hmm . . ." Mr. Jenson rubbed a palm beneath his clean-shaven chin, then scratched absently at a muttonchop sideburn that showed no signs of going gray. "Come to think of it, he was about my size, which is probably why he seemed so interested in me. Takes a skilled tailor to cut a coat to the right proportions." He said this with a smattering of pride, indicating his awareness of his trim physique.

"What else? Hair color and length? Facial hair?" I asked, trying to tamp down my eagerness to hear more. I yearned to mention the man's profile, yet didn't wish to put words into Mr. Jenson's mouth.

"Let me see . . . he was clean shaven. I believe his hair was dark. Couldn't begin to guess the color of his eyes."

"That doesn't matter." Jesse wrote on his pad. "Anything else? Did Mr. Oberlin see him?"

"No, he left before Oberlin returned." Mr. Jenson gave a shrug. "But now that I consider it, the fellow gave me the impression of being a fighter. Had a rough look about him."

"That's it," I murmured to Jesse. "That's our man. It's got to be."

Jesse planned to spend the rest of the afternoon questioning Max Oberlin's neighbors on Spring Street. Meanwhile, I walked to the *Messenger*'s offices and wrote up my preliminary story on the murder at Wakehurst. I also penned a short article on the tailor shop robbery for our new editor-in-chief to review. All the while, I wondered where Ethan was, and whether he had organized his notes from last night for his society column.

Derrick had brought in a man named Stanley Sheppard to replace me as editor-in-chief. I found him in the front office of our tiny establishment, hunched over the same tasks I had rejected only weeks ago. Two desks occupied the room over-looking Spring Street, one for the editor-in-chief and the other for an office manager. The latter chair had remained empty for the past year, except when Derrick occupied it. I had come to hope Derrick would occupy it permanently, instead of dividing his time between Newport and Providence, as he had been doing for several years now.

Mr. Sheppard glanced up when I came through the door separating the front office from the actual workings of the *Messenger:* news, typesetting, printing, assembly, bundling, and storage. The scent of pipe tobacco hung on the air, as it never had when I occupied this space. Not that Stanley Sheppard would ever smoke in a building filled with paper. For that, he slipped outside, but his pipe stood on its stand in a corner of his desk, always ready should he desire to run out for a quick few puffs.

I held out the two sheets of paper in my hand.

"Any breakthroughs yet on the Wakehurst matter," he asked, dispensing with the usual greeting. Mr. Sheppard was like that. Why waste words when in the newspaper business every moment mattered? He skimmed my article even as he asked the question, another of his time-saving habits. Mr. Sheppard hailed from New Hampshire originally, giving him a stronger New England drawl than the one typically heard on the streets of Newport. At about forty, he was young enough to be energetic and resourceful, yet old enough to know when to weigh his options and proceed with caution. Unremarkable in appearance—average height and build, with crow's-feet around the eyes, and appropriately silvered at the temples—he had a sharp mind and a keen sense of fair play.

"Not yet," I replied, "but here's the thing." I moved beside his desk, which faced the street, so we could talk without him having to turn around. "I think the murder and the break-in at the tailor shop might be related."

He had just moved on to the tailor shop story. A *hmm* emanated from his gravelly voice. "Why?"

"Because I saw someone last night who might have been wearing the attire stolen from Oberlin's."

"Interesting." He looked up and met my eye. "All right,

find out. Make sure Ethan has his eyes and ears open everywhere he goes as well. What people won't tell *you*, they might utter in a society writer's presence. Hell, half the time, they barely know he's there."

I was nodding, a faint smile on my lips. "My thoughts exactly. But where *is* Ethan? I'd hoped to compare notes with him this morning."

"He ran out. Wouldn't tell me where."

This, too, indicated Mr. Sheppard's faith in his staff. He knew as well as I did that if Ethan left the building, he had a good reason. "I need to find a way into the Schuylers' cottage, and soon," I said. "I'd like to find out more about Mrs. Schuyler and her daughter."

"Won't be easy, getting in. Not now, with them in mourning." He studied me, his brown eyes deepening with thought. "You're onto something else besides this possible tailor shop connection."

"I witnessed a few things last night that have me wondering."

"You think the wife and daughter are implicated?"

"Let's just say it's an avenue worth exploring."

"All right, Miss Cross. Explore." He turned back to the ledgers and correspondence strewn across his desk. I watched him another moment, taking note of how contented he seemed in the performance of such tasks. With a sense of gratitude, I also acknowledged my own contentment with how matters at the *Messenger* had, at long last, been resolved. When Derrick had announced my replacement, I'd had my doubts. Another man, and nearly two decades my senior? I had assumed that, with a pat on the head, I would once more be consigned to trivial matters. How wrong I'd been. I genuinely liked Stanley Sheppard, with his rough voice and his terse economy of words and his apparent trust in me and my abilities.

I went back to the cramped newsroom and was gathering my things, when Ethan, breathless, came barreling down the hallway. "Miss Cross. I'm glad you're here."

About to pin my hat in place, I hesitated, arms in the air in readiness. "Where have you been? I was hoping to confer with you about last night."

"I know. But I needed to follow up on a lead."

"About last night?"

"Of course about last night. Miss Cross, who at the fete would have been even more invisible than me?"

"Me?"

He rolled his eyes and shook his head. "The jester."

"Don't you think he was more of a spectacle with his many colors and his bells?"

"On one level, perhaps. But, historically, jesters could venture into places denied most ordinary individuals, even managing to sit in a dark corner of the privy chamber as kings discussed momentous matters with their nobles."

"What are you getting at, Ethan?"

"Jesters were allowed entrée where others weren't because they were never to be taken seriously. They were part of the scenery, or, as was the case last night, part of the decorations. Jesters *play* the fool, so people believe them to *be* foolhardy and let down their guard."

"Yes, I see." My heart began to beat a little faster. Could this jester, who would pop up from the shadows ringing his bells when least expected, have seen something important to do with Clayton Schuyler's murder, perhaps without even realizing it? "Then we need to find this jester, don't we?"

Ethan smiled widely. "Already done, Miss Cross. That's where I've been. Finding out where this jester makes his home. His name is Burt Covey, by the way."

"How on earth did you manage to track him so quickly? Did you question Mr. Van Alen?"

"I didn't have to. I went directly to the source of jesters, Miss Cross."

This cryptic explanation left me shaking my head.

"I went to the theater. The Opera House. Burt Covey joined the in-house troupe at the beginning of the summer, and supplements his income by hiring himself out to private parties in a variety of roles."

"*Hmph.* Mrs. Fish could have used him last year to play the role of Prince Otto, rather than that poor little chimp," I dryly observed, remembering last summer's fiasco at the Fishes' cottage, Crossways. Prince Otto, nephew of the Austro-Hungarian emperor, was supposed to have been the Fishes' guest of honor at their Harvest Festival last summer, and when he'd failed to materialize, Mrs. Fish had decided to turn his disappearance into a grand joke rather than face humiliation in front of her peers. A telephone call had procured a substitute from a nearby menagerie, and to everyone's delighted surprise, in walked a chimpanzee wearing a velvet cape and holding a scepter. Unfortunately for Prince Otto, the night had not turned out so happily.

"I suppose you missed my story earlier this summer, then," Ethan said. "Mrs. Fish *did* hire him, but to play a butler who fumbled his every move, yet managed never to spill a drop. He had the guests falling down with laughter."

"As I can well imagine. Leave it to Mrs. Fish. But were you able to find out where this Mr. Covey lives?"

Ethan answered with another smile, or grin, I should say. Within minutes, he and I made our way outside, with a promise to Mr. Sheppard that we'd be back soon.

Chapter 7

Ethan's and my trek out to a small cottage overlooking Easton Bay proved fruitless, as we found Burt Covey not at home. Before leaving the Opera House earlier, Ethan had inquired whether the actors were expected for a rehearsal that morning, and had been told they would not be returning to the building until the next day. Great was our disappointment, then, when one of his housemates, of whom there appeared to be several living in the ramshackle house, informed us Mr. Covey had gone out and left no word where he might be found.

But I remembered something else. Or someone else, I should say. The actress who played Titania on the Shakespearean stage might well be the woman who, according to Imogene Schuyler, drew the attention of Jerome Harrington the night of the fete. Her name remained a mystery to me, but it shouldn't be too difficult to find her, provided she also plied her trade at the Opera House. I added Titania to the list of individuals with whom I wished to speak.

Ethan and I climbed back into his pony cart and returned

to the *Messenger,* where I edited stories sent to us from the Associated Press through the Western Union office. How much smaller the telegraph had made the world, and how much more accessible news from anywhere and everywhere. Someday, perhaps, the telephone would do the same. This endeavor kept me busy for the next couple of hours as I pored through various news stories and chose the ones I thought would most interest our readers. Anything within the scope of high society I handed off to Ethan.

I also rummaged through old Associated Press articles we kept on file, hoping to find a reference to Judge Clayton's recent rulings. I found nothing significant, nothing that would have involved Cornelius Vanderbilt or men like him.

That turned my thoughts to Uncle Cornelius. With a shock, I realized I hadn't spared him a single consideration since last night. Understandable, perhaps, given the circumstances, but guilt nonetheless prodded. And then it occurred to me that if Uncle Cornelius had still been alive, I would not have been at Wakehurst last night and would not now be scrambling to piece together how Judge Clayton had come to be lying among the hydrangeas, an arrow through his chest.

That Uncle Cornelius had been acquainted with Judge Schuyler I knew to be a fact. Yet, I could only guess at the extent of their friendship. Suddenly I wondered if any of my cousins could provide insight into the judge's life and whether there might have been any threats to his life in recent days. Aunt Alice might know, but I couldn't possibly question her now, during the height of her grief.

The Breakers hadn't been properly shut down for the winter, and I hoped Alfred or Gertrude, or perhaps both, might return to Newport to see to the business of settling the household accounts, overseeing the packing of the items that would be returned to New York, and dispersing the excess staff to the family's other estates. I saw no need to bother Neily again, since he would not have been privy to his father's confidences in recent years. I was almost glad of it, in a way, as I didn't think he would be pleased to see me anytime soon.

Speaking with my Vanderbilt cousins would have to wait. In the meantime, I couldn't get the image of the surviving Schuylers, Delphine and Imogene, out of my mind. At the same time, I realized it might not be them I needed to question next. A plan formed in my mind.

"That's about it for me today." I slid the article I'd been working on from the typewriter's cylinder and turned in my chair to regard Ethan. "How are you doing?"

"I'm done here, but I've got to get out to Bailey's Beach for an evening swim race."

I grinned. "Are you going as a reporter or a swimmer?"

His lips formed a smirk. "A reporter, to be sure."

"Give me a ride out? I left my carriage at Stevenson's for repairs. I'll ring up The Breakers carriage house in the morning for a ride back into town."

"That won't be necessary."

Ethan and I both turned our attention to the doorway, and the surprise I saw there brought me surging to my feet with a decided lack of dignity. "Derrick!"

Ethan was grinning now as he, too, rose from his chair. "I'll just be going, then. Mr. Andrews, it's nice to have you back."

"Thank you, Ethan." As Derrick spoke, his gaze never left me. He moved aside to let Ethan pass through the doorway, then once more filled it, beaming at me. I came around the desk and with no further ado found myself in his arms, my cheek pressed to his collar.

"I'm so glad you're back," I whispered against starched cotton.

"So am I. I heard what happened at Wakehurst." He drew back. "And once again, you're involved, aren't you?"

"Not in any official capacity, outside of being a reporter. But trust me, I *will* report."

"I don't understand."

I explained to him about Jesse's replacement, and the reason for it. "I feel dreadful, Derrick, but the whole thing is ridiculous. It's only because I'm a woman that Jesse has to suffer. Those crimes were solved. What should it matter how or by whom? Besides, it's not as though Jesse didn't do his job. I merely helped."

Derrick drew me closer again. "I'd say you've done more than that. But right now, I don't know if I share your indignation or am relieved you'll have to take a back seat in this investigation."

"Not as a reporter I won't. I certainly can't rely on Gifford Myers to pass on the facts to me, so I'll have no choice but to find them out on my own. The public has a right to be informed."

He rested his chin on my hair, the strands stirred by his sigh. "The police department should realize it'll take far more than a new detective to keep you down." Finally releasing me from his embrace, he sat on the edge of the desk and held my hands.

"Do you know the Schuylers?" I asked him.

"Not well, although my parents had become friendly with them in recent years."

"I don't suppose they have any idea of who might have murdered the judge? An enemy, someone with a grudge?"

He shook his head. "My parents' dealings with the Schuylers would be on a purely social level, and not particularly often, at that. I believe they did spend some time together in the South of France last spring, but that's hardly a place where anyone dwells on unpleasant matters."

On the way back to Gull Manor, I asked Derrick to take a brief detour. I had lingering questions about last night, and I thought these could be answered with a visit to Wakehurst. As we approached the front door, I hoped we would find Mr. Van Alen not at home, as it was the house I had come to see, not him. More specifically, the veranda. A footman answered, dressed in a traditional uniform of tailcoat and knee breeches rather than the doublet and hose of the previous night. He ushered us into the Long Gallery and asked us to wait while he climbed the stairs. Even during the day, entering that house felt like stepping back in time and across a great distance to England's baronial past. Ordinarily, I appreciated this harkening back to earlier centuries, but now I found the dark coffered paneling, dusky Oriental rugs, and ancient displays of armor oppressive and ominous. I hoped to accomplish my task and leave as soon as possible.

After a few minutes, Mr. Van Alen came down to greet us. We had obviously interrupted his leisure time, as evidenced by his velvet smoking jacket, with its elaborately embroidered cuffs and lapels and the mock slashing detail on the sleeves, like those on an Elizabethan doublet. His house shoes, I was amused to note, were tied with satin ribbon and came to points at the toes that turned upward, in another attempt to ape Tudor fashion.

He greeted us with a puzzled expression. Certainly, he had not expected visitors on such a day. After making polite inquiries, he asked if he could provide us with refreshments, for which Derrick and I thanked him but declined.

"I'm terribly sorry to disturb you, sir," I said. "It's a trivial matter, really."

"Disturb me? My dear Miss Cross! 'Twas you who found the deceased last night. I'd have thought surely you had taken to your bed today and tried to cast the entire sordid debacle from your mind."

"I lost something last night, a fan that was a gift from my parents. I wondered if I might walk out onto your veranda to see if it's there."

"Of course, of course." He led us down the Long Gallery to the dining room, where we exited onto the veranda. Positioned at the side of the house above the formal gardens, the veranda spanned the width of the south wing from front to back, also overlooking the area where I had found Judge Schuyler. I pretended to search among the wrought iron garden furniture, even on the flagstone floor.

"Are you certain you didn't leave it in your cousin's carriage on your way home, Miss Cross?"

I glanced up to find Mr. Van Alen hovering right behind me, following my line of sight everywhere I looked. How I wished he would go back inside; how I wished he hadn't been home at all. An idea occurred to me. "You know, sir, I might have left it in your den. I wonder, while I continue to look here, if you might check there for me?"

"I remember no such item in your possession whilst you inhabited my den, Miss Cross."

"It's worth checking, though, wouldn't you say?" Derrick put his hand on Mr. Van Alen's shoulder and gave him a little nudge. "Just to put the lady's mind at ease."

I put on as distressed an expression as I could muster.

"At your service, milady." He stepped back inside, and I let out a little huff of relief.

Derrick scowled. "Life is a game to him."

"A harmless affectation," I replied with a shrug. "It's not that I don't wish to tell Mr. Van Alen why I'm really here. I don't like lying, but I wouldn't want him inadvertently repeating the true reason to Detective Myers."

Derrick nodded his agreement, and I hurried over to the railing overlooking the rear garden.

He joined me there. "Where did you find the judge?"

Things looked different from this perspective and in the daylight. I searched the trees and shrubs and attempted to visually retrace my path as I'd followed the sound of the dogs' barking. Finally I stretched out my arm. "There, I believe."

I pointed to where I had circled the shrubbery and came upon the judge. "From the ground," I explained, "he had been hidden, until I'd come within a few feet of him. But from here, from this raised vantage point, he would have been visible in the light from the kitchen windows."

I raised both arms, as if holding a bow, and used the length of my left arm, as I would have with an actual arrow, to take aim at an imaginary target. I dropped my arms to my sides and nodded. "Yes, I believe our killer stood here, or close to it."

"Miss Cross, 'I am not bound to please thee with my answers.'" The sound of James Van Alen's voice startled us both. Shakespeare again. Derrick made a sound of frustration. We turned as that gentleman strode across the veranda to us. "Forsooth, your fan is not to be found in my den."

He saw where we stood and frowned. "Ah, I see. You fear perchance you dropped it in the garden. Seems a likely scenario, but we cannot have you down there again, Miss Cross, I shall not hear of it." His perplexity continued, until he suddenly brightened. "I shall send my footmen to search. Should they find it, I'll have it sent to you posthaste. Gull Manor on Ocean Avenue, is it?"

"Yes. Thank you, Mr. Van Alen." I experienced a wave of guilt over the footmen having to search the scene of the crime. Were there bloodstains on the grass? Would those young men find it a gruesome task? I would have owned up to the truth if not for the prospect of Detective Myers finding out, taking the matter to Chief Rogers, and Jesse landing in more trouble than he was already in.

*   *   *

For a brief time that evening, I found myself forgetting about death—about Uncle Cornelius laid to rest in that mausoleum on Staten Island, and about Judge Schuyler bleeding out among the hydrangeas. Nanny's artful touch in the kitchen did indeed soothe my demons, at least temporarily, and having Derrick there lifted my mood.

After supper, he and I strolled the length of my property, a small peninsula that thrust its rocky edges out into the Atlantic Ocean. The morning's threat of rain had dissipated with little more than a brief drizzle. Under a purpling sky, the lowering sun half obscured behind a thin band of clouds near the horizon, our shadows stretched out long and deep behind us. The spray was up, the waves choppy and edged with golden foam. Derrick seemed uncommonly quiet and I sensed something weighing on his mind. I also sensed it had nothing to do with Judge Schuyler.

"We've barely discussed your time in Providence," I said, hoping to prod him into revealing his thoughts. We walked, hand in hand, our shoulders brushing in a way that felt intimate yet comfortable.

"There's not much to say," he said with a shrug. "We sold off a few smaller newspapers and purchased some larger ones. Business as usual."

I had known that had been part of the reason for his trip to Providence. The Andrews family's newspaper holdings included the *Providence Sun,* but also numerous other papers throughout New England and Upstate New York. "You say it so nonchalantly, but those kinds of acquisitions are important."

"Perhaps, but I needn't have been there. My father and his financial team could have handled the transactions just as easily without me."

I halted and turned to face him. "What are you saying?"

He glanced out over the waves, then back at me. "Claiming to need my help was merely another excuse to bring me to Providence."

"And get you out of Newport." It was my turn to shrug. "It's not the first time. We needn't be surprised."

"Oh, I'm not surprised. But I am angry. And growing weary of such tactics."

Perhaps I should have been, too. Derrick's parents would do anything to separate us. They simply didn't consider me good enough for their son, and rarely missed an opportunity to make their opinions known.

But I smiled, anyway, knowing that while Derrick wouldn't abandon his family, neither would he abandon me. No, if he and I were to go our separate ways, it would be our decision, not theirs. It had taken me some time to fully believe it, and there were moments when I still feared the differences in our social positions would come between us. But so far, he had proven as constant as the tides, and equally dynamic.

"Why are you smiling?" He tried to look annoyed, but smiled as well.

"Because perhaps I understand your parents, a bit anyway. They need you. They're afraid of losing you."

"Then they should stop pushing me away."

"They don't realize that's what they're doing. They believe by creating reasons to keep you in Providence, you'll forget about Newport, the *Messenger*, and me."

"How mistaken they are." His arms went around me. Earlier, he had shed his coat, and despite the chill carried on the evening air, he had come out in his vest and shirtsleeves. Beneath those sleeves, I could feel the ruggedness of his muscles, honed years earlier by rowing and boxing. Those muscles rendered his embrace as sturdy as the bedrock beneath our feet. His lips nudged until mine opened, and he kissed me, soundly and long.

Of course, it was exactly then the kitchen door opened and my dog, Patch, came lumbering out.

Nanny called to us, "Cake's ready!"

I let out a sigh; Derrick blew out a breath that might have carried a mild oath along with it, but we ended with a shared chuckle. Nanny had baked a ginger pudding cake specially to welcome Derrick back to Newport, and we mustn't disappoint her. She was sure to have whipped up some fresh cream to go along with it. It was therefore our duty to go inside and for each of us to enjoy a thick, lovely slice, perhaps two.

Patch reached us after taking a circuitous route across the garden, diverting first to chase something through the long grasses, then over to a stunted crabapple tree to conduct his business, and finally to pause on the rocky bank of the property to bark at the incoming surf. Only after attending to these matters did he trot over to us, happy and panting, to urge us to follow him back to the house.

I started to go, but Derrick grasped my arm and stopped me. The setting sun had cleared the clouds, emerging as a bright copper disc that lit the water and framed his profile, and I blinked from the dazzle of it all. Words formed on his lips, and I found myself bracing with anticipation, longing to hear whatever it was he wished to say. By his very hesitation, I sensed the importance of those words, a matter of great consequence, and I barely drew a breath as I waited. But he smiled once more, delivered a brief kiss to my lips, and started us walking again.

Before Derrick left that evening, I asked a favor.

"How much do you know about the Harringtons?" I began by inquiring.

"Made their fortune in banking. Large mansion on Fifth Avenue, an estate on Long Island, and another one in Hyde Park. What else is there to know?"

"Whether or not they're in financial straits, that's what. Can you find out?"

At this, he showed me the lopsided grin that had initially endeared him to me. "What do you think?"

I grinned, too, as his arms went around me and he kissed me good night. "Let me know what you learn."

The next day at the *Messenger*, I received a telephone call from the wife of the pastor at Trinity Church. Mrs. Lowrie was a good friend of Nanny's, which explained why she thought to notify me about an event that would take place tomorrow at the church.

"A memorial service for Judge Schuyler," she said, "at ten in the morning. They plan to take his body home to Philadelphia, once the police have released it, but seeing as there are so many of the judge's acquaintances currently here in Newport, it was decided something should be done here as well."

"Thank you, Mrs. Lowrie. I appreciate your letting me know."

"Yes, well, I thought the *Messenger* might want to report on it." She paused, yet I sensed her gathering her thoughts to say more. She proved me right. "Do you know if they've discovered anything more about his death?"

"I'm afraid not," I answered truthfully, not that I would have been free to reveal any details about the case.

"Such an awful thing, murder, and in such a way as happened to the poor man. Can you imagine?"

I could, actually. I'd been there and found the body, after all. Had the judge been found lying near an archery target, one might have allowed for the possibility of a novice's arrow having gone tragically astray. But my discovering him among the rhododendrons and hydrangeas beyond the confines of the fete precluded any scenario but murder.

A new plan formed in my mind as I hung up with Mrs. Lowrie, and I cranked the telephone to once more summon the operator. "Gayla," I said when she came on the line, "connect me with Ochre Court, please."

"Goodness, Ochre Court? Got an invitation to tea, did you, Emma?"

"No, Gayla. It's not Mrs. Goelet I wish to speak with, as if she would even come to the telephone. I'm calling belowstairs." Mrs. Goelet, Grace Wilson's older sister, would consider herself far too grand and refined to do anything as vulgar as speaking into a trumpet-shaped mouthpiece.

"Oh, I see. I don't suppose this has anything to do with what happened at Wakehurst the other night, does it?" Gayla Prescott kept Newporters well connected via the wires that crisscrossed their way across town, but she was also the nosiest individual I had ever encountered. Through the years, I'd learned one might as well satisfy her curiosity at the outset, or one's call might never be put through.

"What would make you think that?" I crossed my fingers in my lap and prepared to lie. "If it had to do with Judge Schuyler's death, why would I be calling over to Ochre Court?"

"Oh, true. That wouldn't make sense, would it?"

"Rest assured, I'm only checking on a friend who works there, Gayla."

Having appeased Gayla's insatiable quest for town gossip by assuring her I had none to offer, she put my call through. The butler at Ochre Court answered, and moments later, the person I wished to speak with came on the line, one of the maids who worked in the house

"Miss Cross? Nora Taylor here." A brogue stronger than Katie's filtered across the distance, accompanied by crackles and a low electrical buzz.

"Hello, Nora, and, please, it's Emma." We traded pleasantries, asking after each other and our network of close acquaintances. Nora had been out to Gull Manor on several occasions in the past year and got on quite well with both Nanny and Katie. "Nora, I'm calling to find out whether your chef there is preparing food to send over to the Schuylers' house. You know who they are, don't you?"

"Blessed Mary, all of Newport knows who the Schuylers are, after what happened the other night. Oh, do forgive me, Emma, I nearly forgot you're the one who found the poor man. Such a shock it must have been. You poor dear, are you all right?" I could all but see Nora pressing a hand over her heart.

"It was a shock, to be sure, Nora, but I'm fine. About that food . . ."

"Oh yes. Mrs. Goelet did instruct Monsieur Geroux to prepare some of his specialties for the Schuylers and their servants. She says the house staff must be as upset as the family, and what's more, there's going to be a memorial and they should be allowed to attend and not be stuck in the kitchen preparing food all day."

"I'd hoped as much. I'm wondering, Nora, if you could facilitate a favor for me."

" 'Facilitate'? I'm not sure I understand."

"Do you have some free time later?"

"Around five o'clock, yes."

"Perfect. I'll come by the service entrance then."

Ethan reappeared after a short absence around lunchtime. "I've been back to the Opera House. The actors were rehearsing. All except our Mr. Covey. Appears he's ill today."

My eyes narrowed at this news. "If I didn't know better, I'd say our jolly jester doesn't wish to be found."

"His housemates must have told him we were at their cottage inquiring yesterday."

"Yes, they must have . . . but why would he avoid us?"

"He's got something to hide?" Ethan suggested.

"*Hmm.* What about Titania? Did you look for her?"

"I did. She warmed to the idea of speaking to me, once I'd told her I was with the *Messenger.* I started off complimenting her performances at Wakehurst and asking about her career. Where she's from, how she started acting. Her training. All of that. But as soon as I brought up Mr. Harrington's name, she issued me the cut direct and stalked off."

"Goodness. Perhaps Imogene Schuyler was right."

"I'm sorry, Miss Cross. I suppose I wasn't very discreet. Perhaps you should try."

"Don't worry, I will. You did get her name, didn't you?"

"Clarice O'Shea."

"A stage name, no doubt. Not that it matters." I gave a decisive nod. "Clarice O'Shea and I shall meet soon."

Before leaving town that afternoon, I once again used the telephone, this time to ring up Jesse. It took several minutes for the desk officer to track him down in the building, and when he came on the line, he sounded harried.

"I won't keep you but a minute, Jesse. I just thought it only fair to let you know what I'm planning, and with whom."

"Why don't I like the sound of that?"

"It's nothing dangerous. But it involves Nora."

A long pause followed this disclosure. Jesse and Nora had met the previous year and had enjoyed a light courtship ever since. Jesse cleared his throat. "Must it involve Nora?"

"I'm afraid so." I explained my plan. When he finally agreed that it didn't sound overly dangerous, I changed the subject. "Anything new in the Oberlin case?"

"Not much. I'm no closer to learning the identity of the man you believe you saw wearing the stolen clothing. Not a single one of Oberlin's Spring Street neighbors remembers hearing or seeing anything unusual between when Oberlin closed the shop and the fete at Wakehurst began."

I thought about that a moment. "Once darkness fell, it would have been difficult for anyone to have seen anything behind the shop. There isn't much lighting back there."

"I'll keep inquiring."

I told him of Ethan's theory about the jester, relaying the man's name, Burt Covey, and where he lived. "Ethan tried at the Opera House, and we went out to his cottage near the beach, but he wasn't there either."

"Interesting. Have you had another chance to check the Opera House?"

"Ethan did, this afternoon. Seems Mr. Covey wasn't well today, so he didn't come in. But Ethan took the opportunity to speak with another of the actors. Or actress, in this case. A Clarice O'Shea. She played Titania at Wakehurst."

"Do you think she might have seen something?"

"Perhaps," I replied, "but I'm much more interested in why Miss Schuyler accused Mr. Harrington of flirting with this woman. She might be able to shed some insight into the state of the couple's relationship, not to mention Jerome's finances."

"When are you planning to approach her?"

"Sometime after tomorrow. In the meantime . . ."

"In the meantime," he continued when I paused, "I'll check our records and see what I can find out about our jester and our actress. Possibly nothing, especially if those are both stage names. But you never know."

"It sounds to me as if Burt Covey is deliberately making himself scarce. But I can't think of a reason why, unless he simply doesn't wish to be involved in a murder case."

"Perhaps he's our murderer."

The idea jolted me. Could a small-time actor have a connection to Judge Schuyler, one that could prompt him to commit murder? "When you look into his past, see if he's left any trail in Pennsylvania."

"I'll let you know what I find out." With that, Jesse rang off, and I left the *Messenger*.

The repairs on my buggy hadn't been completed yet, but I had borrowed a small trap from Stevenson's Livery, and my horse, Maestro, seemed only too happy to be pulling less weight. I drove out to Ochre Court, explained my idea to Nora, and arranged to meet her there again the following morning.

With Nanny's help the next day, I prepared to carry out my plan. She and I rose extra early, and she fitted me into one of my great-aunt Sadie's dresses, a simple, dark gray muslin day dress with a homemade lace collar. The garment hailed from a good decade ago, but that didn't matter. Over this, I pinned an apron, Nanny securing the ties around my waist. My flat walking boots completed the outfit. I climbed into my borrowed trap and drove over to Ochre Court to collect Nora.

"You certainly look the part, don't you?" Her Irish brogue asserted itself as she surveyed the effects of my disguise. "But here, you'll need this."

She handed me a starched linen cap and a couple of hairpins. Only weeks earlier, I had sent Ethan Merriman to Kingscote disguised as a butler. Now here I was, about to steal into the Schuylers' leased summer cottage as a maid. The family and much of the staff would be leaving about midmorning for the memorial. Before they went, I hoped to be able to strike up conversations with some of them, because I knew from experience that servants, from the highest to the lowliest, could provide insight into their employers' lives, provided they were willing to chat. I also hoped for an opportunity to do a bit of snooping upstairs.

Nora hefted a large covered basket onto the seat between us. "For the Schuyler ladies and the servants," she said.

"Both sweets and savories. I hope it brings them some comfort."

"I'm sure it will." I had known that families up and down Bellevue Avenue would be sending gifts meant to console the Schuyler household today. Neighboring servants might even offer their services temporarily to allow more of the Schuylers' staff to attend the memorial. This gave me the perfect excuse for arriving at their home, as I couldn't very well have knocked on the front door and expected to be admitted. Especially not when I planned to ask questions. I only hoped none of the servants hailed from Newport, or if some did, they'd be willing to play along with me and not expose my ruse.

The house sat on the landward side of Bellevue Avenue, a short walk south of my aunt Alva's Marble House. Set at the end of a curving driveway and surrounded by a sweeping front lawn, it was a large Queen Anne–style house with a turret on one side, a square tower toward the rear, and a wide veranda out front. We drove around to the service entrance and I helped Nora down with the basket.

"Now, if it looks as though I'll be here a good while, take the buggy and return to Ochre Court," I told her. "I don't want you getting in trouble with Mrs. Goelet. Can you manage the horse, do you think?"

"Your Maestro is spirited, to be sure, but he's a good lad as long as one keeps a fair and gentle hand on him." Since Nora had become a regular visitor to Gull Manor, she and Maestro, as well as Patch and my aging roan hack, Barney, had become fast friends.

"Good." I glanced up at the house, smoothing Aunt Sadie's dress and making sure my cap hadn't slipped askew. "I hope they don't balk at there being two of us. I realize they might find it unusual for a pair of maids to deliver one basket."

Nora shrugged. "If we walk in as if nothing is odd, no one

should question us. We'll head straight for the kitchen, as though we both belong there."

"You head for the kitchen," I said. "I'll start asking around."

"Just like that?"

"Of course not. First I'll ask if there's anything I can do for them. You know, one maid concerned about another. They're bound to be shocked by their employer's death, and some of them might be sincerely grief stricken. I'll lend them a sympathetic ear." Did I feel a twinge of guilt about that? Yes, I surely did, but I reminded myself it was all part of finding justice for Clayton Schuyler.

Nora conceded my point with a nod. "It's possible some of them might be genuinely sorry about his passing. I've never had much more than a quick word with any of them, so I don't know how the staff here felt about Judge Schuyler, or any of the Schuylers, for that matter."

"That's what I intend to find out." I pointed to the entrance. "Shall we?"

Chapter 8

The housekeeper admitted us with no sign that she found the pair of us at all unusual. Nor was she anyone I recognized; I therefore assumed she had traveled from Philadelphia with her employers. "Thank you for coming. The kitchen is through there." She pointed the way with a thin, bony finger.

Nora started ahead, but I lingered. "I'm very sorry about the judge."

The housekeeper, who had also started to walk away, stopped and turned. "Thank you. It's come as quite a shock to us all. I'm afraid it isn't business as usual around here. Far from it."

"I can stay to help out, if you need me to. My mistress said it would be all right."

"Perhaps you might fill in for one of our kitchen girls during the memorial. We need a few servants to remain behind to ready things for when Mrs. and Miss Schuyler return with the guests who attend the service."

"I would be happy to."

She started to turn away again.

"Did you know him well?"

Once more, she stopped and turned. "Who? The judge? He and I spoke little through the years. I report directly to Mrs. Schuyler." I perceived a slight defensiveness in her manner. Perhaps she believed I was hinting at some sort of impropriety.

"Yes, of course. I only thought . . . well, a housekeeper's position is a sought-after one. Most remain with the same family for ever so long." I found myself using turns of phrases I often heard from Katie, except without her melodic brogue.

"Oh yes, that's true. I've been with the Schuylers a dozen years now." She compressed her lips and cast her gaze at her feet. When she looked back up, her eyes glistened. "While I cannot say I knew the judge well, he was a good employer and I've made my home with the family."

"Mrs. Schuyler and her daughter must be distraught."

She hesitated, a shadow of uncertainty crossing her face. "Yes . . . they certainly are."

"If there's anything I can do for them, please say so . . ."

"I don't see what you could do for the mistress and her daughter. But thank you for offering. Now, if you wish to help out, please see Mrs. Keston, in the kitchen. Through there." She pointed again.

Her brisk steps dismissed me. She reached a doorway and turned in, entering her parlor, I assumed. What had her hesitancy meant? That she wasn't sure Mrs. Schuyler and her daughter were distraught? Or that she shouldn't be speaking of such matters with a stranger?

I moved on to the kitchen. Here I found Nora standing at a work counter unloading her basket. Her offerings were not the only sign of well-meaning neighbors. It looked as though entire cooked meals had been brought over as well, along with fruits, vegetables, and anything else the household might need to create meals with a minimum of fuss. Several kitchen maids were busy sorting and finding room in the larders and cupboards for this extra bounty. None of them were familiar to me. They wore their typical garb, but with black armbands, just as I had taken to wearing. Today, however, I had omitted it from my wardrobe.

"Let me help you." I approached a girl, still in her teens, who was hefting a crate filled with apples and pears. I moved beside her and took hold of one side of the crate.

"Thank you," she said a little breathlessly. "I've got to bring it down to the cold storeroom, through there." She pointed with her chin at a doorway across the kitchen. "Have you brought food from your employers, too?"

"Yes. I came with Miss Taylor from Ochre Court."

"Goodness, Ochre Court? That's one of the big ones." She matched her steps to mine as we walked sideways into a small square hall. A tall window let in a burst of sunlight, and I blinked in the glare. The maid directed us to a cement staircase, and we descended to the coolness of a cellar. We placed our burden on a countertop, and she unlocked and opened a storeroom door. "I can take it from here."

"No, I'll help you bring it in and set it down. It's no trouble."

Her look of gratitude both warmed my heart and inflamed my guilt in deceiving her. However, it was for a good cause, and I wasted no time in attempting to draw her out. "Are you planning to attend the memorial?"

"I'm afraid I can't be spared, not with so many of the others going. I don't have seniority, you see."

"I've offered to stay and assist, so you should be able to go if you wish."

She compressed her lips, frowning slightly. "No . . . it's all right. I'll stay."

"How long have you been with the Schuylers?"

"Only since the spring. They hired me right before they decided to lease this house for the summer. I hadn't expected to be going so far from Philadelphia." She sighed with longing.

"Family back there?"

"Lots of family. I'm one of eight. There's an army of aunts and uncles and cousins, too. This is my first time away from home." As she spoke, she turned to straighten items on the storeroom's shelves. "Are you from here?"

"I am. I'm Emma, by the way." I didn't see any harm in telling her my real name, as Emma was common enough.

"I'm Cathy," she said shyly.

"I suppose working for a family like the Schuylers was an opportunity you couldn't pass up, even if it did take you away from home for a spell."

"I couldn't have turned it down." Another sigh conveyed what I perceived to be a misgiving. I pretended not to notice.

"Such a prestigious family. And Mrs. and Miss Schuyler are both so beautiful. You must be proud to serve in such a household." Inwardly I acknowledged that I was baiting her, and regretted having to do so.

"Yes . . . they're lovely to look at."

"Oh?" I studied her a moment. "Do I detect something of a qualm about your mistresses?"

"No!" Her expression turned wary, even fearful. "Of course not."

Reaching out, I placed a hand on her shoulder to reassure her. "It's quite all right. I understand. It's not always easy, is it, being in service?"

"If only they weren't always arguing." Her voice dropped to a murmur. "We can hear them down here, you know. My home was always crowded, but almost always happy. It upsets me to hear it. I wish . . ."

"You wish you could go home," I said, lowering my tone

to match hers. She nodded, and a tear formed at the corner of her eye. She quickly wiped it away with the back of her hand.

"I'm sorry. You didn't come here to watch me fall apart." She gave a weepy chuckle.

"Don't be sorry. I certainly didn't come here expecting to see everyone smiling. This is a very trying time for all of you."

"I only wish I could be sorry about Judge Schuyler." Her hand flew to her mouth. "I didn't mean it like that, truly. I *am* sorry he died, but maybe now the shouting will stop."

"Do you know what it was about?"

She shook her head. "Sounded as if Mrs. Schuyler would start it, and the judge would tell her she'd better hold her tongue, but what it was about, I couldn't tell."

"It sounds like theirs wasn't a very happy marriage."

"No, I don't think it was. But when I tried asking the others, no one would tell me anything. Said to mind my business if I knew what's good for me. They're right, of course. Asking questions can get you tossed out without a reference."

"Cathy, where are you, girl?"

At that impatient summons from the kitchen, she gasped and scampered away. "Coming!"

When I returned to the kitchen, I saw no sign of Nora and assumed she'd driven the buggy back to Ochre Court, as we had agreed. I continued asking questions and gleaned similar information from others belowstairs, at least from the ones willing to speak to me. Not all of them were, yet their tight-lipped reticence told a story as well. This was not a contented home, generally speaking, nor had the judge and Mrs. Schuyler been a happy couple.

But as for Imogene, I could find out little more about her,

or her engagement to Jerome Harrington. It seemed the staff had no opinion on the matter. Strange.

An unexpected boon presented itself when another kitchen assistant was told to bring tea up to Imogene Schuyler's personal maid in her room on the third floor.

"I was just going to get ready to go to the service," the girl protested to the housekeeper.

"Do this first, and then you may get ready." The housekeeper had already changed her clothes from the plain cotton she had worn when she admitted me earlier to a more tailored black broadcloth, probably her Sunday best. She wore a felt hat with a low brim and a netted veil.

The girl pouted, but I came to her rescue. She and I had spoken only minutes ago, while I'd helped her put away the scrubbed pots and pans from breakfast. "I could carry up the tea, ma'am," I said to the housekeeper.

"Good, that settles it. Thank you. Laura, you may go and get ready. Be quick about it. The carriages will be leaving shortly."

With a cup and saucer in one hand and a plate bearing a cornmeal muffin in the other, I made my way carefully up the back stairs to Miss Powell's room beneath the eaves on the third floor. I'd also been told to hurry, as Miss Powell hadn't had time for breakfast before getting Miss Schuyler ready for the memorial, and now she wished a quick repast before boarding the carriage with the rest of the upper servants.

"It's about time," she called out when I knocked on her door. She swung the door open and did a double take upon seeing me. "Who are you? I've never seen you here before."

So much for a thank-you. "I came from Ochre Court to help out this morning."

"Did you, now?" She surveyed me up and down, no doubt taking in my out-of-date dress and deciding by some standards of her own that I had passed muster. "All right, bring it in and put it there." She pointed to a dresser near the foot of the bed. Dressed in severe black, her hair pulled back in an equally stern coif, Miss Powell was not an unattractive woman—quite the opposite. But like many a lady's maid, she had taken pains to minimize the fact. After all, it wouldn't do for a maid to rival her mistress in beauty.

"I'm so sorry about your employer," I said as I set down the teacup and plate. Folding my hands at my waist, I turned to regard her. "Quite a respected gentleman, Judge Schuyler."

"Good heavens, yes. A remarkable and eminent gentleman. Many of the Four Hundred families sought his advice on a great many matters."

"I can well imagine." I attempted to sound slightly awed. "You must be very proud to work for the Schuylers." Yes, *proud,* I decided, was exactly the right word, for I detected no grief in her countenance, only self-satisfaction to be connected to such an illustrious family.

"Of course I am. The Schuylers are old money. They're wildly wealthy and exceedingly genteel." I moved aside as she approached the dresser, dragging a chair away from the wall first. Using the dresser top as a table, she sat and broke off a piece of her muffin. She popped it into her mouth and spoke around the crumbs as she chewed. "Mrs. Schuyler has assured me my job is not at risk, now that her husband . . . well . . . you know."

"That's very good of her. Is she a very congenial lady?"

"Mrs. Schuyler?" Miss Powell looked almost affronted by the question. "She's everything a great lady should be. Her family is also an old one, originally from France and settled in the South. Lejeune is her maiden name."

I nodded, feigning interest. "But it's her daughter you serve, isn't it?"

She conceded this with a nod and devoured more of her muffin, washing it down with a hearty draft of tea. A portion of her enthusiasm seemed to have waned as she said, "Miss Imogene, yes."

Perhaps she perceived less prestige in serving the daughter rather than the mother. I sighed wistfully. "I understand there was to have been a wedding soon." I waited for her half-hearted nod, and went on. "I suppose Miss Imogene must be terribly upset to have to put off her marriage plans. Or perhaps she hasn't had time yet to even consider such things, being deep in mourning as she is."

"Hmm. I suppose."

She avoided my gaze, so I took the opportunity to study her. A haughtiness had entered her expression, making her appear imperious, rather like her young mistress. For the first time, I wondered about Miss Powell's background. Did she hail from a once-prosperous family who had fallen on hard times? I brushed the thought aside as irrelevant to my present purpose. "Who is the young man? I remember reading about the engagement. A Mr. Harrison, is it?"

"Harrington. Jerome." She said the name without enthusiasm. She seemed about to say more, but hesitated. I waited, hoping she would enlighten me further, and was rewarded for my patience. "He's not good enough for her, if you ask me."

I raised my eyebrows in a show of surprise. "Are the Harringtons not a good family?"

"In background, yes. But there's something about the son, Miss Imogene's affianced, that irks me. In my opinion, he's weak. Not nearly as strong a personality as Miss Imogene herself." The pride had returned to her voice, almost as if she were speaking of her own daughter.

"You think she could do better."

"Much better, indeed."

"What does she think? Would she agree with you?"

Miss Powell drained her teacup and set the cup and saucer on the dresser beside the plate, empty of all now but the crumbs. She came to her feet and went to a coat stand in the corner. "She hasn't said."

"She doesn't confide in you?"

The question raised a scowl as she turned back to me. I feared she considered my query impertinent and would summarily dismiss me. Rather, she mulled over her answer before saying, "Often she does. But not about her engagement. And that makes me suspect she isn't entirely happy about it."

"Perhaps she favors another." I thought of my cousin Consuelo, who had loved one man while being forced by her mother to marry someone else. According to the argument I had overheard at the Elizabethan Fete, Jerome Harrington would be dependent on the money Imogene brought to the marriage, and I had assumed this lay at the root of her objections to him. But such arrangements were not at all uncommon. In fact, Consuelo had married the Duke of Marlborough under those exact circumstances. It happened all the time in society, and if Imogene had felt any affection for Jerome Harrington, the arrangement wouldn't have deterred her. Perhaps they simply didn't suit, or perhaps, as I had suggested, Imogene favored another man, as Consuelo had.

Who could he be?

Miss Powell had taken an overcoat from the stand and swung it around her shoulders. "If she has her sights set on someone else, he's a mystery to me. Come here. Help me on with my hat."

She held out a derby-shaped hat with a netted veil that would cover her face. We stood in front of the mirror as she directed me to tip it this way, tilt it that way, until she was satisfied, and then I slipped the pin through to hold it in place.

"I'd best be getting downstairs before the carriages leave."

Her chin came up, her nostrils flaring slightly. "I shall trust you to be discreet about our conversation . . . What did you say your name was?"

"Emma."

"Emma." She gave me an arch look. "You are to repeat none of this. Do you understand?"

If our conversation worried her so much, why had she confided in me in the first place, instead of sending me on my way, once my errand had been accomplished? "Yes, ma'am," I assured her. "Not a word to anyone."

"Good. Now I must go. Come along."

I gathered up the tea things and followed her down the back staircase. She turned off at the first floor and hurried out through a door that opened onto the service drive. I continued down to the kitchen and deposited the china in the scullery. Then, after ensuring no one saw me, I turned around and retraced my steps.

Chapter 9

I hesitated partway up the back staircase. I had waited to be sure Cathy had ample tasks in the kitchen to keep her occupied. Who else might still be in the house? A lower maid, perhaps collecting the morning laundry and taking advantage of an empty house to catch up on the dusting? There was also a pair of footmen even now setting the finishing touches in the dining room for when the Schuylers returned with their guests. For what I planned to do, I needed to be careful—and quiet.

Satisfied Cathy kept no supervisory eye on me, I tiptoed up to the first floor. There, I felt tempted to pass through the swinging door and have a look around. What might the main rooms of the house tell me about the Schuylers as a family? Wishing to avoid the footmen, I resisted the urge and kept going to the second floor, where the main bedrooms were located.

Three doors opened onto the service landing. Through one of them, I spied a sewing room. The second door was locked, and I assumed it was the linen closet. Linens, like the silver, were often kept under lock and key to prevent the servants from being tempted. The third door, unlocked, gave entry into the main corridor. My surroundings immediately and dramatically changed from the plain white walls and wide oak floorboards of the servants' landing to carved plaster ornamentation and a gleaming herringbone-patterned floor over which stretched a costly Persian Heriz runner of deep reds, blues, and greens.

Pausing in the doorway, I stood listening for some moments. All seemed utterly still, the kind of silence only possible in rooms devoid of people. I heard no rustling of bedcovers, no humming of a maid who knows there is no one to hear her.

Closed doors flanked either side of the corridor. For a moment, a sense of defeat swamped me as I considered those doors might be locked. Nevertheless, I proceeded, and to my relief, the first knob turned easily in my hand. I glanced into what appeared to be a guest room, evidenced by an utter lack of personal touches. I closed the door and kept going. Knowing such houses as I did, I found it safe to assume the master's and mistress's bedrooms would be found closest to the main landing, which I could see ahead of me. Directly opposite the stairs was usually a sitting room, often with the owners' bedrooms to either side. I deduced that Miss Imogene's room was one of these here in the corridor.

When I peeked into the room lined in pale green silk accented by lovely white woodwork, I inhaled a floral scent and knew I had found the room I'd been looking for. A bed, with a tall, carved headboard whose center had been upholstered in the same green silk as the walls, dominated the room. I moved past it, searching for insight into the young woman who spent her time here. The room's decorations wouldn't provide that insight, I knew, as the Schuylers were only leasing the house. This wouldn't be the first time I'd opened drawers and peered into cupboards.

And yet, a quick search uncovered no diaries hidden beneath frilly underthings, no photographs tucked away inside well-worn volumes of favorite books. In fact, there were no books at all in the room, not even on the bedside table. The wardrobe revealed an exquisite array of dresses and ball gowns, but nothing secreted behind them.

I went into the adjoining bathroom, where the drawers of a dressing table practically burst with all the usual beauty products—scented soaps and bath salts, facial creams and powders, tinted lip salves and other subtle cosmetics. All were of the finest quality, as were her perfumes, brushes, and combs. I went back into the bedroom, stood at its center, and glanced around me.

The word *temporary* came to mind. Imogene treated this room as the very temporary dwelling it had been meant to be. In my experience, however, it was a rare young woman who didn't bring reminders of home on her travels. My impression became one of an utterly unsentimental individual, one with few or no bonds with either her past or her present. A woman who simply existed, who stood back, indifferent and untouched by the world around her.

Could that be true? I had witnessed her temper, her indignant anger at her fiancé's supposed shenanigans with the actress. Had Imogene merely seen him speaking with her, and decided to use the opportunity to escape a marriage she never wanted? Or had she discovered an ongoing relationship between Jerome and the actress, or multiple women? Whatever Jerome's actions, they had certainly affected Imogene Schuyler.

A second possibility occurred to me: Imogene had taken pains to conceal her true self from whoever might enter this room. Perhaps she merely had her parents in mind, or perhaps she had sought to protect herself from prying eyes outside the family. Why? What did she have to hide? Or was I reading more into it, and her room's lack of individuality only revealed a woman who believed in traveling light?

Based on the array of toiletries in her dressing table and the number of dresses in her wardrobe, I doubted that very much. I'd also come to doubt Miss Powell's claim that her young mistress confided in her about most things. The very nature of this bedroom led me to suspect Imogene Schuyler confided precious little to anyone.

With a sigh, I let myself out of the room. When I perhaps should have retreated downstairs, I went forward, instead, toward the main upper landing.

Upon finding the room that obviously belonged to the lady of the house, I stole inside. The curtains had been closed, and swaths of black fabric draped the mirrors above the mantel, mounted on the dressing table, and the full-length mirror beside it. The rest of the room was in perfect order, much like her daughter's. The bed had been expertly made, the dressers and tabletops cleared of clutter. However, unlike her daughter's room, there were photographs in gilt frames, several books lying on tabletops, and in the pigeonholes of an elegant, gilded writing table, I found both incoming and outgoing correspondence.

I looked through both, sorting through them like decks of cards. Many were letters from friends and family back in Philadelphia. Others regarded household expenses, while still others concerned orders for clothing and accessories. They came from as far away as New York and even Paris. One in particular caught my eye, not because of the contents, an order for a traveling wardrobe that included a good number of pieces, but because of the dates involved. The invoice and accompanying message indicated Mrs. Schuyler would be traveling to Paris in a mere few weeks and would collect her new attire there.

Traveling to Europe in the fall. This struck me as unusual. The time for European trips was in the spring. Nearly the entire Four Hundred left our shores at the first sign of the spring thaw, flocking to France, Italy, and other ports on the Mediterranean.

Had she planned this trip with her husband? With Imogene?

Alone? Leaning over the desk again, I rifled through once more, searching for travel plans. I didn't know if the Schuylers owned a yacht. If not, Delphine might have booked passage on a transatlantic liner. I found no indication of such plans, but that wasn't to say a ticket didn't exist.

Indeed. If Delphine Schuyler had scheduled a trip to Europe without her husband, she might not have wished him to know about it. I suspected her husband would never look through his wife's daily correspondence, and so would not have noticed the invoice and note about her upcoming trip. Travel tickets were another matter. Those she might have believed she needed to hide from prying eyes. But where?

All that was, of course, supposing they hadn't been planning to travel together. Briefly I considered searching the judge's bedroom, but time had passed since I had begun my hunt, and I feared the memorial service would end and everyone would soon return to the house. I'd already pushed my luck as far as I deemed prudent. Then again, I would not have another chance like this one.

Slipping out of the room, I listened for footsteps, voices, or other signs that someone might be sharing the second floor with me. When no sound came, I crossed the landing. As I'd expected, I passed a sitting room, its double doors wide open, the interior furnished with comfortable, overstuffed chintz in bright floral patterns. Another pair of double doors stood to the left of the sitting room, and making nary a sound, I hurried to them.

Neither door budged in response to my efforts. I blew out a breath of disappointment. Mrs. Schuyler must have ordered her husband's rooms locked, perhaps unwilling to have his things disturbed. Some people kept the bedrooms of lost loved ones like shrines, changing nothing, keeping the personal effects just as the deceased had left them. Again my doubts chased that possibility away. If Delphine Schuyler loved her husband so completely, why those dry eyes at Wakehurst when she learned of his fate?

Before I'd relinquished my hold on the polished brass knob, a sound reached my ears. Quickly I darted a glance over my shoulder to the staircase. Seeing no one and hearing no ascending footsteps, I turned away from the doors and started to retrace my route to the back stairs.

A rustling stopped me in my tracks. Once again, I looked behind me and saw nothing. But I decided to waste no further time in looking and hurried along, as fast as I could, without making undue noise.

"You there. What are you doing up here?"

The female voice startled me. It didn't sound like Cathy. Had the housekeeper returned early? I ground to a halt and turned slowly around. The sunlight from the windows at the half landing obscured all but the outlines of the figure standing at the top of the stairs. I could make out no features to put to the voice. Only that she wore all black, the skirt tiered and ruffled, with a tall hat adorned with ribbons and feathers.

Not a servant.

"I asked you a question. What are you doing up here?"

"I . . . um . . . came to straighten up Miss Imogene's bedroom," I stammered, grateful for the shadows of the hallway. This woman's voice sounded familiar . . .

"I was told no one should be upstairs at this time of day. Your mistress is coming shortly with her guests, and you should be below, helping to make sure everything is ready."

"Yes, ma'am." Could she be a relative of the Schuylers'? That would make sense. Only, I hadn't heard of there being

That made me smile, in spite of my current mood. "No. But you're different. You wouldn't let anyone get the best of you, ever. You're strong, Nanny."

"So are you, my lamb, and you know it."

"Usually." I shook my head, unable to quite explain the sensation of powerlessness that had gripped me in that corridor. A horrid notion lodged itself in my brain, along with the memory of a frantic knocking at my door four years ago. "This is how Katie felt, when she worked at The Breakers."

Nanny nodded, but said nothing. Anger simmered behind her spectacles as she, too, remembered the night Katie had been thrown out of The Breakers. Katie's fate had been that of many maids, and many more to come, unless society changed.

But I hadn't gone to the Schuylers' residence to prove a point. I had gone to see what I could find out about the Schuyler women. I told Nanny about the two bedrooms I explored, and about what I had found in Delphine's writing desk.

"An off-season trip to Europe could signify any number of things," Nanny observed. "But I agree, it's unusual."

"Do you think it could mean she'd been planning to leave her husband? Especially in light of what some of the servants insinuated. Cathy in particular. The arguing she heard from upstairs bothered her more than it did the others."

"She wasn't used to it." Nanny's expression turned sad. "Poor dear. It can't be easy for her, being so far from home. But aren't you forgetting something, Emma? Something about Mrs. Schuyler?"

"I'm not sure what you're getting at." I removed one of the pins in my apron that had been pricking my skin through my dress. "I know her mostly by reputation. I haven't had much direct experience with any of the Schuylers."

Nanny raised a finger and tapped it at the air. "Think back to when your aunt Alva left her first husband."

I thought back to that great scandal of four years ago, and then gasped. "My goodness, I *had* forgotten. Delphine Schuyler was one of Aunt Alva's most vocal critics at the time, as much as Aunt Alice. She put the blame for the divorce squarely on Aunt Alva's shoulders and said women like Aunt Alva would be responsible for the unraveling of America's moral fabric." I came to my feet, spurred by indignation. "Society would have shunned Aunt Alva, anyway, but Mrs. Schuyler made matters worse by bringing up Aunt Alva's 'shame,' as she described it, every chance she got."

Nanny reached up and took my hand, drawing me back down on the couch beside her. "It's unlikely, then, that she would risk becoming a social outcast herself by leaving her husband."

"Perhaps she thought that by simply leaving him, but not divorcing him, she could avoid a scandal." But I quickly discounted that notion. "No, if she had done that, he could have cut her off without a cent. No, the only way out of an unhappy marriage for Delphine Schuyler would have been . . ."

My gaze met Nanny's, and she finished my thought. "As a widow."

Chapter 10

The next afternoon, I sat near the statue of Oliver Hazard Perry in Washington Square and kept my eye on the Opera House doors. There was to be a performance in a week's time. The marquee advertised John Philip Sousa's comic opera *The Bride Elect*. I knew only that it involved two rival kingdoms on the Isle of Capri, and that it included a large cast.

I hoped Burt Covey was one of them.

While I sat, a parade of individuals marched through my mind. Imogene Schuyler, who didn't wish to marry Jerome Harrington. Delphine Schuyler, who had been heard to argue with her husband, and who had plans to be in Paris within the next few weeks. Jerome Harrington, who perhaps acted out of rage if Judge Schuyler had agreed to call off his daughter's wedding. The mystery guest at James Van Alen's fete, who may have stolen the clothing he wore from Max Oberlin's tailor shop. I added another name: Clarice O'Shea, who might have wished to sabotage the marriage of Miss Schuyler and Mr. Harrington.

Had Burt Covey seen anything that night? Had he deliberately avoided Ethan and me out of fear of angering a killer?

The doors opened and men and women streamed out onto the sidewalk. I sighed with relief. I had risked missing them if they had exited by the rear stage doors, but I had wagered on their wishing to catch the trolleys or shop in town. They came in twos and threes, their voices and laughter drifting to me where I sat. The afternoon sun lit the square, much as theater lights lit the stage, and I studied each face as it appeared. But it was Burt Covey's stocky build that identified him to me.

He walked with a man and a woman, both of whom towered over him. I supposed his shorter stature and muscled frame was what allowed him to perform somersaults from a standing position without any apparent effort. Once they'd cleared the park, they separated, the man and woman heading north on Thames Street, and Mr. Covey crossing the square toward the trolley stop. I waited until he reached the far sidewalk before hurrying out of the park gates.

When the trolley came, I watched Burt Covey board it and hand his coin to the trolley master. I jumped in through the rear and silently praised my good luck, as most of the seats were vacant. The driver rang the bell and we glided forward on the tracks.

After paying my fee, I moved closer to Mr. Covey. As a matter of fact, I sat right next to him. He attempted to contract his person to put space between us, as I had no doubt annoyed him for sitting so close in an almost-empty vehicle.

I turned to his profile. "Mr. Covey?"

He started and whipped his face around toward mine. "What? Who are you?"

"Sorry to startle you, Mr. Covey. My name is Emma Cross." I spoke in a low voice to avoid attracting the interest of the few other passengers. "I attended the fete at Wake-hurst the other night. Perhaps you remember me?"

"No, I don't remember you. There were a lot of people there." He seemed to recognize his mistake as soon as he finished speaking, for a look of regret fell over his features.

"Then you *are* the actor who played the jester."

He exhaled and faced front again. "Yes. Now leave me alone."

"I'm sorry, Mr. Covey, I only wish to ask you a few questions."

"You're not a policeman."

"No, but I *am* a reporter. For the *Newport Messenger*. Perhaps you've read it?"

"I'm not much for newspapers."

The response, although not an uncommon one, never failed to raise my hackles. How could someone live in this world and not care to know what was happening in it?

Gathering my patience, I said, "It doesn't matter. What does is that you were everywhere that night. You might have seen something significant, even if you don't realize it. I only wish to ask—"

With a lurch, the trolley paused at its next stop, near Bowen's Wharf on Thames Street. Burt Covey leaped to his feet, squeezed by me, and, without another word, exited to the street. I had barely a moment to recover before the trolley started to roll forward again. Grabbing a nearby pole, I sprang up and made for the door, leaping down to the cobbled street from the moving car and nearly tumbling to the ground. As it was, I barely kept my footing and managed to twist my ankle in the process.

"Mr. Covey!" I cried out.

He had reached the sidewalk and was barreling along, heedless of the individuals who had to sidestep him or be struck down. With little choice, I bit down against the pain gripping my ankle and took off after him—not quite at a run, but at a painfully brisk walk.

"Mr. Covey, I will follow you home if you do not stop and speak with me. I'll be at the theater again tomorrow. Please stop."

About a dozen yards ahead, he came to a halt, his back to me, his shoulders heaving from his effort to evade me. I limped along until I reached him. "What was that all about? One would think you had something to hide, Mr. Covey."

He looked everywhere, but at me—at the storefronts to one side of Thames Street, then across wharves on the other side and out over the ships bobbing in the harbor. "I'm a simple actor, Miss Cross. I don't want any problems."

"I don't intend to give you any."

At this, he finally swiveled his head until he faced me. "Really? You already are, I'll have you know."

"Mr. Covey, if you tell me what you witnessed that night, I promise I'll leave you in peace."

"And if I did happen to see something, which I didn't, but if I did, and I tell you, do you think that man's killer will leave me in peace?"

"Yes." At his contemptuous expression, I clarified, "Because he'll be in prison. As it is now, he's free to murder again. Are you saying you saw who killed Clayton Schuyler?"

He stared into my eyes a good long moment. I noticed his were blue and razor sharp in their intensity. I had no doubt Burt Covey was a keen observer of the world, as many actors are, and reporters are as well. He knew something from that night at Wakehurst; of that, I was certain.

"I am *not* saying that. Fine, you may ask your questions, Miss Cross. But on my terms and where I say."

"All right. Where shall we go?"

He took off along the waterfront again, forcing me to

limp after him at a quicker pace than my poor ankle would have preferred. He easily skirted a puddle of spilled fish guts, while I nearly went down. Only the sheer force of my will, and a strong disinclination to stink of fish for the rest of the day, prevented me from falling. I pleaded in vain for him to slow down, and received no response when I again inquired where we were going. He gave me no choice but to keep up or go home.

We were nearing the corner of Bath Road when he abruptly stopped and waited for me to catch up. When I had, he gestured with his elbow to the door on his left. "In here."

He'd brought me to a pub called the Topside Tavern, not the roughest one in Newport, but not a place I would have patronized had I been alone. He opened the door and waited for me to precede him inside.

"Why have you tried to dodge me, Mr. Covey?"

He raised his pint of ale and drank, then lowered it to the tabletop. I sipped my tea. We sat in a corner near the front window. At the bar, several men sat, quietly talking; a few of the other tables were occupied by both men and women, who were eating lunch. It was a group of workaday people enjoying some time to themselves.

Burt Covey leaned slightly forward, as if to drive his point home, and repeated his concern. "I don't want trouble."

"I don't mean to give you any," I replied a second time. "But a man was killed at Wakehurst, and we all need to do our part to see justice done for him."

"Why?" He raised his pewter mug to his lips and peered at me as I groped for a reply.

"Because that's what honest people do, Mr. Covey."

"Honest people mind their business, Miss Cross. I'm an actor, and not a well-off one. I certainly don't need my name showing up in the newspapers for the wrong reasons. You want to review one of my performances? You go right ahead. Other than that, I want to be left alone."

I crossed my arms in front of me. "For a jester, you certainly can be surly."

"I'm not a jester. I'm an actor who was paid to play a jester. If you like, you can pay me to play the part of an eager witness."

"Mr. Covey, what harm could it do you to tell me whether or not you saw something suspicious that night?"

"I could tell you I didn't, and whether I did or didn't, you'd have to take my word for it, wouldn't you?"

Stubborn man. He was leading me in circles, and he knew it. I narrowed my eyes at him and realized I should have expected to be bested by a man who utilized words to make his living. As a reporter, I did as well, but I used words to relay facts and tell the truth. Burt Covey used them to create illusions and entrance his audience.

Tamping down my frustration, I inhaled a deep breath and started again. "Mr. Covey, let's start with the argument you helped me break up near the stage."

He frowned and shook his head. "What argument?"

"It was between my cousin, Cornelius Vanderbilt the younger, and a tall, rather rough-looking man in a suit of clothes that fit him a bit too tightly. I was attempting to draw my cousin away before things took a violent turn, and when he wouldn't budge, you suddenly appeared and distracted him. After that, I was able to extricate him from the situation."

"Oh, that argument." He waved his cup in the air, a signal to the barkeep to bring a refill.

"Did you happen to notice where that man went immediately afterward?"

"Your cousin?"

"Mr. Covey, please—"

He laughed and leaned over the table on his crossed arms. "All right, Miss Cross. Let me think . . ." His exaggerated show of considering the matter sorely taxed my patience. I was about to give up and storm out, when he frowned slightly and opened his mouth to speak. "As a matter of fact, I did notice him again—the gent whose clothes didn't rightly fit him. It was while the rest of the guests were hurrying over to see the joust. He seemed to be going in the wrong direction. At the time, I didn't think much of it." His gaze suddenly sharpened. "Come to think of it, I also saw you moving in the wrong direction. Where were *you* going?"

His tone did more than insinuate, it accused. But again, I realized he sought to bait me and undermine my confidence. It wouldn't work. "I didn't wish to see the joust," I told him. "The idea of putting animals at such a risk is appalling to me. But tell me more about what this man did, and where he went."

"I saw him climb the steps to the veranda."

My pulse quickened at this news. "When? Was it before or after the joust began?"

"Before, I'd say. When everyone was still heading to the other side of the hedge."

"Where were you at the time?"

"By the stage, talking to the other actors and taking down the set."

"Did you see how long he stayed up there?"

"Sorry, no. Never noticed him again. Maybe he left. Maybe he made himself invisible."

"Very funny." I sat back and thought. The man in the ill-fitting suit had attended the fete under suspicious circumstances. Why had he gone up to the veranda? To leave the fete by exiting through the house? My guess was, he hadn't come through the house upon his arrival, but instead had sneaked in somewhere along the perimeter of the grounds. It only seemed logical that he would leave by the same means.

That brought me back to his reason for being there. To commit murder? Even a killer could not have imagined the coming together of events to provide such an opportunity. First the archery equipment was stowed on the veranda. Then Judge Schuyler went behind the house to smoke his cigar . . .

Then again, who gave the judge that cigar? The murderer, most likely, someone who knew his wife wouldn't have approved and that he would have to smoke it in secret. Perhaps it hadn't been divine providence at work that night, but a clever killer who had learned of Mr. Van Alen's plans and took full advantage of them.

"You're certain it was the same individual who argued with my cousin?" I asked Mr. Covey.

"Reasonably certain. It was dark near the veranda."

"*Hmm*, true." I decided to change the subject, for the moment. "How well do you know Miss O'Shea?"

"Clarice O'Shea?"

"Yes, the actress who was dressed like Titania that night."

"Is she a suspect?"

"No, Mr. Covey, she is not." I said this with absolutely certainty—in my voice. However, if Clarice O'Shea had been carrying on with Jerome Harrington, she could not be ruled out as a suspect. She might have seen dispensing with the judge as the only sure way of stopping Jerome's marriage to Imogene. "Do you know if she has been seeing a young man named Jerome Harrington?"

" 'Seeing'?" He scowled. "Is that your polite way of asking if she's been sleeping with him? That's what most of you upright citizens think of actors, isn't it?"

"I don't mean that at all." At least, not necessarily, I acknowledged to myself. "I merely wish to know if she and Mr. Harrington are friendly."

He smirked. "You'll have to ask her."

"Fair enough." I had little doubt Mr. Covey would warn his theater mate to expect me soon. I could only hope I would find her in a cooperative mood. "Did you see anyone else walking away from the joust to another part of the gardens?"

"Come to think of it, there was that young fellow, the one who looked like he walked into a door." He placed his palm against his cheek.

Jerome Harrington, who had been struck by Imogene Schuyler only moments earlier. "And where did he go?"

"Couldn't say for sure. Toward the house, at least that end of the garden, but I didn't pay attention after he passed the stage."

"Anyone else?" When he shook his head no, I switched back to the subject of my initial queries. "About that man who, you say, climbed the veranda steps. Did you happen to notice him at other times during the evening? Did he seem to have issues with anyone else?"

"Not that I saw. But he certainly didn't seem to think highly of Mr. Vanderbilt."

"No, he didn't. Are you sure you didn't see him approach Judge Schuyler?"

"Not that I saw, no." He studied his ale, then sighed. "What a medieval way to go." He pantomimed holding a bow and shooting an arrow. "But fitting, considering the night's theme."

"Yes, I suppose whoever murdered Judge Schuyler possesses a keen sense of the dramatic." Someone like an actor, I couldn't help thinking. I came to my feet. "Thank you, Mr. Covey, I appreciate your taking the time to speak with me."

"Did I have any other choice?"

I smiled down at him. "Good luck at the performance next week. I understand it's a rousing musical. You are to perform in it, yes?"

"As an extra. Why don't you come?"

"Hmm. Perhaps I will, if there are any tickets left."

Before I took a step to leave, he stood. "You going to give my name to the police?"

"No, Mr. Covey. The police have made it quite clear they don't need or want my advice on whom they should interview."

His smirk reappeared. "If that's what they think, they're fools."

Questioning Clarice O'Shea would have to wait. A stack of Associated Press articles delivered from the telegraph office kept me busy during the remaining afternoon hours. The day before, there had been a riot in Carterville, Illinois, involving union and nonunion miners, that had ended in several deaths. Besides many of our summer cottagers being heavily invested in coal, what made this of special interest to Newporters was the connection to Mr. Stuyvesant Fish of Crossways. Mr. Fish served as president of the Illinois Central Railroad, and it seemed the shooting had occurred in the Carterville terminal of the Illinois Central.

The very word *union* resonated inside me. Judge Schuyler had pronounced judgment in favor of union demands, to the detriment of business owners and investors. Perhaps this incident yesterday had no connection to that judgment, but the coincidence nudged at my instincts.

After gathering and writing up the facts that came in from several sources, I collected Maestro and my borrowed trap and set out for Ocean Avenue, as Crossways sat not far from my own Gull Manor. I took Bellevue Avenue south and made the turn onto Ocean Avenue, near the tip of the island.

Beachmound, a white mansion that gazed down on Bailey's Beach from a high perch, looked so like Crossways, with its grand portico and wide columns, that visitors often mistook one for the other and arrived for balls at the wrong house. I passed Beachmound and soon arrived at the long driveway of Crossways.

Mr. and Mrs. Fish were expecting me, as I had telephoned ahead and spoken with the butler. Had I been anyone else, I doubt they would have seen me, but Mrs. Fish and I had forged a kind of friendship the previous summer. I supposed she persuaded her husband I wouldn't take up too much of his time.

I was shown into the enclosed porch at the west side of the house. The windows stood open to the ocean breezes, and the scents of late flowers drifted in from the adjoining garden—the same garden where a body had been found last summer. Mr. and Mrs. Fish joined me a few minutes later; Mrs. Fish wore a diaphanous afternoon dress of autumnal oranges and golds trimmed with lace. She sat across from me, while Mr. Fish, looking weary and solemn, took the seat beside mine.

"What can I do for you, Miss Cross? I suppose you'd like a quote about the Carterville incident?"

I regarded the signs of sleeplessness in his shadowed eyes and nodded apologetically. "I'm sorry to bother you now—"

"No, it's your job, and it *was* my railroad where the executions took place."

I flinched at the word he used to describe the deaths. "Is that how you see it?"

"These union disputes in Illinois have been going on for a long while, but especially the past year," Mrs. Fish put in. She sounded angry. "No one has done anything to defuse the situation."

"Yes, but 'execution'?"

Mr. Fish cleared his throat loudly, but Mrs. Fish waved a hand at him. "Perhaps the information you saw didn't mention this, but the union and nonunion miners were divided according to race. Only white workers were members of the union. Only Negro men were killed."

This disclosure struck me like a slap to the face. "No, what I read didn't include that."

"Well, it should have." Mrs. Fish harrumphed.

That certainly explained Mr. Fish's pained expression.

"Sir, would you like to add anything? I understand the Illinois Central isn't at fault in this matter, but will the company be taking any precautions to make sure nothing like this ever happens again at one of its facilities?"

"I'm afraid there's not much we can do." He stared down at his feet before meeting my gaze. "But there is something I can do personally. I own stock in the Carterville mine, and a lot of other mines around the country."

I nodded. Most of the Four Hundred owned stock in all types of mining.

"As an investor, I can put pressure on shareholders and management to address union issues." He shook his head as if disgusted by the matter. "I don't know if it'll do any good, but any fool should be able to see a mine can't turn a good profit if its workers are shooting each other."

"Do you think they should stop hiring the nonunionists?" I asked him bluntly. I waited in some apprehension for his answer. If the circumstances had caused racial tensions, weren't union policies in not extending membership to Negro workers to blame? It seemed to me the problem ran deeper than simple mine management and extended further afield than the mining industry.

Could matters of race have played into Judge Schuyler's decision as well?

"What I think, Miss Cross, is that men—all men—should

recent—he had angered someone enough to commit murder. Could it have been a member of his own family? A friend or acquaintance? Or, perhaps, a leader of industry, who hadn't appreciated the judge's ruling that favored the workers over profit? And that included just about every gentlemen of the Four Hundred.

Chapter 11

I left Crossways feeling listless and unsettled, and wondering why, when the wealthy and poor mixed in any way, the poor always suffered to one degree or another. Yes, the wealthy put the poor to work and supplied them with the means of earning a wage, but too often the problems accompanying that employment were ignored until something terrible happened.

Something like seven men lying dead of gunshot wounds.

When I arrived home, Katie came out to help me unhitch the trap and settle Maestro with a cooling sponge bath, a thorough brushing, and a hearty meal of oats and hay. We spent some time with Barney as well. Poor Barney, too old and frail now to pull a carriage, but still my sweet boy. I had refused to "put him out to pasture," as the polite euphemism put it, but for a time, I had also fretted over the expense of keeping an animal that no longer served a practical purpose. Nanny had helped me settle the matter.

"Emma," she asked me bluntly one day last spring, "do you love that horse?"

"I do, Nanny. He's been a loyal companion to me, and to Aunt Sadie before me."

"Then he serves a purpose, doesn't he?"

I had contemplated her lined face; her steel-gray hair, which she still bothered to set in rags every night so it would curl; and her kindly, if near-sighted, eyes. Whenever I looked at Nanny—really looked at her and acknowledged how much she had aged in recent years—my heart would ache. Yes, whether horse or human, my old friends were precious to me and I would do everything in my power to see that they were happy and well cared for.

Thanks to Uncle Cornelius, keeping Barney would no longer be cause for financial concern.

"The carpenter was out this morning, Miss Emma," Katie told me as we finished up with the horses and headed to the house. The setting sun ignited the waves and tossed a lovely golden hue across the rear of the property. Katie shielded her eyes with her hand. "Those shutters won't bang in the wind anymore."

I nodded absently, my thoughts drifting back to my conversation with Mrs. Fish.

"And he offered to come back and attend to anything inside the house that might need fixing. Miss Emma?"

"What?" I shook my head to clear it, breathing in the briny ocean air, heavily laden with the scents of the outgoing tide. "Sorry, Katie. What was that? Something about the house?"

Katie put her hands on her hips. "Miss Emma, is something wrong?"

I shook my head, and we went inside. After pecking Nanny's cheek in greeting and allowing Patch to prop his front paws on me so I could pet him and give him a hug, I wandered to the front of the house. A sensation niggled at me, though I felt hard-pressed to identify it.

I moved into the dining room doorway and began surveying the contents of the room. There had been a fire in here
last summer, and quite a lot of restoration work had been
necessary to rid the walls and furniture of the reek of smoke.
New curtains, new cushions on the chairs, all compliments
of Nanny's sewing talents. The window had been refitted
with new woodwork. The walls had been freshly painted.
We rarely used the dining room, preferring to take our meals
either in the morning room or at the wide, round kitchen
table. Now, as I studied the improvements, I couldn't help
considering how that money might have been better spent.

Next I crossed the hall, entered the parlor, and lit a kero-
sene lamp. Here was quite a different story from the dining
room. With the damage not having extended this far, there
had been no need to refurbish. The hooked rug in front of
the sofa showed worn patches and frayed edges. The sofa itself sagged here, bulged there, while threads hung loose and
the upholstery in places had faded beyond recognition.

I turned around, viewing the scuffed floorboards of the
hall, partly hidden by another faded and worn area rug. A
decision was forming in my mind.

"Deciding on what you'll replace first?" Nanny shuffled
down the corridor from the kitchen, smiling at me as she approached. "You can afford to make this place shine now,
Emma."

"I can," I agreed, and turned once more to view the parlor.
"Aunt Sadie refurnished this place after she inherited it from
my great-grandparents. Oh, she didn't replace everything,
but she made modifications here and there that made the
house her own."

"You told me she packed up everything that reminded her
of her sister."

"Yes, her twin," I said with a sigh. "Aunt Sadie couldn't
endure the reminders after my grandmother died." Aunt

Sadie and my maternal grandmother, Abbie, had been fraternal twins, but had looked so much alike that people had often confused them. Aunt Sadie had remained single by choice her entire life, but Abbie married my grandfather, Jonathan Stanhope, and had my mother and then her younger brothers and sisters. Only my mother had reached adulthood, and shortly after she married Stuart Braden Gale III, my half brother's father, my maternal grandparents left Newport to move west, to Ohio.

Mother told me a telegram had arrived only two weeks later, telling of a train accident . . .

"So, what have you decided to do first?"

Nanny's question cleared the cobwebs from my mind. I blinked and brought the room back into focus. "Nothing."

"Whatever does that mean?"

I took Nanny's hand and led her to the parlor sofa. Once we'd settled, I said, "It means what you think it does. Nanny, I've realized that, other than necessary repairs to keep the place from falling down around our heads, I can't spend Uncle Cornelius's money on luxuries. Not even to make this house presentable to outsiders."

"I see," she said quietly. Her gaze traveled the room, stopping here and there for a moment before moving on. "It's certainly your decision to make, and I've always been happy with the house as it is. But I'm curious. What changed your mind?" She looked me directly in the eye. "Is it because you don't feel you earned that money?"

I chuckled at how well Nanny knew me. "Yes, partly." I stared down at her wrinkled hand, still lying in mine. "A story came over the wire today." I explained about the miners' dispute and the men who had died. And then I related my conversation with Mrs. Fish. "It all reminded me that money like this, whether it's from Uncle Cornelius or some other member of the Four Hundred, was made at the expense of others. Yes, the Vanderbilts have done a lot of good with their wealth, but while they've helped some people with their philanthropy, they've hurt others, or at least ignored their needs."

"That's the way of the world, I'm afraid."

I nodded at the truth of that. "How can I fancy up my house with that money? How can I think about luxuries when others are deprived of their basic necessities because they're paid too little or excluded from the unions that control the workers' rights to earn a living?"

I'd leaned my cheek against Nanny's shoulder as I asked this last question, and now the loose curls that escaped her coif tickled my brow as she shook her head. "You can't. Other people would, but not my Emma. Not my lamb."

"You don't mind?" I raised my head from her shoulder.

"Didn't I just say I've always been happy with this house the way it is? Who would we be impressing, anyway? Derrick? He doesn't care, he only sees how beautiful you are."

"I'm not," I protested with a snort. "I'm plain, as plain as this parlor."

"Don't argue with me, child. Nanny knows best."

I embraced her for that.

"So, what *are* you going to do with the money?" Nanny asked. "Give it back?"

I shook my head. "Alfred and the others would consider it a mere pittance, nothing compared to their millions. And it would hardly make a difference to Neily's situation. No, I'm going to increase my donations to St. Nicholas, for one." St. Nicholas Orphanage in Providence housed both boys and girls and was always in need of funds. I'd been supporting them for years whenever I could, whether it be sending small sums I could spare or encouraging Newport's wealthy population, especially the ladies, to raise funds for them. "Perhaps something like a scholarship fund for women, or . . .

I don't know. I must think about it. But, Nanny, I'm feeling better already. That money had been weighing heavily on me and I didn't even realize it until today. I only knew I didn't like thinking about the money, or talking about it."

As I left off, Patch came streaming into the room and went straight to the front window. Rearing up on his hind legs and propping his front paws on the window seat, he craned his neck and barked. Not a full-out bark, but half under his breath, as though he were assessing a situation that made him uneasy.

Nanny and I exchanged glances. We had learned never to dismiss Patch's warnings. But *was* this a warning, or merely a few birds or squirrels Patch believed needed a good talking-to?

I rose and went to the window. With my hand on the back of his neck, I moved the lacy curtain out of the way and peered outside. Dusk had draped the front yard in soft tones of purple and gray, yet I could make out enough to see that nothing seemed out of the ordinary. Patch's hackles rose and a growl vibrated against my fingertips.

"What is it, boy?" I glanced at Nanny over my shoulder. "He must hear something that worries him."

"I don't hear a thing," she said with a shrug. "It's probably a hawk or a fox skulking about."

"Perhaps. I'm going to have a look. Come on, Patch." I hurried around to the front door. Patch kept pace with me, and when I opened the door, he sprang out and bounded down the drive. I followed, kicking at my skirts with my rapid steps.

We were halfway to the road when I heard it—an urgent clopping, underscored by a rumbling that could not have been caused by the wheels of a carriage. An automobile, to be sure. I'd heard enough of them during the year I spent living in New York City, and only weeks ago, Newport had seen its first auto parade, organized by my aunt Alva. Many of those vehicles continued to inhabit the island, often speeding along our lanes and screeching around corners, startling people and animals alike. No wonder the sounds, inaudible at first to human ears, had set Patch on alert.

Through the trees that bordered the front of my property, I glimpsed a single-horse curricle as it sped by. It appeared to be driven by a man in a top hat, his hands fisted around the reins. In the evening shadows, I could make out no more than that. Man and vehicle quickly disappeared from my view as they headed east along Ocean Avenue toward Bailey's Beach. A few seconds later, the motorcar whizzed in and out of view at the end of the driveway. Patch had almost reached the road, but now he yelped and pulled back, his feathery tail curling between his legs. I ran to him, took hold of his collar, and continued to the road. A terrible apprehension gripped me.

At the pace the two vehicles were traveling, this could be no friendly pursuit. Motorcars did not, in my experience, race with carriages. Nor did they speed along winding, twisting ocean lanes riddled with sudden hills, potholes, and blind corners—at least, not when driven by responsible individuals. All this added up to a dangerous situation in my opinion, and my hunch proved correct when a terrible crash reached my ears.

"Emma, what is all that racket?" Nanny called to me from the open doorway. Katie stood behind her, peering over her shoulder.

"I'm not sure, but I think there's been an accident," I called back. With that, I hoisted my skirts and started along the road at a run. Patch once more kept up with me, but this time rather than springing ahead, he stayed at my side. The road brought me around a corner and up a hill. Then, turning once again, the road sloped downward and opened onto broad views on both sides. The motorcar raced along a good quarter mile away now, while the carriage . . .

I surged forward with a burst of speed. Horse and carriage had veered off the road and tipped onto a narrow strip of rocky beach, which would not have existed at high tide. The horse, on its side, thrashed against the sand and fought the traces and shafts that held it to the vehicle. I experienced a moment's indecision. The man lay on his side as well, having been thrown several feet from the carriage seat. At first, he lay unmoving, and a horrible dread filled me, but then he stirred, his movements crunching against the shell- and pebble-strewn sand. He placed the flats of his hands beneath him to lever himself upright.

Seeing that he was at least conscious and capable of moving, I followed my instincts and went to the horse. It continued to struggle, and my fears mounted that it would harm itself. To the man, I called out, "Are you hurt? Is anything broken?"

He had managed to sit up, albeit shakily. His head sagged between his shoulders and he shook it with jerky motions. "I . . . I don't think I'm badly injured. Wh . . . what happened?"

I didn't take the time to explain. Urgency drove me as I crouched beside the horse and ran my palm down its broad and muscular neck. "There, there. It's all right. I'm here to help you. Patch, come." When my dog complied, I gently nudged him near the other animal's head and bade him to sit. I hoped blocking the horse's view of his surroundings might help calm him.

"Sir, can you stand? Can you help me?" I'd gone to work unbuckling the many straps, girths, and backbands that connected the horse to the gig. "We need to reach beneath him if we're to free him from his harness."

"Good heavens, yes." Without coming completely to his

feet, the man scrambled crablike across the sand until he crouched across the animal's bulk from me. The horse had ceased its thrashing, but continued to strain against its bonds. Its master did as I had, stroking its neck and speaking soothing words in a voice that hadn't quite regained its steadiness. He winced as he dug his hands down into the sand and shells to unbuckle the straps beneath the animal. "There, there, girl, it's all right."

"I think that's everything now," I said as the last strap slid free. "She should be able to move safely." The man nodded, and I had a clear view of his face for the first time. I gasped in recognition. "Mr. Gould?"

He nodded as he grasped the mare's bridle and carefully rose to his feet, gently urging the horse to do likewise. I stepped back out of the way as the animal maneuvered her feet beneath her and heaved her body to a standing position. As soon as she had, she instantly calmed. Patch let out a friendly bark and wagged his tail.

George Jay Gould ran his hands over the horse, from her nose to her rump, and down each leg in turn. Despite blood trickling from cuts on two of her legs, she patiently endured his probing. "Good God, it's a miracle, but I don't believe she's broken any bones."

"The backs of your hands are bleeding," I pointed out. He raised his hands to glance at them and shrugged.

"It doesn't matter, as long as she's all right." Handsome George Gould, his normally neatly cropped brown hair standing up every which way, even his carefully trimmed, curling mustache askew above his lip, continued comforting his horse. The fact that such a man—the principal shareholder of three railroads, yachting sportsman, and youthful millionaire—had been run off the road this way filled me with astonishment.

"It's a miracle neither you nor the horse was killed, Mr. Gould. What on earth was that all about?"

He seemed only now to take an interest in me, or, rather, in who I might be. "Do I know you? You seem familiar."

"You have probably seen me at events here in town. Or perhaps at the homes of my relatives, the Vanderbilts. My name is Emma Cross."

"Ah, yes, the lady reporter." His gaze swept my length. If it held judgment, I couldn't decipher it. "And how do you come to be here, at just this right time?"

Did I hear a note of suspicion in his question? Did he believe that, having spied his wild chase, I had followed for the sake of a story? "I live nearby," I said defensively, my dander up. I pointed to Patch. "My dog heard the ruckus your carriage and that motorcar were making, and when I looked out . . . well . . . I couldn't believe what I saw. Carriage or automobile, it's madness to drive so recklessly on this particular road. I would think you'd know that, Mr. Gould."

"I do know it, Miss Cross," he countered with a grimace. "Believe me, it wasn't by choice. At least, not on my part."

I couldn't fault him for sounding peeved with me. More gently, I asked, "Who was in that motorcar? Why was he following you so closely?"

"I wish I knew. I had turned out of the Morgans' place, Beacon Rock, and was on my way to Greystone for a dinner party with the Wysongs. My wife was to join me there later. Suddenly I noticed the motorcar pull up behind me. I tried slowing and pulling to the side, but he showed no interest in passing me. For a while, he seemed bent on harassing me, pulling up close and then backing away again. My first thought was that it was Reggie Vanderbilt—your own cousin, Miss Cross. I'd heard the young whelp had managed to persuade his father to buy him a . . . but no . . . I realized it couldn't be him, not with the funeral only days past."

"No, there you are right, Mr. Gould. None of the family, except Neily, is in Newport at the moment. Then you have no idea who chased you? Who sent you off the road?" *Who might have been trying to kill you?* I left that particular thought unspoken, but it nonetheless lodged firmly in my brain. As firmly as . . .

An arrow hitting its mark. Chills traveled down my back, and I wrapped my arms around myself to conceal them. I also realized that as the last of the sun dipped below the horizon, a chill edged the ocean breezes.

"I haven't the foggiest," he replied. "But when I find out . . ."

"As I said, Mr. Gould, I live nearby. We should get you and your horse there and call the police. And a doctor. You said your wife is in town with you? She'll want to know about this as well."

"The devil take the doctor, but I'd feel worlds better if a veterinarian looked over Maribelle. A deuced good carriage horse, she is. I'd surely loathe seeing her lamed from some unseen injury."

"All right, then, we'll telephone Dr. Ashford. He lives not far from here and operates his surgery from his home. About your wife, sir," I persisted.

"Yes, Edith—Mrs. Gould—is here on the island with me. She's been at Ochre Court all afternoon. A charity gathering. As I said, she was—is—to meet me at Greystone later."

"I'll make sure we send a message to her, then."

"Yes, very good, Miss Cross. Now, do lead the way. The sooner my mare is seen by a veterinarian, the better." With a cluck to Maribelle, Mr. Gould took a step, uttered a groan, and clutched his left side.

"What is it?"

"Blasted ribs. Didn't hurt until just now."

"You might have broken one or more in the fall. Perhaps they're only bruised. If you wait here, I could hurry home and telephone for an ambulance wagon."

"No, no. There's not a thing to be done for broken ribs except to bind them. No, Miss Cross, we'll stick to my plan." He sucked in a breath and slowly straightened. Even in the growing darkness, the strain showed in the tightness of his features and the perspiration that beaded his brow. Quite unapologetically, he slung an arm around my shoulders. With his other hand, he reached out to grasp Maribelle's bridle. "Come along, girl."

The horse moved willingly enough, but before we had stepped back onto the road, Mr. Gould stopped. "See any sign of my hat, Miss Cross?"

I scanned the beach, then looked out over the darkened waves and realized it might be forever lost. "No, I'm afraid I don't. Perhaps we'll find it along the road on the way to my house."

"I do hope so." His voiced hitched as his ribs apparently pained him again. "It's a damned fine beaver hat and I'd hate to lose it."

Katie gently cleaned the abrasions on the backs of George Gould's hands and wrapped them in linen strips in a way that still allowed him the use of his fingers. Poor Katie blushed the entire time, disconcerted at being in such close proximity to a man of George Gould's social stature. To his credit, he neither said nor did anything to increase her chagrin, but submitted to her ministrations calmly and without fuss.

But then, Mr. Gould had taken a decidedly cavalier attitude toward his accident—if one could call it that, which I did not. He claimed his side no longer ached as much as it initially had; so, yes, the ribs probably were only bruised, and he had declared that no real harm had been done. Dr. Ashford spent nearly a half hour examining Maribelle and, to both Mr. Gould's and my vast relief, he had confirmed an absence of broken bones and declared the animal to be in fit health.

Nanny supplied us with a pot of strong tea and included a

batch of raisin scones. Accepting the tea, but waving away the offer of food, Mr. Gould soon apparently had a change of heart and consumed nearly the entire dozen Nanny had arranged on the plate. While he ate, he speculated on why his mystery pursuer had behaved in such an uncivilized manner. A drunkard? A youth out to prove some ridiculous point or to rebel against his father's rules? A thief who had stolen the vehicle and was desperate to get away?

It took some persuasion on my part to finally convince him of the wisdom of summoning the police. He had dismissed my urgings until I finally reminded him that Maribelle might have been seriously injured or worse, and shouldn't the culprit be brought to justice? Only then did he consent to my telephoning into town.

With the police promising to be on their way, Mr. Gould remembered that he had been expected somewhere tonight. "I must tell the Wysongs not to hold up dinner for me and to let my wife know I've been delayed. Have you a footman you can send, Miss Cross?"

I chuckled. "I'm afraid I don't have any footmen, but you're welcome to use my telephone."

"Ah." He strode from the parlor into the hall, one arm holding his side. He had seen me use the device to telephone Dr. Ashford, so I needn't direct him to the alcove beneath the stairs. When he arrived there, however, he lifted the ear trumpet and spoke into the receiver. "Hello? Hello?" I had followed him into the hall. After a moment, he turned to me. "It doesn't appear to be working."

I suppressed a smile at the thought that George Jay Gould, like many leaders of American industry, did not know the proper way to operate a telephone. Whether at home or at his place of business, Mr. Gould would have a secretary perform the task of making the connections before handing the call over to his employer.

Joining him in the alcove and making it necessary for him

"He certainly may have been, Mr. Whyte, but there are many investors in my companies. I cannot be expected to know the name of each and every one."

"Then it's safe to say he was not a major stockholder," I suggested.

"Not a major one, no. Those I am aware of." Mr. Gould toyed with the edge of the linen bandage on his left hand. "But see here. Surely, you're not suggesting this prankster tonight wished to 'do me in,' as they say?"

Jesse answered his question with another one. "Who knew you were to dine with the Wysongs tonight?"

"The Morgans of Beacon Rock. My wife. Whomever else the Wysongs invited. My valet. I assure you, none of those people would wish to see the last of me."

Jesse folded his arms over his chest. "Are you certain of that, Mr. Gould?"

Chapter 12

After Mr. Gould and Maribelle left us that evening, Jesse, Scotty, and I discussed new possibilities. We began with what I had learned from Mamie Fish.

"If what both Mrs. Fish and Detective Myers said is true about Clayton Schuyler ruling in favor of workers' rights," I said, "it makes it less likely the person who shot that arrow into him needed to steal evening attire. He could have afforded to purchase his own."

Jesse nodded, but Scotty looked dubious. "You believe the killer is a member of the Schuylers' own class?"

"They kill, too," Jesse reminded his assistant.

"When they have what they believe is a good enough reason," I agreed, and added, "like anyone else."

Scotty remained unconvinced. "If his own people were unhappy about the ruling, why not simply use their money to influence the next election and have him removed from the bench?"

I considered that. "It could have been a matter of seizing an unexpected opportunity, that of the archery equipment having been left on the veranda. Anyone could have seen the footmen carrying it up there. Then when the judge walked behind the house . . ." I held up my hands in reference to what happened after that.

Nanny came through the parlor doorway and made her way to the sofa. Jesse shifted to give her more room.

"I couldn't help overhearing, but maybe the judge went behind the house for more than a cigar."

I regarded her from my seat across from her. "What do you mean, Nanny?"

"We all know what goes on at these affairs." She pursed her lips and gave us a knowing look. "*Affairs* being the operative word. You believe Delphine wasn't happy in the marriage, that she might have been planning to leave her husband. Perhaps the judge was no angel."

"A tryst," I concluded, and remembered Delphine Schuyler's accusation toward me. Wryly I said, "Yes, that did already come up."

Beside Nanny, Jesse was nodding. "Emma, did you see him spending time with anyone in particular that night?"

I shook my head. "For the most part, he seemed to be enjoying the company of his gentleman friends. At one point, he attempted to rein in his daughter, but she would have none of it. It was after her argument with Jerome Harrington and she was in a high temper."

"What about one of the actresses?" Scotty suggested.

Jesse sat a little forward in his chair. "The woman who played Titania. What was her name?"

"Clarice O'Shea," I supplied.

"Perhaps Miss Schuyler had it wrong." Jesse's eyes narrowed as he thought it over. "Perhaps this O'Shea woman wasn't carrying on with Jerome Harrington, but with Clayton Schuyler."

"I don't know," I said. "I saw how Miss O'Shea watched

Miss Schuyler when she stormed through the garden. If Miss O'Shea and Judge Schuyler were engaged in any sort of dalliance, Miss O'Shea would have stared daggers at *Mrs.* Schuyler, not the daughter."

"It could have been another of the actresses"—Nanny smoothed a wrinkle in the skirt of her cotton dress—"or one of the wealthy ladies. But it's something to consider, isn't it? Because whoever that woman is, if she exists, she might have seen something, mightn't she?"

None of us could argue with that. Nor could the man in the ill-fitting suit be ruled out at this point. Clayton Schuyler's judgment in favor of union workers only widened, rather than narrowed, the possibilities of who might have wished him dead.

"Good morning, Emma. I have news."

Thus did Nanny greet me the next day when I entered the morning room for breakfast. An open newspaper lay beside her plate, and I wondered what new disaster had occurred the night before. Would I have to rush off to gather the facts and write up an article for the *Messenger* before having even a bite to eat? For an instant, I lamented having missed the opportunity to be the first to report on the matter, and wondered whether Ed Billings, a rival reporter at the *Newport Observer*, had beaten me to the scoop.

Across the table, Nanny sat facing me. Her expression held no hint of disaster. Moreover, she pushed the newspaper aside, as if it were of no consequence at all.

I took my seat opposite her. "Am I to guess, then?"

"Your cousins arrived late yesterday afternoon. Alfred and Reggie." She grinned, and I remembered hearing the telephone ring about a half hour earlier. Little happened in this town that Nanny didn't hear about from her extensive network of friends who worked in the various cottages.

"Goodness, I hadn't expected any of them this soon. Aunt Alice must be eager to settle The Breakers for the winter and have one less matter on her mind."

"You wish to talk to Alfred, don't you? I wouldn't wait. You don't know how long he'll be here."

"I'd like to talk to Aunt Alice, but that's out of the question right now. So, yes, I most certainly do wish to speak with Alfred. Too bad Gertrude didn't come as well, but I suppose she's with her mother." I pondered going directly to The Breakers after breakfast, before I went to the *Messenger.* "Nanny, would it be terribly ill-bred of me to go over this morning? I'll, of course, offer them any help I can with the house."

"This is no idle matter you wish to speak with him about," Nanny said earnestly. "A man was murdered."

"Yes, and a possible attempt was made on another man's life. You're right, Nanny. I'll go as soon as I've eaten."

Before I left the house, a knock sounded at the front door. I opened it to behold a footman in the Wakehurst livery, a carriage parked behind him on the drive. He bade me a polite good morning and handed me a sealed note and a small roll of linen, tied closed with a ribbon.

I carried the note and package into the kitchen, where Katie and Nanny were washing up the breakfast things. Nanny looked surprised to see me. "I thought you'd left. Didn't I hear the front door open and close?"

"You did. One of Mr. Van Alen's servants brought a message." I broke the seal and unfolded the page:

> *My dear Miss Cross,*
> *I fear your fan has fallen prey to thievery. It has been discovered that some other items have gone missing from my dining room, presumably on the night of the fete, and I fear your fan might be among*

them. Though I cannot hope to replace a gift from
your parents, please accept this token in its stead,
along with my deepest apologies.
　　Your servant always,
　　James J. Van Alen

Oh dear. Quickly I untied the ribbon and unrolled the linen
to reveal a fan of silvery gray silk embroidered with gold
vines, the blades of carved tortoiseshell. A wave of guilt engulfed me. "Oh, Nanny. Good heavens, I have to return this."

Katie, standing at the sink, craned her neck to see. "Oh,
Miss Emma, that's lovely."

"If you return it, you'll have to admit you deceived him."
Nanny took the fan from my hands and held it up to the
light from the window. "It surely is a beauty."

"It might have been his wife's. Or his mother's. I wish I'd
never lied to him. I was afraid he might let slip to Detective
Myers that I was there, and that would get Jesse in trouble
again."

"Your heart was in the right place, my lamb." Nanny
handed the fan back to me. "Perhaps you might wait until
the murderer is in custody."

I thought that over, but concluded it would be wrong to
wait. "No, this needs to go back immediately. As soon as I
have a chance to stop by Wakehurst." I dropped the fan into
my handbag, bade Nanny and Katie good-bye, and left the
house.

When I arrived at The Breakers, I found Alfred in the library, a corner room of dark wood and rich green brocades.
Most of the rest of the downstairs looked like a house of
ghosts, with sheets draping the furnishings and light fixtures.
A team of servants was busy packing items to be transported
to the New York town house, and sorting others that would

be put in storage. Only in my memory, happy voices echoed against the marble walls and soaring ceiling of the Great Hall. The servants spoke in hushed tones and the house already had an abandoned air that caused my heart to squeeze.

Pen in hand, Alfred sat at the writing table, hunched over some papers. Mason, the family's longtime butler, stood at Alfred's shoulder, ready to hand him another sheaf of pages to be signed. I'd found my way to the library on my own, with no one to announce me. I knocked softly on the door frame.

"Alfred, am I disturbing you?"

He looked up in surprise. Then, seeing it was me, he came to his feet. "Emmaline. No, you're not disturbing me. In fact, I could use a break from all this paperwork. Closing up the house and all."

Mason beamed at me. I had once helped him regain not only his position here at The Breakers, but his life as well. "Miss Cross, it's lovely to see you. I hope you are well?"

"I am, thank you, Mr. Mason. It's good to see you, too." I addressed Alfred again. "How is your mother?"

"Holding up. You know Mother. She's a brave soul and as strong as bedrock, when she must be." He smiled sadly.

I nodded. "She is that. Have you ... spoken to Neily since the funeral?"

"No. I know he returned to Newport about the same time you did. Have you seen him?"

"I did. At Wakehurst a few nights ago." As soon as I'd spoken, I wished I hadn't.

Alfred's expression darkened. "A social affair? He went out to enjoy himself with our father only a few days in his grave?" At some unspoken signal between them, Mason bobbed his head, first to Alfred, then to me, and left the room.

"It wasn't like that, Alfred," I said, but stopped. What *had* it been like? Grace had tried to persuade Neily to stay home that night, but he had refused. He had gone to Wakehurst intending to enjoy himself, not that I believed he found one moment's true enjoyment at James Van Alen's Elizabethan Fete. "Alfred, Neily was—and is—terribly upset by your father's death. By all that's happened in the past few years. He's feeling ostracized by the family and very much abandoned."

"He's got Grace, hasn't he?"

The disdain in Alfred's voice both saddened and disappointed me. "Not you, too, Alfred. I thought you understood his position where his marriage is concerned. I thought you sympathized."

Alfred pushed away from the table and paced to the fireplace of carved white marble. Against the room's dark paneling, the stone stood out like a shroud, or so it seemed to me in that moment. "Hang it, Emmaline, I *am* sympathetic. But you don't know how it's been these past years, with our father ill and our mother frightened and angry. All of it could have been avoided if . . ."

"If Neily hadn't married Grace," I finished for him.

"If he had met and married someone else, yes." Alfred paced again, this time to the window overlooking the gardens on the south side of the house. "I do need to speak with him. He left New York so quickly, I didn't get a chance to tell him I have every intention of restoring a good portion of his inheritance. Whatever isn't tied up with the ownership of the New York Central. *That* I can't return to him. The board of directors won't go against Father's wishes."

Suddenly whatever reason I'd had to be annoyed with Alfred vanished. "That's wonderful of you. I know he'll be grateful."

"Yes, if he'll ever agree to see me." He gave a quiet laugh and turned to face me. "Is there something I can do for you, Emmaline?"

"Yes, actually, there is." Before I went on, I became aware of the murmurs of the servants working in the other rooms and decided I didn't wish what I had to say to become fodder for gossip. "Can you take a brief walk with me?"

"I can think of nothing I'd rather do at the moment." He smiled. "Anything is better than signing all of these legal documents concerning the house and everyone who is employed here."

"I do hope you aren't letting any of them go," I said as Alfred and I traversed the Great Hall toward the loggia doors.

"Dear Emmaline, always concerned with the less fortunate." I heard the good-natured teasing in his voice. "No, you may rest easy. We're transferring most of them to the other houses and are retiring a few on pensions that should keep them comfortable in their later years."

"I'm grateful for that. Your father would be happy, too."

Alfred opened one of the doors and we stepped out onto the mosaic floor of the loggia, then down the wide steps to the lawn. The ocean stretched in deep blues and greens beyond the cliffs, forming an unbroken line against a cloudless horizon. The air had turned crisp and fall-like, the kind of weather that turns colors brighter and increases visibility for miles. The sails of several pleasure yachts flashed in the sun.

We walked in silence toward the hedges that lined the property along the Cliff Walk. The cries of the gulls echoed against the cliffs, and far below us, the waves made that distinctive clapping sound as they broke against innumerable layers of pebbles. I stopped and faced my cousin. "Alfred, have you heard about the murder of Judge Schuyler?"

"It was in the papers, yes. Quite a shock. Mother didn't wish to discuss it, but I know it upset her. More than she already is, I mean."

"How well did your parents know the Schuylers?"

"They socialized occasionally. As I'm sure you know, the Schuylers are from Philadelphia. But they came to New York fairly often, and, likewise, my parents sometimes traveled to Philadelphia. They had many acquaintances in common, I believe."

"And did they ever speak about the Schuylers' marriage?"

"Their marriage? Emmaline, what are you getting at?"

"I've heard rumors that they hadn't been getting along well, that they did a fair amount of arguing. And that . . ." I halted, pondering the wisdom of revealing what I'd learned when I nosed through Mrs. Schuyler's bedroom. But if I wanted to learn the truth of her intentions regarding her husband, I couldn't shy away from difficult questions. "I have reason to believe Mrs. Schuyler was planning a trip to Europe next month, and that she might not have wished her husband to know about it."

Alfred held me in his gaze, his eyes narrowing. "And just how did you find this out?" He put up a hand. "Never mind. Yes, there had been talk previously, according to Mother, that trouble was brewing between the judge and his wife."

"Could he have been having an affair?"

"No!" After blurting out the denial, Alfred pinched his lips together and shoved his hands in his coat pockets. "Perhaps. I honestly don't know. But even if he had been, it doesn't mean his wife murdered him, Emmaline."

"I didn't say she did."

"No, but you're implying it. What do the police say?" Alfred raised his eyebrows, and I knew his question had been meant to make a point, being that I should leave matters alone.

It was not advice I intended to heed. "The police have taken all such investigations out of the hands of Detective Whyte and given them to a new detective, who knows nothing about Newport or its citizens."

"Perhaps they feel a new perspective would be beneficial."

I chose to ignore that comment. "Alfred, has there ever

been any hint of another man in *Mrs.* Schuyler's life? Especially in recent months."

"A dalliance on *her* part?" Alfred sounded scandalized by the very notion. "Emmaline, what sorts of novels have you been reading?"

"Really, Alfred, just because your parents doted on each other doesn't mean the rest of society is behaving itself. Not everyone enjoys the marital bliss your parents shared."

"No, you're quite right there." He smiled, again sadly. "What a shame they didn't have many more years together. It's very unfair, Emmaline."

"Yes, it is. But, Alfred, if you can shed light on anything to do with the Schuylers, it could help. Think about it. If they were unhappy, and Mrs. Schuyler *did* entertain the affections of another man, that man might have devised a way for them to be together sooner rather than later. And remember, unlike our aunt Alva, Delphine Schuyler does not consider divorce an option." As long as the other lived, they were each trapped in the marriage.

Another thought occurred to me. The man in the ill-fitting suit—could *he* be Delphine Schuyler's lover? A man driven to murder, not because of a social injustice, but out of passion? It seemed unlikely that a woman such as Mrs. Schuyler would take any interest in a man not of her social standing. But then again, who better than someone utterly unknown to her circle of acquaintances?

I had obviously given Alfred reason to consider as well; for now, he said, "I believe there *had* been talk of the Schuylers being estranged in recent months, of essentially living separate lives. My mother might know more, but—" He gave me a warning look.

"Don't worry, I have no intention of worrying her with any of this. But I do have another couple of questions." The beginnings of reluctance clouded his face, but I pressed on.

"There was a man at Wakehurst that night with whom Neily argued. When I asked him about it, Neily became terribly evasive."

"And? I assume my brother had been drinking and forgot to mind his manners. The other fellow as well. It wouldn't be the first time young men argued."

"This was different. I feared they'd come to blows and went to intervene. Even the jester recognized the need to separate them."

Alfred blinked. "'The jester'?"

"Never mind. The point is, I don't think the other man belonged at the fete. I believe he came in uninvited." I went on to explain the break-in at Max Oberlin's and the missing suit of evening clothes.

"I'll admit this is all very curious." Alfred lifted his face to the ocean breeze, frowning into the morning sunlight. "But I cannot imagine who this fellow is."

"Are you quite certain there haven't been any threats against the family? Any accusations?"

He turned his gaze back to mine. "There are *always* threats and accusations, Emmaline. The Vanderbilt family members are well-known public figures. The New York Central employs thousands. We're investors in countless other companies and institutions. Someone, somewhere, is always bound to take some issue with one or all of us."

"The New York Central..." I murmured. "George Gould is a railroad man as well..."

"I'm sorry, Emmaline. What was that?"

"Apparently, your father and Clayton Schuyler landed at opposite sides of a labor dispute not long ago. The judge apparently ruled in favor of the workers, and your father, among others, was not happy about it. Were you aware of a recent rift between them?"

"I really couldn't say. Father never mentioned it. And if

you're asking me about specifics to do with the dispute, I can't help you, not off the top of my head. I'd need to look into the records. But, undoubtedly, it had to do with companies being compelled to honor union agreements in terms of pay and work hours. Nothing unusual."

"Would your father have objected to such an agreement?" The idea of Uncle Cornelius attempting to circumvent his obligations saddened me and made me more resolute than ever not to use my inheritance for frivolous purposes.

"No, Father would not have, but don't forget, there are shareholders and board members, and beneath them, department managers, overseers, foremen . . . you understand. Company policy is not always carried out as it should be. Sometimes it takes a legal jolt to set matters on the proper course again."

Alfred's explanation seemed awfully pat to me, a way to brush off the guilt of shirking one's responsibilities. Was Alfred like that? Had Uncle Cornelius been? Was I terribly naïve to hope my relatives held themselves to a higher standard than most businessmen of their stature?

The answer, I acknowledged, was yes.

"Just one more question, and I'll leave you to your work." I paused, and Alfred nodded his consent. "Can you think of anything George Gould and Judge Schuyler had in common? Something that might make them both targets of the same killer?"

"I don't understand."

I started back toward the house, and Alfred kept pace beside me. "This isn't common knowledge yet, but last night someone in an automobile ran George Gould off Ocean Avenue. His carriage tipped over onto the sand. Somehow, neither he nor his horse was seriously injured. Although, had the tide been in, he might have drowned and been washed out to sea."

"Gad! Do you think the two incidents are related?"

"I hope not, Alfred, but it's certainly possible. Especially if there is something that connects Mr. Gould and Judge Schuyler."

"If so, then Mrs. Schuyler could have had nothing to do with it. Whether her marriage was happy or not, she could not have a reason to make an attempt on George Gould's life."

Other than verifying claims that the Schuylers hadn't enjoyed a happy marriage, I left Alfred, having learned little else. I did come away feeling happier on Neily's account, with renewed hopes that he and his siblings would soon reconcile.

Rather than climb back into my borrowed carriage and continue my trek into town immediately, I decided to amble over the grounds, gazing at the house from the outside. I had happy memories of The Breakers, where I had been invited during the summer months to visit with my cousins when we were young. But it hadn't been *this* Breakers. Not this monolithic structure of stone and marble that mimicked the Italian palazzos of Renaissance Genoa. No, I had played in the shadow of an older Breakers built in 1878, a turreted, peak-roofed house in the Queen Anne style.

Indulging in my memories, I wandered around the house and down the service driveway, where the children's playhouse stood nestled in trees and shrubbery kept every bit as sculpted as that of the main house. I smiled at the figures carved into the posts holding up the overhang as I walked up the porch steps. Peering in through the wide front window, I was surprised to see Reggie Vanderbilt sitting inside.

He must have heard my tread on the porch, for he gazed out at me through the window and came to his feet. A moment later, he met me outside. "Hello, Em. Want to come in?"

Chapter 13

❧

ntered the *Messenger*'s front office, I found Der-
tanley Sheppard with their heads together dis-
siness. For an instant, I experienced a stab of regret.
t resigned from the editor-in-chief position, it
e been me sitting closely beside Derrick, planning
or the well-being of our growing enterprise. Had
ol to give up such an opportunity? Didn't I owe it
er members of my sex to make the most of such

my remorse stem simply from not being the indi-
o, at this moment, shared Derrick's goals, as well
:imity?

o men looked up as I came in, then briefly came to
Derrick smiled. Mr. Sheppard frowned.
late, Miss Cross."

looked rather taken aback at the editor-in-chief's
but he didn't intervene.

v, Mr. Sheppard. I stopped at The Breakers to
iy cousin Alfred about Clayton Schuyler. I thought

I shook my head. "What are you doing in there, Reggie? Something you shouldn't?" I was thinking back to a time several years ago when I'd found him in the playhouse, drinking some of his father's whiskey on the sly. He had been a youth in his teens then. He was twenty now, all grown up. Or so I hoped. Certainly, he stood taller than me and had filled out from his former youthful slenderness. I detected the beginnings of a mustache as well. If Neily and Alfred favored their father in looks, I saw more of their mother in the fullness of Reggie's face and the shape of his eyes.

"Just sitting and thinking," he said. "It's such chaos up at the house right now." Despite his implied denial, I smelled the liquor on his breath, but I said nothing about it. "What are you doing here?"

"I came to see Alfred about a matter. Judge Schuyler's murder."

"Same old Em. In it again, aren't you?"

"I can't seem to help it, Reggie. You see, I found the body that night."

His features tightened, as though he felt a sudden pain. "Rotten luck. But why did you need to speak to Alfred about it? We weren't even in Newport when it happened."

"Let's walk," I said, and slipped my hand into his offered arm. I couldn't help smiling at the gentlemanly gesture. I was so used to thinking of Reggie as a child, but he was a man now and would soon look to marry. "It's good to see you away from New York, Reggie. Away from . . . well . . . you know."

"Mother's grief. Yes, I feel I can breathe again here, whereas I seemed to be stifling in Manhattan. I do wish Mother had come with us, though. The ocean air would have done her a world of good, I think. But she wouldn't have it."

"No, I don't suppose she would."

"Now, tell me what you spoke about with Alfred."

Ordinarily, I wouldn't have shared those thoughts with Reggie, or with anyone I considered too young or innocent to be involved in such matters. But I once again reminded myself that Reggie had grown up, was certainly no innocent, and what was more, he had a way of finding out other people's secrets. He always had.

Still, I kept my reply vague. "I was curious about the Schuylers. I wanted to see if Alfred knew anything about them."

Reggie studied me, a grin playing about his lips. "You suppose Mrs. Schuyler did the old boy in?"

It was on my tongue to deny it. But I said, "I don't know. As I said, I'm curious about them. All of them."

"Even Imogene?"

"She's about your age. Do you know her well?"

Reggie gave a half shrug. "I'll tell you this. I was surprised when I heard she intended hitching herself to Harrington."

"Why? Do you think the Harringtons aren't good enough for the Schuylers? Her father seemed to believe they were."

"It isn't that. I'd been under the impression Imogene had set her cap for someone already."

This information, the first I'd heard of it, made my pulse jump. "Who?"

"Don't know exactly. But last spring in Paris, it certainly seemed the case. Mutual friends were all speculating. And Imogene would only smile slyly when asked."

I compressed my lips as I turned my head to regard him. "Think, Reggie. You must have seen her with someone. Or heard a name mentioned."

"You can be assured she was as discreet as can be. And I don't believe I heard any names, only that Miss Imogene Schuyler had attached her hopes to some mystery man. Her friend Eliza Denholm would probably know. But, really, you can't think Imogene had anything to do with her father's demise. That would be absurd."

Would it? Women committed murder, perhaps not with

the same frequency as men, but with the same [...] termination. There were still three people in [...] night with whom I had not yet spoken. Imo[...] her mother, and Jerome Harrington. The for[...] be inaccessible for the moment, but I consi[...] fair game. And now I added another name to[...] sons I wished to meet: Eliza Denholm.

Leaving The Breakers, I realized Wake[...] short distance down Ochre Point Avenue. [...] return the fan. Oddly, Maestro didn't heed [...] to turn in at the gates and we continued int[...]

he might know if the judge had received any threats. Alfred's parents are—were—acquainted with the Schuylers."

"And did he?"

"Unfortunately, no. But he *had* heard about the Schuylers' recent estrangement. All was not well in their marriage."

Mr. Sheppard scrutinized me with his keen gaze "Is this what you meant when you said the Schuyler women were 'an avenue worth exploring'?"

I nodded.

"Be careful with that line of thinking." His New Hampshire pronunciations sharpened. "We don't want to stray into the realm of yellow journalism."

It was Derrick's turn to scowl, his indignation evident. "Sheppard, I don't think that's at all what Miss Cross has in mind."

"It's all right," I said, raising my hands. "I agree, Mr. Sheppard, and I shall proceed with the utmost caution. I discovered something else interesting as well, from my younger cousin Reggie. Apparently, Miss Imogene might already have had an understanding with another young man when her parents arranged her marriage with Jerome Harrington."

With a glance first at Derrick, Mr. Sheppard rubbed a hand beneath his chin. "Reggie Vanderbilt isn't the most reliable source, though, is he?"

"That may be true," I replied with a chuckle, "but this has a slight ring of truth to it. It bears further inquiry, I should think."

Mr. Sheppard conceded this point by inclining his head. "Did you find out anything about that mysterious man who might have broken into the tailor shop?"

"The man in the ill-fitting suit, as I've come to think of him." I let out a sigh. "Not yet. I haven't been able to find him or discover who he is."

"Keep trying." Mr. Sheppard raised a forefinger in the air. "My money is on him. If he stole those clothes in order to attend the fete, it's likely he killed Judge Schuyler. The only question is why."

"That's *if* the tailor shop thief and the man I encountered at the fete are one and the same." I turned my attention to Derrick. "What about the Harringtons? Have you been able to check into their financial situation?"

Derrick set down his fountain pen. "I can't find a thing to indicate they're having difficulties. They did sell off some shares in a coal-mining company recently, but there's nothing unusual about that."

"Perhaps they sold out because they needed the cash," I suggested.

"It looks as though they reinvested in real estate in North Carolina."

"Really. Hmm . . ." I had been about to ask whether they might also have sold off some of their property—again for cash—but if they were buying real estate, it wasn't likely they were short of ready money. Then another thought struck me. "Coal. This isn't the first time that commodity entered a recent conversation."

Derrick looked puzzled. "What do you mean?"

"There was trouble only yesterday in Illinois, in a town called Carterville."

"On our front page today," Derrick and Mr. Sheppard said almost simultaneously, and Mr. Sheppard continued with, "union against nonunion workers. Good job picking up on that one, Miss Cross."

I nodded. "I spoke to Stuyvesant Fish about it yesterday afternoon, because when the shooting broke out—"

"It occurred at a terminal of his Illinois Central Railroad." Mr. Sheppard made an impatient gesture. "We read your story. What are you getting at?"

"It's rather coincidental, don't you think?"

"Hardly." Mr. Sheppard made another gesture of impatience, accompanied by a scowl, neither of which I took personally. "Coal is the life's blood of our society. Most people of means are invested in it, to one extent or another. It runs our railroads, our industries, and our homes. Why, the Berwinds are building that newest monstrosity up on Bellevue with coal money, and they plan to run the whole house on electricity generated by their coal. What of it?"

"If coal is so lucrative, why did the Harringtons sell their stock?"

"Because some mountains in North Carolina tickled their fancy and they decided to free up some cash in order to purchase the land," he said.

"Well, I also talked with *Mrs.* Fish yesterday, and she confirmed what Detective Myers knew about Clayton Schuyler recently ruling in favor of union workers. Which means he might have angered more than a few wealthy investors and industry owners. I'm wondering if those workers were miners."

A shrug and a thoughtful *hmph* was Mr. Sheppard's only reaction.

"Not only that," I continued, "George Gould's carriage was run off Ocean Avenue last night by an automobile. He might have been killed. I believe he may have been targeted by the killer."

"There's many a reckless driver on this island," Mr. Sheppard reminded me with a shrug. "Damned vehicles. Dangerous thing in the hands of the wrong person. Don't go reading more into this without firm evidence."

Perhaps he and I had reached a bit of an impasse. But just as I had learned not to discount the warning barks of dogs, I had also learned not to ignore my distrust of coincidences. The connection might be minuscule, but experience had taught me that the most gossamer threads could lead to a killer.

"Well, I have work to do," I said. "I'll let you two get back to business."

"Miss Cross!" Mr. Sheppard called to me as I was about to leave them. When he saw that he had my attention, he said briskly, "Continue exploring."

"Yes, sir." With a grin, I pushed through the door leading to the back rooms. Footsteps behind me brought me to a halt before I reached the office Ethan and I shared. I turned to see Derrick filling the narrow corridor.

When he reached me, he grasped my hands. "Is he always like that? Have I made a mistake bringing him on?"

The question, and the earnestness with which Derrick asked it, truly puzzled me. "Mr. Sheppard?"

"Yes. Emma, perhaps I should have spoken up more, but I thought I'd discuss it with you privately first. I didn't like the way Sheppard spoke to you. Not at all."

"Don't be a goose. Mr. Sheppard didn't do or say anything wrong. It's just his way."

"I don't understand. He's brusque and rude and talks to you as though you were some kind of underling, and he's done nothing wrong?"

"If anything, he treats me like a real reporter."

"You *are* a real reporter."

"Yes, and Mr. Sheppard knows it." I found myself enjoying Derrick's concern as much as I enjoyed the warmth of his hands around mine. I gave our joined hands a playful swing. "He plays devil's advocate and I have no problem with that. Keeps me on my toes. I have no need of molly-coddling."

"If you're sure . . ."

"I'm positive." After a quick glance to make sure there was no one else in the hallway, I reached up and pressed a bold kiss to his lips. "Now, we've both got work to do, don't we, Mr. Andrews?"

"Indeed we do, Miss Cross."

I felt his gaze—no, I felt his *smile* on my back as I turned away and entered my office. I never made it to my desk; the wall telephone summoned me with its impatient ringing.

"Newsroom," I answered succinctly.

"Emma, it's Jesse. I thought you might be interested to know an automobile was reported stolen last night. Belongs to a local family, very well-to-do."

My eyes opened wide. "Do you think it could be the vehicle that ran George Gould off the road last night?" I blew out a breath. "I wish I'd gotten a better look at it so I could identify it."

"That's all right, I'm fairly certain this is the one. Our men found it on the side of the road near Forty Steps. No clue yet as to who had been driving it." He paused, then said, "I have more. There's been another incident."

"Not Mr. Gould?" My hand went to my throat, and I pressed the neat linen tie that held my collar closed.

"No, nothing like that. A break-in. Max Oberlin's Gentlemen's Outfitters. Again."

"It is the strangest thing," Max Oberlin said after unlocking the shop door for Jesse and me. "The clothes and hat have been returned, and with them, payment. Three dollars. Oh, that's not nearly what they are worth—good heavens, no. But I can have them cleaned and resell them. I do not believe Mr. Jenson will want them, now that someone else has worn them, but some gentleman will, surely."

This speech amazed us both. Mr. Oberlin led the way to his main counter, where the garments lay draped; beside them, the small pile of coins winked up at us in the light.

"He paid for use of the clothing." I reached out and fingered the white dress shirt. What it lacked in frills, it made up for in the quality of the fabric and the expertise in tailoring.

"It appears we have an honest thief," Mr. Oberlin agreed.

"How did he get in this time?" Jesse asked him.

"Same as last time, through the back entrance. Broke the new lock I had installed only the other day. Perhaps part of the money he left is to replace the lock again."

"And do you know if anyone saw anything?" Jesse took out his tablet and pencil.

Max Oberlin shook his head. "I called the station as soon as I opened this morning and saw this." He gestured at the clothing. "I have had no time to speak with my neighbors."

"All right, I'll take care of that," Jesse said.

"The thought of someone breaking in." Mr. Oberlin gave shudder. "It distressed me. Very much. I did not like to be here before the other shops were open and the streets filled with activity." His expression eased and he almost smiled. "But now, this has happened—the return of the clothes, the payment. I think it is not so dangerous to be here now."

Jesse and I exchanged glances, and I said, "I believe Mr. Oberlin is correct that he has nothing to fear from his thief. I've never heard of one who made restitution, and so quickly."

"Nor have I." Jesse didn't seem pleased by the prospect, however. Something about the scenario clearly bothered him, as it did me, to be honest. Yes, for Max Oberlin, I believed the incident had ended agreeably enough, and he no longer needed to fear his intruder returning. But the thief himself? I wondered if his business in Newport had concluded, or if he remained here to attend to other matters.

Or other murders. Had he shot that arrow into Judge Schuyler's chest? Had he run George Gould off the road? Who might be next?

I left Jesse to examine the rear door of the shop—again—and finish questioning Mr. Oberlin. Spring Street ran parallel to Thames Street and was lined with private homes, shops, and businesses. Many of the buildings hailed from the previous century, some well before the Revolution. It didn't surprise me that our thief had had an easy time breaking into Oberlin's shop.

I headed south but didn't have far to go to reach my destination. A bell jingled when I entered a dress shop several doors down. The front room presented a scene very much like Oberlin's, but instead of dark serge, checks, and stripes, colorful silks, muslins, and linens, along with ribbons and lace, met my gaze. The main room was empty, but a voice called from somewhere in the back.

"Coming." A few seconds later, the proprietress, Molly Sayers, parted the curtains separating the shop from the back corridor and stepped through. "Emma, what a delight to see you."

"Hello, Molly. How are you? How has business been?" I felt slightly guilty for not having stopped in on Molly for some time now. This shop had been a favorite of my mother's when she lived in Newport, but it wasn't often I spent money for an entirely new dress. Mostly, I wore older garments freshened by Nanny's sewing talents, taking trim off this frock and the buttons off that, and combining them on yet a third to create an entirely new look. Perhaps, though, with my newfound wealth, I might bring both Nanny and Katie here for a special treat. They both deserved it.

"Business has been rather brisk this season," Molly said in answer to my question, setting my conscience to rest. "I've had steady orders all summer, and already our local women are thinking about their holiday outfits." She spoke to me from across the counter. Now she leaned over on her elbows, stretching closer. "I was sorry to hear about Mr. Vanderbilt, Emma."

"Thank you, Molly." I could think of nothing more to say to that.

She brightened. "How are your parents?"

"Very well, thank you. They spent the summer in Marseille."

"Oh, how splendid."

"They're back in Montmartre for now, but are thinking of wintering in the South of France, in Avignon. My father wishes to paint a series of scenes from throughout the city."

"Ah, the bohemian life. Sometimes I envy them." With a wistful look, Molly straightened. "But what can I do for you today? Time for something new?"

"Not today, but soon." I glanced over my shoulder at the street door. Seeing no one about to enter the shop, I turned back to Molly. "Have you heard about the break-in at Oberlin's?"

"Of course. All of us along this stretch are afraid we'll be next."

"I don't think you will be. Did Jesse Whyte speak to you after the first break-in?"

Molly's eyes went wide. "You mean there's been another?"

"Yes, but it's not what you think. The thief returned the clothing—with payment."

"How very odd. So he only wished to borrow them, then. Or *rent* them, I suppose one could say."

"Exactly. Have you seen anyone lurking about? He would be large. Not overly tall, about average height, but muscular and a bit stocky. A strong-looking man."

"Jesse asked me that question the day after the first break-in, and I hadn't seen anything—or anyone—significant."

"Think, Molly. He's been back again. What time did you arrive at your shop this morning?"

"About two hours ago."

"And can you picture the people you passed on the street? Were they known to you? Was there anyone who fit the description I just gave you?"

"I'm afraid that description fits many of our townsmen, Emma. Especially the workingmen."

I thought back to the individual I'd seen at Wakehurst, and I hit upon a detail that might make him stand out. "His nose had obviously been broken. Perhaps more than once. It made him look very much like a fighter. A boxer." I had become familiar with men who engaged in the sport earlier that summer, and now, when I thought about it, Neily's nemesis at the fete might have spent time in the ring. If not, he almost certainly kept rough company and engaged in fisticuffs from time to time.

"I'm afraid not," Molly said.

"Keep your eyes open for him. Please."

"I most certainly will. It's so odd, though," she said again, shaking her head in mystification. "Why would someone steal something and return it? Why not simply keep the clothing, or dispose of them somewhere? Why take such a chance on returning them when he might have been caught?"

"I can't answer that. But if you do see him, contact Jesse or me right away. Don't approach him. Don't speak to him."

Molly studied me with a puzzled frown. "Why do I suddenly have the feeling this man did more than steal clothes from Max Oberlin?"

"No one is sure of anything at this point, but he might be dangerous."

Her frown persisted. "There was a murder in Newport only days ago, at Wakehurst . . ."

I nodded. "Yes, there was. And this man we're looking for

was there that night. That's all I can say, but it's enough to warrant the utmost caution."

"Good heavens, Emma. Perhaps for once, you should leave things well enough alone."

We both knew I wouldn't.

After leaving Molly, I decided not to return to the *Messenger* right away, and went in the opposite direction, to Washington Square. I entered the Opera House, hoping to find Clarice O'Shea.

Even in the lobby, the walls shook from the music booming from the theater proper. Brass, woodwinds, and drums pulsated up from the floor to fill the air around me. Above my head, the crystals hanging from the chandeliers clinked against each other.

There was no one in the lobby to stop me, so I pushed my way through the swinging doors into the main part of the theater. Gaslight and conical reflectors illuminated an elaborate set meant to portray a mythical kingdom from the past, the backdrop extending as high as the gold-painted proscenium arch that framed the stage. A full orchestra occupied the pit. This being only a rehearsal, the actors wore their everyday clothes, but performed their stage directions and used the fullness of their voices as though a paying audience packed the seats.

I scanned the stage, looking for the woman who had played Titania at Wakehurst. But there were too many actors and too much activity to distinguish one woman from another. She did not appear to be playing the lead part, at any rate, for the woman presently standing near the edge of the stage, and singing as though her life depended on it, was noticeably stouter than the actress I sought. I also realized that I had seen Titania that night in full theatrical makeup and most likely a wig. That would certainly make picking her out of a crowd much more difficult.

Several people occupied seats in the fourth or fifth row, watching the progress of the rehearsal. I noticed one making notes. No one spotted me, so I slipped into the shadows of the very last row. It wasn't long before I became caught up in the storyline of the piece, which apparently involved an arranged marriage and an uncooperative daughter who wished to wed another man.

How apropos, I thought. But what about our hero? Did he have feelings for his young betrothed, or did he have eyes only for her fortune? The music swelled, crested, and crashed with an emphasis only John Philip Sousa could achieve with such excitement and gaiety. It brought a broad smile to my face. My feet tapped against the floor.

Suddenly the music and voices ceased with an abruptness that left my ears ringing. One of the men observing from the orchestra seats stood up and clapped his hands several times, calling for attention. He wore a vest and shirtsleeves, the latter rolled up to the elbows. I assumed he must be the director.

The conductor in the pit turned around to face him, and the next several minutes were spent in giving directions, asking questions, and yelling at a few select individuals on the stage. I had always heard anyone engaged in a career in the arts needed a thick skin, and I could certainly see why.

"And just what do you think you're doing here?" I gasped at the cross voice just off to my left and whipped my head around to face the aisle. A man stood at the end of my row with his hands on his hips and a frown that matched his curt tone. "You're not supposed to be in here. No one is, unless you're with the show." His eyes narrowed and he craned forward, scrutinizing me. "And I'll wager you're not with the show."

"I'm sorry, there was no one in the lobby and I thought it would be all right to slip inside."

"Oh, you did, did you? Can't a man answer the call of nature without someone taking advantage? Thought you'd see a free show, did you?"

"That's not why I'm here. I—"

"What's going on back there?" The man I had assumed to be the director had turned full around. The others in the row beside him came to their feet as well. The actors onstage squinted and shaded their eyes from the stage lights to see what the commotion was about.

"We've got us a stowaway, Mr. Comstock," the man near me said.

"A what?" The director, apparently named Mr. Comstock, scowled.

I came to my feet. "I'm terribly sorry. I'm not a 'stowaway,' as this man puts it. I came to speak with one of your cast members."

"I know you." A stocky man came forward from among the actors. "Mr. Comstock, she's a reporter for a local paper."

"Come to review our musical, have you?" The director's scowl didn't ease. If anything, it grew blacker. "Well, you can get out. We're not ready. *Obviously.*" He gestured behind him.

"I'm not here to review anything. I wish to speak with—"

"We've already spoken, Miss Cross, and I said all I have to say." Burt Covey's voice echoed against the theater's walls.

"Miss O'Shea?" I moved to the end of the row, side-stepped the man from the lobby, and proceeded down the aisle. "Is there a Miss O'Shea among you? That's whom I'd like to speak with. If you please."

A woman came forward from the crush of her fellow actors and went to the edge of the stage. "I'm Clarice O'Shea." She peered at me with those striking eyes I had noticed at

Wakehurst—large and heavily lashed—but I saw now that her hair was not the silvery blond of that night, but an ordinary light chestnut, rather like my own. "Burt told me you'd be looking for me." She smirked. "I suppose talking to you is the only way to be rid of you. Mr. Comstock?"

The director again clapped his hands. "Twenty minutes, everyone. But not a moment more."

Chapter 14

Miss O'Shea led me backstage to a private dressing room, which I assumed at first to be hers. When she caught me examining the shelves of wigs and cosmetics, she chuckled. "If you're thinking this is my dressing room, you're wrong. I'm just a chorus girl, for the most part. I only brought us here so we'd have some privacy. Since we're not in costume today, it won't be needed." She gestured at a spindly wooden chair in the corner. "Sit. Talk."

She chose the seat at the dressing table, but sat facing me, rather than the mirror. She was indeed beautiful, and I saw now that her eyes were a remarkable color, neither green nor blue, nor hazel like mine, but a rare combination. Her features, while even and feminine, were nonetheless strong, traits that could cast an expression to a theater's back row, even the last row of a balcony. I found myself slightly mesmerized by her, and thought if she wasn't a leading lady yet, she would be before long.

"Now," she said, sounding businesslike and impatient, "what is this about? Or need I ask?"

I shook my head, puzzled.

"Wakehurst. I remember you there that night. Oh yes, like you newspaper reporters, I have keen powers of observation, Miss . . . ?"

"Cross. I'm Emma Cross."

"I noticed you when you intervened between those two men who appeared close to blows."

I nodded. "That's right. You wouldn't happen to know what they were arguing about, would you?"

"Me? Hardly. I just wanted them to stop or go away. They were distracting from the performance." She studied me a moment. "I hope you don't believe *I* murdered that man?"

"Goodness, no. Why would you have?" Not that it would have been impossible. For all I knew, Miss O'Shea had performed in Philadelphia, encountered Judge Schuyler, and, for one reason or another, vowed to kill him. Or, as I'd theorized earlier, she might have believed killing the judge would prevent Jerome Harrington's marriage to Imogene Schuyler. For whatever reason, however, my instincts didn't lead me in that direction. "I *am* here about a matter that could be related to the judge's death. Do you know his daughter, Imogene?"

The actress's hesitation was palpable; so much so, I already had my answer. To her credit, she didn't attempt to deceive me. "I have not had the pleasure of Miss Schuyler's acquaintance, but I know *of* her. Rather well."

"Through Jerome Harrington? I assume you've made his acquaintance?"

Another hesitation, this time accompanied by a flush of color, there one instant and gone the next, but unmistakable. "Yes."

I waited for her to elaborate. When I realized she wasn't going to, I pressed on. "Are you and he . . ." I compressed my lips and began again. "How close acquaintances are you?"

"Do you mean, are we lovers?"

I replied with a quirk of my eyebrow.

She laughed softly. "The answer is no, we are not. Not that it's any of your business." She appeared to consider a moment, then continued. "But I suppose a reporter can dig up such information easily enough if she wishes. So I'll save you the time and simply tell you. Jerome and I *were* lovers. Almost two years ago now. It was the late fall of '97, during the New York theater season. He saw a burlesque I had a prominent role in, and he wished to meet me afterward. Oh, he was so young, barely a man, but I assure you, Miss Cross, he was not without his charms. But when the season ended, so ended our liaison. Jerome went to Europe for the spring, while I traveled up and down the East Coast performing."

"And you've had no contact since?"

"Not until the other night at Wakehurst." She leaned her head to one side. "It's funny, but he recognized me immediately, even in my wig and makeup. We talked for a few minutes, and he told me of his engagement."

"Was he unhappy about it? Did he express dissatisfaction with the arrangement?"

Her brows drew inward as she appeared to weigh her words. "He was matter-of-fact about it. As those people often are."

By "those people," I understood she meant the Four Hundred. But the briskness with which she made that pronouncement gave me pause. I felt certain she had left something out. "What else did you discuss?"

"Not that it's any of your business, but what else could there be? We spent a few minutes catching up. He asked about my career. That's all."

A member of the Four Hundred "catching up" with a minor actress with whom he had had a brief affair? It surprised me that he had bothered to acknowledge her at all. Then again, considering Jerome Harrington's age, it was likely Miss O'Shea had been his first paramour. And she *was* a striking beauty. She must have made quite an impression on him. "You say you spoke for a few minutes. Long enough for his fiancée to grow suspicious?"

Miss O'Shea shrugged and made an elegant flourish with her hand. "If Imogene Schuyler is the suspicious sort, then, yes, I suppose so. Was she jealous?"

"I'm not sure *jealousy* is the right word for it." I almost added that Imogene Schuyler had other reasons for opposing the match, but I would have been gossiping and I had no right to do so.

"Well, she had no reason to be, truly. And she's a fool if she doesn't marry him." Miss O'Shea compressed her lips as if realizing too late that she shouldn't have made that last comment.

"Then you think highly of him," I said.

"Didn't I already say that?"

I shrugged, not quite sure if she had or not. "Did he express doubt that the marriage would take place?"

"Perhaps."

"He did," I concluded out loud. Which meant that, even before their argument, and before Imogene saw Jerome speaking with his former lover, the match had been on shaky ground. I decided to take a chance. "Do you know anything about his prospects? His inheritance? Did he ever confide in you?"

Her cheeks pinked again—subtly and briefly. "Not really. He . . . made clear to me that he'd prefer to make his own way in life, rather than live off an inheritance."

"Did he have any plans for doing so?"

"Oh, you know how the young men of his class are. Full of plans and bravado. I only know he wished to make a name for himself and not live off his family's legacy. Perhaps it was a matter of not wishing to remain under his father's thumb. And he told me he found banking a colossal bore. Who could blame him?"

"What does he have against his father?"

"I didn't say he had anything against his father." Her lips twitched with irritation. "Can't a young man wish to strike out on his own?"

"In my experience with the Four Hundred, there's usually a reason. A good one." I was thinking of Neily. "Have he and his father argued? Perhaps over business?"

"I couldn't say." She stood up, a signal that our time had reached its conclusion. "I think if you have any other questions about Jerome, Miss Cross, you'll have to ask *him*. I've said more than enough."

Chapter 15

Clarice O'Shea stood up to end our conversation, but I wasn't yet ready to go. She glared down at me in consternation. Was she considering pulling me out of the chair?

"I only wish to know if you saw anything unusual that night," I said quickly, to placate her and assure her I would ask no more questions about Jerome Harrington. She sank back down onto the dressing table bench.

"I saw many unusual things. Those people don't do anything by half, do they?"

"No, they don't." I chuckled. "What I mean is, arguments, or anyone stealing off alone to a part of the garden where they shouldn't have been. Or hurrying up to the veranda while everyone else assembled for the joust," I added, hoping to spur her memory.

She gave a shrug. "By then, our part in the evening had ended and we were packing up our stage props. I hadn't time to be watching anyone. Besides, we were under the glare of Mr. Van Alen's electric garden lights by then. It was difficult to see anything beyond them from the stage."

"I see." I pondered that a moment, remembering Burt Covey telling me he saw Wakehurst's mystery guest, the man in the ill-fitting suit, running up the veranda steps. Was Miss O'Shea protecting that man? Had Burt Covey been lying? With no ready answer, I rose voluntarily this time, and Miss O'Shea followed suit. "If you do think of anything, please contact me. You can find me at the *Messenger*."

After my talk with Clarice O'Shea, I went directly back to the *Messenger*'s offices—and met with trouble. I realized as soon as I stepped into the front office that I should have heeded Mr. Sheppard's frantic hand signals through the window and kept going.

"That's her. Arrest her at once."

I halted just inside the door, staring mutely back at two faces aiming unmistakable hostility in my direction. "Mrs. Andrews . . . what are you doing here?"

"Seeing justice done," Derrick's mother snapped in return. "What are you waiting for, Detective Myers? She broke into the Schuylers' Bellevue cottage. She deserves to go to jail."

The detective took a step closer to me, inciting me to back up until the closed door came up against me. "Miss Cross, where were you two mornings ago?"

"She was skulking around the Schuylers' home is where she was." Lavinia Andrews managed to look both menacing and gleeful at the same time. "That's right, Miss Cross. It took me a little while, but I finally realized who that nervous little maid was upstairs at the Schuylers' house. What were you doing? Stealing?"

The door bumped against my back as someone from outside attempted to enter the office. I stepped away and turned, and felt buckets of relief wash over me when Derrick walked in.

"Mother? What are you doing here?" He took in Detective Myers's presence and glanced over at Mr. Sheppard, who had come to his feet. "What's going on here?"

"What's going on, darling, is your little doxy is being arrested for breaking and entering."

"Mother, you will not—"

Before Derrick could continue, I broke through my astonishment and found my voice. "I did no such thing. I accompanied a friend to the Schuylers' home to bring gifts from Ochre Court."

"Dressed as a maid?" Mrs. Andrews challenged. "As if *that* wasn't meant to deceive anyone."

"There was someone there I wished to speak with, and dressing as a maid ensured I'd be admitted."

"Then what were you doing upstairs?" Derrick's mother compressed her mouth into a bold line of triumph. She obviously thought she had me.

"I stayed for a time to help out, while the servants were getting ready to leave for the memorial service. When you saw me, I had just gone upstairs to bring Miss Schuyler's personal maid a cup of tea."

"Aren't you considerate?" the woman said with a scoff. "I very much doubt Imogene Schuyler's maid has a room on the second floor. At least, not the part of the second floor where I caught you."

"I'd lost my way." Somehow I managed to answer calmly, though my insides quivered.

"Lost your way, indeed. The only reason I didn't inform Mrs. Schuyler about this and bring her along to see you incarcerated is that I don't wish to add to her burdens and upset her further. She has enough to endure at present." Mrs. Andrews turned her attention to her son. "Do you see now, Derrick? This woman is a criminal. She cannot be trusted. Detective Myers has no choice but to arrest her."

"Mrs. Andrews—" I began, but Derrick cut me off.

"You're not only being ridiculous, Mother, but you're also slandering one of the most decent and selfless people I've ever known." When she started to respond, he turned the whole of *his* attention to the detective. "As you can probably see for yourself, my mother has no liking for Miss Cross and never has, despite Miss Cross having once done her a very good turn. I can't fully explain it, but there it is. I'm afraid you've been brought here for no good reason, Detective."

I was surprised to see that the past few minutes had left Detective Myers befuddled and ill at ease. "Perhaps," he said, "but I've no choice but to bring Miss Cross to the station for questioning. The Schuylers will have to be contacted to see if they've discovered anything missing. If so—"

"They won't," I said firmly, at the same time hoping neither Imogene nor her mother had noticed anything moved among their belongings. Had I left something amiss?

The door opened again, this time hitting Derrick on the backs of his legs. He stepped out of the way and opened the door wider. We gaped to discover Jesse standing on the threshold. He removed his hat and stepped inside. "I understand there's been a complaint against someone here?"

Detective Myers waved a hand at him. "I'm handling it, Whyte."

Jesse frowned in what appeared to be genuine puzzlement. "You're our new homicide detective, aren't you? Petty theft and such are my line now. I'll take it from here." He smiled amiably at his fellow policeman.

"This seems highly irregular to me." Mrs. Andrews fingered the embroidered edge of her silk glove. "If I'd wanted Detective Whyte to handle the matter, I would have asked for him. I believe I shall have to file a complaint."

Detective Myers surprised me again. "Detective Whyte

does have a point, ma'am." He set his hat on his head. "I'll leave this matter in your capable hands, then, Whyte. I've more important matters to attend to. Good day."

Mrs. Andrews rounded on him. "You cannot simply leave. Detective Whyte isn't about to do a thing about this."

"I'm sorry, ma'am, but if I don't want him interfering in my business, I can't be interfering in his." He turned a warning glare on me. "But if I find out you, Miss Cross, were attempting to worm your way into my investigation of Judge Schuyler's death, you will be very sorry. I'll have my eye on you. Now, if you'll all excuse me." He hurried out the door before Mrs. Andrews could stop him.

Having lost one champion, she appealed to her son by grasping his arm. "Derrick, you're making a dreadful mistake. Why will you not listen to reason?"

"When I hear reason, I listen." He extricated his arm from her hold. For an instant, his jaw hardened, a sign of his effort to rein in his anger. "Please, Mother, let's not end up saying things we'll regret. You must have somewhere more pleasant to be right now. And while it would please me no end to give you a tour of our offices, I honestly don't think it would interest you much. Or perhaps it would?" He held out his arm to her, an obvious offer to escort her through the building, as well as a peace offering.

"Another time, thank you," she replied stiffly. With a tug on each of her gloves, she stalked to the door. Derrick moved to open it for her.

"Good-bye, Mother," he murmured as he watched her set off along Spring Street. Then he shut the door. I realized how much it pained him that he would not be showing his mother the business he had built from a foundering broadsheet to a growing and respectable newspaper.

That he and *I* had built, for although I had finally admitted that being editor-in-chief was not the ideal position for me, while I *had* occupied that chair, I had put my full efforts into making the *Messenger* successful.

The four of us let out a collective breath of relief. Mr. Sheppard sank back into his chair. Despite our audience, Derrick put his arms around me.

"Are you all right?"

"A bit shaken, to tell the truth. But I'm fine." I eased away as I offered him and the others a rueful smile. "She wasn't wrong, you know. Oh, about stealing she was *absolutely* wrong. And about the breaking part, if we're being precise, because the housekeeper herself admitted me. But I did enter the Schuylers' house under false pretenses and I did go snooping through Mrs. and Miss Schuyler's things."

"All in the name of justice," Derrick teased.

"Indeed." Jesse chuckled. "I don't think I'll be hauling you over to the station."

My legs feeling suddenly shaky, I went to sit in the unoccupied desk chair across the office from Mr. Sheppard's. "Jesse, how on earth did you know to come here?"

"Ethan," he replied with a grin. "Apparently, he came in just after Myers and Mrs. Andrews, heard what they were saying, and telephoned me from the newsroom. He's come a long way from shy young man to your willing partner in crime, Emma. I'm not entirely sure it's a good thing."

As if he'd been listening, and perhaps he had been, the inner door opened and Ethan joined us in the front office. "Is everything all right? Miss Cross, I see you haven't been dragged down to Marlborough Street."

"Thanks to you." I went to him and gave his hands a grateful squeeze. The gesture made him blush, but he also looked genuinely pleased. I turned back to the others. "Now, then . . ."

I spent the next several minutes relating what I learned at the Opera House from Clarice O'Shea, and what she had told me about Jerome Harrington. "She spoke so highly of him, it's difficult to believe their affair has been over for nearly two years," I said. "And yet she insisted it was."

"Do you think she was lying?" Derrick asked.

I shook my head and sighed. "No, but I have nothing to back up that opinion besides instinct. She seemed entirely sincere."

"She *is* an actress," Jesse pointed out.

"Very true." I had given up my chair and now paced the small office. "But she also seemed in favor of Jerome marrying Imogene. She said Imogene would be a fool not to marry him. But if he's so wonderful, why the rift with his parents?"

"Do you think less of your cousin for being disowned by his parents?" Ethan had taken the swivel chair I'd vacated and sat turning it gently from side to side.

"You know I don't." I paced some more. "Then the question is, what caused the rift? Perhaps Jerome is taking the high road when it comes to living off his father's money. Perhaps he sees any potential inheritance as ill-gotten gains." I was, of course, thinking of my own situation with my inheritance from Uncle Cornelius and how conflicted the matter left me. I had truly loved the man and had seen him not only as an uncle, but often as a second father. He had always treated me with kindness and respect. And yet . . .

"Sometimes I'm glad my family has relatively little, at least compared to these cottagers." Ethan shook his head. "Life seems much easier this way."

I couldn't have agreed more. The situation with Derrick's mother would not exist if he had hailed from an ordinary, working-class family. But I'd had the choice of an ordinary, peaceful life—with Jesse. And I had decided to travel the more difficult path with Derrick—or, rather, my heart had made the decision.

I turned to Jesse now. "Do you know if Detective Myers has any good leads?"

"He's focusing on Judge Schuyler's past cases. He's convinced it's someone the judge ruled against in the past, so he's going over the records and compiling a list of possibilities."

"Not a bad strategy," I conceded. "Has he found any evidence that one of those possibilities could be in Newport now?"

"As a matter of fact, Myers spoke with someone you've already questioned. The jester."

"Burt Covey? Was he ever sentenced by Judge Schuyler? Does Detective Myers suspect him of the murder?" I tried to remember if he had been missing from the vicinity of the stage that night, but I had been watching Neily, not him.

"No," Jesse said, "Myers doesn't think Covey did it. But Covey told him the same thing he told you, about the man he saw climbing the terrace steps. Myers's attention is on finding that man. He believes he could be an ex-convict with a grudge against Judge Schuyler. So, oddly, he and I are looking for the same individual, but officially for different reasons." He narrowed his eyes on me. "Speaking of that night, I'm on a new case. Apparently, murder was not the only crime at Wakehurst that night."

"Theft," I said as a wave of heat rose in my cheeks.

Jesse nodded. "I understand a fan of yours might have been stolen?"

That heat intensified as the others turned their gazes on me. I opened my handbag and slid out the folded fan. "No, Jesse. Derrick and I used that excuse to make our way back into Wakehurst the next day. I wanted to see if the arrow could have been shot from the veranda. I had no idea Mr. Van Alen would discover things missing from the house. Apparently, he believes my fan was taken as well."

"A fan that never existed." Jesse reached for the one I

held, and I passed it to him. He opened it and examined it from all sides. "Costly."

"He gave me this to make up for the one he believes was stolen," I explained, and hastened to add, "I plan to return it at the first opportunity. Unless you wish to give it to him."

"Oh no. Not me." Jesse snapped it closed and dropped it back into my hand. "I'll let you explain your way out of this one."

Derrick smiled at me indulgently, clearly amused, while Mr. Sheppard and Ethan looked as though they had questions they knew better than to ask. I tucked the fan back into my bag and asked Jesse, as much to change the subject as out of curiosity, "Have you found any leads about the identity of the man in the ill-fitting suit?"

"Not yet, although I'm checking the boardinghouses nearby." He made a moue of frustration. "But if you ask me, it's too easy an answer to consider him the killer. Too pat."

"Why had he been there, then?" Derrick's question was a rhetorical one, a question I'd asked myself countless times. "And why did he argue with Neily?"

Mr. Sheppard toyed with the memo spike on his desk, running a fingertip up and down the edges of the papers impaled on it. "Do you think their argument had anything to do with what Emma dug up about miners and union rights?"

"I wonder . . ." I faced the window, gazing out onto Spring Street. "Coal and railroads go hand in hand, don't they? That could be why Neily wouldn't talk about it. He might be ashamed of his family's involvement." I let go another laugh, an utterly mirthless one. "At least Detective Myers isn't accusing Neily, although he practically did that night at Wakehurst."

"Your cousin could have been threatened." Derrick's quiet pronouncement drew the attention of the rest of us, and all gazes converged on him. "Doesn't that make the most sense, Emma? That Neily wouldn't wish to speak of the argument in order to protect you, his wife and child, and anyone else he cares about?"

"Good heavens, perhaps he wasn't being difficult or evasive, he was being protective." I blew out a breath. "Which means I'll never get it out of him. Not unless I can find out enough to corner him with the facts and coerce him into confirming my conclusions."

Questioning Jerome Harrington would prove tricky for me, at least if I attempted to do so alone. As a bachelor, he tended to frequent places denied to me: the Reading Room, the card rooms on the second floor of the Newport Casino, the homes of other bachelors. At none of those places could I move about freely. Quite the contrary, I'd once stood on the front step of the Reading Room, Newport's most exclusive gentlemen's club, and suffered grave consequences as a result. Not that I intended to give up on the idea of finding the young man, but I would most likely need Derrick's or Jesse's assistance in tracking him down. In the meantime . . .

I had done Grace a service in attending the Wakehurst fete. Would she return the favor? With little doubt, I stopped at Beaulieu that evening on my way home from the *Messenger*. I took a chance that I would find her home, and I was correct. But it had been an easy assumption. She and Neily surely regretted attending the fete; it was highly unlikely they would venture out anytime soon after that fiasco.

I found her alone on the rear veranda, enjoying a cup of tea as daylight faded and the ocean waves took on deep blue and purple tones. Seeming pleased to see me, she set her teacup aside and jumped up to embrace me. Of Neily, I saw no sign.

"How are you feeling?" I inquired.

"Oh, quite well, thank you." She smoothed a hand over

head. "But a murderer with conscience enough to return stolen clothes with payment?"

"I don't know what part he played, but I don't believe his being at Wakehurst was purely coincidental. But there's more, and I want you to take heed. Did you hear about George Gould's mishap on the road last night?"

"'Mishap'? No, I haven't."

Her eyes widened and her color rose as I related the events of the previous evening. "It seems whoever murdered Clayton Schuyler might be planning more to come." I reached over to grasp her hand. "Please, you and Neily have a care."

"Gracious," she repeated in a whisper.

"I'm sorry to worry you. There may be no connection at all between the two occurrences. But I do want you and Neily to take precautions to stay safe. Most likely Neily would not become a target, anyway, given that he's not part of the decision making at the New York Central."

She made a disparaging sound I knew wasn't aimed at Neily, but at his family. "*That,* he is not."

I felt a pang at having not been completely honest with her; at least for not having related Derrick's theory about Neily trying to protect those he cared about. If it were true, then Neily might indeed be in the potential path of a killer. But telling Grace would only distress her, and she had a tiny new life to think about.

"I came for another reason, Grace," I said. "I need a favor, if you're able to grant it."

"Anything for you, Emma, you know that."

I smiled, my gaze drawn to a brilliant star in the purpling sky. "Do you know a young lady named Eliza Denholm?"

"Why, yes, I do. She's English, but she lives here now. Her mother married the Earl of Brocklehurst some twenty years ago, but they've since divorced. She and Eliza moved back to America about three years ago, and Eliza goes by Miss Denholm, though she is entitled to be *Lady* Eliza. The son, Roderick, remained in England with his father. He's the heir, so one understands why he stayed." Her brows drew inward. "Why do you ask?"

"I need to meet her. I'm told she's a close friend of Imogene Schuyler's." I tipped my head, thinking. "Do you happen to know if she attended the Elizabethan Fete?"

"As it happens, she did."

I nodded, remembering the girl I had seen watching the archery competition, Miss Schuyler's plain friend. "Do you know where I might find her?"

"As a matter of fact, the day after tomorrow there's a donations luncheon at Castle Hill. Alexander Agassiz is raising money for a project at the Harvard Museum of Comparative Zoology."

My pulse quickened with hope. "Are you invited?"

"I am," she said with a grin. "Neily and I, and my parents, all received invitations. None of us had intended going, under the circumstances, but if you need me . . ."

"I wouldn't ask if it wasn't important."

"I cannot guarantee that Eliza will be there."

"Do you think there's a good chance she will be?"

"Her mother received a sizable settlement in the divorce—to ensure her silence about why she left the earl, of course—and she is known to take an interest in the sciences, as does Eliza. They're rather a pair of bluestockings, truth be told. But, yes, I don't think Alexander would have let an opportunity for a generous gift slip through his fingers. They're almost certainly invited."

At the *Messenger* the next day, I sat busily tapping away at the typewriter keys. Despite Judge Schuyler's murder monopolizing the greater share of my attention, there had been other news to attend to. Another break-in downtown, apparently unrelated to the one at Oberlin's; a boating accident; an assault with a deadly weapon—the latter occurring at one of the dockside taverns, late last night, between two sailors who had consumed more than their share of grog. None of these events seemed in any way linked to the murder at Wakehurst, but instead were simply the kinds of disturbances one expects to encounter in a seaport as diverse and bustling as Newport. I knew from my own reading that Newport had rarely been a peaceful hamlet at any time during its history, with crime and vice plaguing the city from its earliest days.

Suddenly my fingers stilled, and I raised my face to sniff the air. The office had one window that overlooked the narrow space between our building and the one next door. Not much of a view, admittedly, but the room had felt stuffy earlier, so I had raised the sash. Now a scent drifted to my nose, one that prompted me to my feet. The article I had been working on forgotten, I snatched up my small notebook and a pencil, hurried down the corridor to the front office, and bounded out to the street. I heard both Derrick and Mr. Sheppard call after me.

Derrick joined me on the sidewalk a moment later. "What's the emergency—"

He broke off, and together we said, "Fire."

We had no sooner spoken than bells began to clang from not far away. The pedestrians on either side of Spring Street, hurrying along on their errands, suddenly paused and smelled the air. Murmurs went up, audible even over the sounds of carts, carriages, and the approaching trolley.

I gazed up and down the street. "Which way do you think?"

Derrick shook his head.

I continued listening to the fire bells, their urgency like a stormy tide rushing at the shore. "That way," I finally deter-

mined, and pointed north. Others had reached the same conclusion, and Derrick and I joined the collective flow along
the street.

A dreadful fear lodged beneath my breastbone, and as we
hurried along, I prayed it wasn't Trinity Church going up in
flames. But before reaching the church, those ahead of us
poured around the corner of Mill Street. We followed and
were brought up short by the dancing flames and billowing
black smoke consuming a small hotel. The fire crew was
hustling people out of the front door, adding them to a small,
dazed-looking crowd huddled near the fire department's
steam engine. The flames must have spread so quickly, the
guests hadn't had time to evacuate on their own. It was a
blessing for them that the closest fire station was only a short
distance away at the junction of Touro Street and Whitfield
Place. The fire brigade had been only minutes in arriving.

I began jotting down notes and talking with onlookers,
herded well to the opposite side of the street and several
doors down. The hoses were turned on the neighboring
buildings first to prevent further spread of the flames, and
then, with the hotel apparently empty, efforts to douse the
fire began in earnest. I acknowledged with a sinking heart
that the building, a timber-framed Georgian structure faced
in white clapboard, would not be saved. As I watched smoke
and ash spiral against the sky, I thought about guests' belongings, the owner's investment, the workers' livelihood.
My eyes burned, but I forced myself to keep watching and
recording.

For a time, I lost track of Derrick, but I knew he was
somewhere close by. I saw reporters from rival newspapers
milling about as well, their tablets and pencils at the ready.
Policemen had arrived on the scene and set about ensuring
the onlookers continued to keep their distance. Upon spotting
a young woman dressed in a maid's uniform leaning against a

tree and watching with a bewildered expression, I approached her, hoping she might know how the fire started. I never made it to where she stood. Another face came into view, one with craggy features and a nose that had been broken a time or two. As my heart sped up beneath my stays, his gaze locked with mine for the briefest instant. Then he pivoted on his heel and set off at a brisk stride toward Spring Street.

Chapter 16

I looked about for Derrick. Not seeing him in the kaleidoscope of faces and colors surrounding me, I hurried after the man I believed to be the very same from the Elizabethan Fete. Though he had quickly turned away, that second or two he'd been within my sight had been enough to convince me I needed to follow him. I had no intention of confronting him; I wished only to see where he went.

On Spring Street, I experienced a moment of panic when I saw no sign of him. Had I lost him among the foot traffic? Had he turned in at a doorway? I strained my eyes, still burning from the smoke, which drifted in fine clouds even here. Then—there he was, about a block away, striding north. I set off, but despite an urge to run after him, I forced my feet to maintain a steady but sedate pace, keeping the man's back in view at all times.

Once, he appeared to look over his shoulder, and I quickly sidestepped behind a pair of ladies in large hats. Counting off a second or two, I moved out from behind them and once again spotted my target up ahead. Though I had focused mainly on his face back on Mill Street, my impression of his clothing had been of sturdy, store-bought quality. Nothing fancy, nothing expensive. Not what Derrick would have worn, but Jesse—yes. A workingman, then, but perhaps not a laborer. At least, not someone who lived hand to mouth. Unless he had also stolen the clothing he wore today.

At Mary Street, he turned east. I hurried to catch up before I lost him. When I reached the corner, I hugged tight to the building and peered around. Would he keep going to Touro? Was he aware of my tailing him and leading me in circles? Perhaps he planned to double back all the way to Mill Street; perhaps he had been lodging at the burning hotel.

Soon, however, he crossed over and stopped before a house on the corner of Mary and High Streets. He gazed back the way he had come, prompting me to press flat against the brick wall beside me. I lamented the dirt and coal soot finding a new home on my snowy shirtwaist and in the folds of my skirt, but didn't dare move. Did he see me? He searched the distance for another moment, then turned and ran up the couple of steps to the front door.

Marlborough Street became my destination, and I wasted no time in crossing Washington Square and making my way over to the police station. Once inside, I asked for Jesse and had only moments to wait before he came to the front counter to escort me back to his desk.

"I have information, but I must be quick about it," I told him in a breathless rush, "or Derrick will worry about where I've gone." I experienced a sharp doubt concerning the wisdom of having come here before returning to find Derrick at Mill Street, but what I had to tell Jesse had seemed too important to wait. "I know where he's staying. At least I believe I do." Another doubt struck me. I hadn't waited long enough to make certain the man remained at the house on

Mary Street, nor could I be sure he hadn't simply gone there to visit someone.

"Catch your breath, Emma," Jesse urged me. He left me a moment and returned with a cup of water. "Here, drink this before you keel over and fall out of that chair. Now, who are you talking about?"

Surprised to discover that I still held my notebook and pencil, I set them down and accepted the cup from Jesse. I took a couple of sips and set it, too, on his desk. "That man at Wakehurst who argued with Neily. Who might have broken into Max Oberlin's shop."

Jesse's eyes sparked with interest and he snatched up a fountain pen. "Where did you see him?"

"At the fire on Mill Street." I knew I needn't explain about the fire, as Jesse would already have heard. "Our gazes connected briefly, and then he immediately left the scene. He must have recognized me. As he made his escape along Spring Street, he looked back a couple of times. I don't think he saw me, though. I'm hoping that while he might have recognized me from Wakehurst, he doesn't believe I recognized him. Not in any significant way, at any rate."

"Where did you follow him to?" Here Jesse set his pen to a scrap of paper.

"Mary and High Streets. Southeast corner, the large Colonial with green shutters."

He nodded as he wrote this down. "I know the house. Owner takes in lodgers."

I retrieved my tablet and pencil and came to my feet. "Then you'll go soon?"

"Right away."

"I wish I could accompany you."

"Derrick must be frantic by now. Go find him and come back here. I might need you to identify him and the clothing from Oberlin's."

That sent me on my way, as did the realization that involving myself in apprehending the man in the ill-fitting suit would reflect badly on Jesse. While I wouldn't say Derrick had grown frantic by the time I returned to him, he looked distinctly concerned, and then vastly relieved to see me. He had stayed on Mill Street, surmising I would be back eventually. I apologized for not waiting for him before following our mystery man, but he understood, especially when I explained the circumstances. Then we boarded the northbound trolley, alighting once more near the police station.

Like good citizens, ones who did not interfere in police business, Derrick and I waited in the station lobby until Jesse escorted us to the interrogation room. On the way there, he informed us of what he had learned so far.

"Precious little," he said with a sardonic slant to his lips. "He says his name is Ernest Kemp and he's simply visiting Newport. Claims to have a keen interest in Early American architecture."

Jesse gave a snort. We reached the interrogation room, guarded by a uniformed officer, who opened the door for us and closed it after we stepped inside. Derrick took up position against the wall beside the door, conveying his intention to merely observe—and perhaps to ensure my safety. He hadn't been at Wakehurst that night, nor had he been to Oberlin's, so he could have little to add. Still, I was glad of his presence, now that I stood in such close proximity to the muscular Mr. Kemp.

His eyebrows twitched at the sight of me; his eyes lit up with recognition. Yet, he said nothing. I immediately noticed the coat he wore—the very same from the night of the Wakehurst fete. There could be no mistake, as it fit him in exactly the same manner: a bit too tight through the shoulders and upper arms.

I questioned Jesse with a look and he nodded. "I had a man run over to Oberlin's for the coat that was stolen and returned. Is it the same one you saw at Wakehurst? And is this the same man wearing it?"

"Most definitely *yes* to the second question." I frowned, attempting to study the garment to make absolutely certain, while ignoring the disparaging looks Mr. Kemp was sending me. Finally I met his gaze. "May I ask you why you seemed so hostile toward my cousin that night, Mr. Kemp?"

"Your cousin? And who might that be?" His voice was gruff, his pronunciations not those of a schooled gentleman, yet still firm and confident. A man used to giving orders, perhaps.

"Cornelius Vanderbilt," I replied.

"He's dead, isn't he?"

"I'm speaking of Cornelius the younger. And, yes, his father recently passed away."

The man shifted his gaze to Jesse. "Is she allowed to ask me questions?"

"You may remove the coat now," Jesse informed him rather than answer the question. While Mr. Kemp stood to strip the coat from his arms, Jesse regarded him, his lips skewed to one side. "What did you and Cornelius Vanderbilt argue about the night of the Wakehurst fete? You see, you *do* have to answer *my* questions, Kemp."

The man grunted, clearly not amused. "Restitution. For miners' families. I'm a foreman at the Clearwater Mining Operations, outside of Scranton, Pennsylvania."

Jesse and I exchanged startled looks. Jesse's eyes narrowed as he tossed the coat over an extra chair. "Restitution for what?"

"For the deaths of twenty-five men who went down a shaft one day and never came out."

I neither doubted his word nor meant to challenge his assertion. I simply didn't understand what he was getting at. "How was that Mr. Vanderbilt's fault?"

"Not his fault alone. The New York Central is just one of several companies that banded together to keep operations running—despite needed repairs."

"You said you're a foreman," I pointed out, not unkindly. "Could you not have stopped those men from going down?"

"I spoke my mind, a bunch of us foremen did. The supports were aging and we recommended an inspection and full repairs. The union shut us up and overrode our concerns." He crossed his arms over his chest, huddling into himself. "Said those men had to make a living, and by not working, they risked being fired. They'd just won a major victory that ended a strike. But now, they were acting under pressure from investors."

I gasped. "Is this the case I've heard about? Did Judge Schuyler make the ruling in favor of the workers?"

"He did. There was a dispute over wages and long hours. Judge Schuyler ruled the men had to be paid for those extra hours, and that the wage asked for by the union was a fair one. The investors didn't like it. They applied pressure to make sure operations resumed immediately. So down those men went."

"And the shaft collapsed." A lump of sorrow lodged in my throat.

Mr. Kemp nodded. "Your bigwigs didn't want Clearwater to take the time away from production for the repairs to be made."

"Isn't the union equally at fault?" Jesse pointed out. "They chose to follow the wishes of the investors, not the foremen."

"Only because they feared losing the small victory they'd gained." His mouth curled downward at the corners. "And I believe cash changed hands."

Jesse unbuttoned his coat and leaned forward toward the

other man, hands on his hips. "What exactly did you mean by restitution?"

"The miners' families need a settlement to survive now. How's a widow supposed to feed her children? Men like Vanderbilt have everything. Their families lack for nothing. Their wives and daughters parade around in silks and jewels. They can darned well provide financial relief to the people who need it, to the people they wronged."

"Mr. Kemp, you spoke to the wrong Vanderbilt that night." I offered him a sympathetic look. "Cornelius Vanderbilt is no longer a decision maker at the New York Central."

"He's his father's heir, isn't he?"

I shook my head. "I'm afraid not. His brother Alfred is."

Ernest Kemp swore, which brought Jesse surging to his feet.

"I'll thank you to watch your language, Kemp." His gaze shifted to me.

So did Mr. Kemp's. "Sorry. Just seems if I hadn't made that mistake, I wouldn't be sitting here now."

"Did you threaten anyone else that night?" I asked him quietly.

"I didn't 'threaten.'" His face darkened, and he looked away again. "All right, perhaps I *threatened* a little, but they deserve to have the fear of God put into them."

"You didn't answer my question," I said.

"A few others. Man named Gould."

My heart thudded. "Who else?"

"John Astor. Felix Mathison. Edward Berwind. A few others."

Good heavens, I thought. Other than his run-in with Neily, I hadn't witnessed any of this. My focus that night had been too narrow to notice much of anything other than my cousin's behavior. Beyond that, and overhearing the tiff between Imogene Schuyler and Jerome Harrington, I had moved about in a daze of grief and disbelief. My body was there, but unaccompanied by either my heart or my mind. For the first time in my adult life, I had been rendered incapable of summoning my reporter's instincts.

How had those other men reacted to Mr. Kemp's charges and demands? Had they, like Neily, bickered in return, perhaps making counterthreats? Or had they ignored Mr. Kemp and walked away?

"None of them had you thrown out." My query was more of a musing, as I already knew the answer. They'd been too ashamed to bring Ernest Kemp's accusations to light, just as Neily had been. I believed that, in Neily's case, his combined anger and grief over his father's death rendered him both unwilling and unable to discuss the matter, even with me. For the rest . . . they knew Mr. Kemp spoke the truth, and if word of it reached the newspapers, their interests would suffer. There would be a public outcry, a demand for a reckoning, worker rebellion, falling stock prices . . .

"Mr. Kemp." Jesse resumed his seat and leaned forward again. "Did you murder Clayton Schuyler?"

"No!" The man nearly shouted the denial. "Why on earth would I? He ruled in favor of the workers. It was those soulless investors that robbed them of their lives."

My gaze met Jesse's again. Mr. Kemp's story seemed logical, at least to me. If anything, Judge Schuyler had proven a friend to the miners, defending their cause against those who would take advantage of them. Men like my uncle Cornelius, and now my cousin Alfred; men like George Gould and John Astor, and countless others known for their coldhearted business policies and callous treatment of workers who complained.

I had also toyed, briefly, with the notion that this man and Delphine Schuyler had been lovers. Now the notion struck me as absurd. If Delphine Schuyler had wished to be free of her husband, it would not have been because of Ernest Kemp. But a question still needed to be asked.

"Mr. Kemp," I began, "were you on the veranda at Wakehurst at any point that night?"

"No, I was not. I came in through . . ." He hesitated, obviously debating his answer. "I forced my way in through the hedges on the side of the property."

"Because you had no invitation," I pointed out unnecessarily.

The man *hmphed*, slinking lower in his chair.

"And you stole the clothes from Oberlin's in order to fit in," Jesse added.

Mr. Kemp raised his eyebrows. "I also returned them, with a very generous payment for their use."

"That's beside the point." Jesse shook his head. "So you dressed the part and gained access to a private party for the sole purpose of confronting men you believed responsible for a mining accident."

"A mining disaster!" Kemp blurted.

"All right, yes." Jesse nodded his agreement, then shook his head. "Do you expect me to believe that's all you were after?"

Mr. Kemp's eyes narrowed, transforming his face into a mask of fury I would fear to encounter on a dark street. "What do you mean?"

I interjected with another question. "Mr. Kemp, where were you two nights ago?"

His lips flattened into a tight line of defiance; he crossed his arms over his chest.

"Stubborn." Jesse regarded him with a mixture of irritation and respect. "I'll repeat the question, and you had better answer me. Where were you the night before last, around sundown?"

"Down at some pub on Thames Street, near Long Wharf. Having supper."

"Which pub?" Jesse pressed.

"The Rusty Wheel."

"Anyone see you there?"

Mr. Kemp held up his hands. "Of course people saw me there. I wasn't the only one in the place."

"They'd better be able to vouch that you were there at dusk. Not before, and not later," Jesse warned him. "In the meantime, you aren't going anywhere until we've sorted this out." Jesse stood and went to the door, opening it to admit the officer, still standing guard outside. When Jesse turned to us again, his face was grim. "Mr. Kemp, you're under arrest for the burglary of Max Oberlin's Gentlemen's Outfitters."

"I *borrowed*, I didn't steal."

"You broke in and took something without the proprietor's permission. It's for a judge to decide if you're guilty of a crime or not. You're also under suspicion for the theft of an automobile, reckless driving and endangering the life of George Gould, and for the murder of Judge Clayton Schuyler."

"I didn't do any of that. You have the wrong man. And I certainly had no reason to kill Judge Schuyler."

If everything he had told us had been the truth, I saw no reason for him to have murdered Judge Schuyler, either. Yet, he had incriminated himself by stealing, no matter what he called it; by entering Wakehurst under false pretenses and threatening Neily and the others; and by attempting to evade me this afternoon. Not that the last one was a crime, but he had seemed awfully determined to avoid me.

"What's this? Who is this man? And who did he kill?"

At the sound of this new voice, Jesse and I turned to find Gifford Myers framed in the doorway. He nudged the officer aside and stepped into the room. "I asked a question,

Whyte. Who is this man?" His gaze lit on me. "And what is *she* doing here?"

"Miss Cross is here as a witness," Jesse said; his effort to remain calm was visible, at least to me.

"Witness to what?" the detective demanded.

"The break-in at Oberlin's," Jesse replied. "Indirectly. Miss Cross saw Mr. Kemp here wearing the stolen clothing at Wakehurst the night of Van Alen's fete."

" 'Indirectly,' my foot." Detective Myers came closer, forcing both Jesse and me to step out of his way as he approached Ernest Kemp. He glared at Mr. Kemp, but continued speaking to Jesse and me. "You've been withholding information, the two of you."

"That's a serious charge, Myers, and you'd better think twice before you make it." Derrick's throaty warning startled me. I had all but forgotten his presence in the room.

The detective whirled about to face him. "You again? I think your mother was right about her." To clarify the identity of *her*, he thrust his finger in my direction.

"Don't you dare speak of Miss Cross that way," Derrick warned in a low growl.

The detective dismissed the admonishment with a shrug, and demanded of Jesse, "You allowed a newspaper owner in here? Have you taken leave of your senses? It's bad enough *she's* here."

"The break-in is my case, Myers." Jesse's chin came up. "I'll conduct my investigation as I see fit."

"If Miss Cross"—he pronounced my name with sizzling disdain—"saw this man at Wakehurst, it becomes part of my case. I don't appreciate being kept in the dark, especially when it was done on purpose. Thought you'd cheat me out of the arrest and take your job back, did you?"

I wanted to tell him that was exactly what we'd had in mind, but I wisely kept silent.

Detective Myers turned his attention back to Ernest Kemp.

"You wore stolen clothes to attend an affair held by one of the cottagers. I assume you had no invitation?"

"Myers, we've already been over this," Jesse began, but the other detective cut him off.

"So, then, no invitation? And stolen clothes. And a man is dead, murdered in Wakehurst's garden. And then there are these three, attempting to keep everything among themselves. It's obvious, isn't it?" He beckoned the policeman standing guard. "Handcuff this man. He's being charged with murder."

"Now wait a minute, Myers." Jesse stepped into the uniformed officer's path. "I'm arresting him for breaking and entering, and holding him on *suspicion* of murder. There's not enough evidence at this point to charge him."

Detective Myers smirked. "You obviously take me for a fool, Whyte. You're going to regret that. And as for *her*—" That forefinger of his shot out again like the muzzle of a pistol, nearly prompting me to duck.

Derrick reached the detective in two strides, took hold of his wrist, and forced his arm to his side. "I'll thank you not to refer to Miss Cross as 'her.' You'd better learn to mind your manners, or you will have a problem. A serious one."

"I could have you arrested for assaulting an officer of the law." Gifford Myers looked Derrick up and down, his lip curling ever so lightly.

Derrick released him, but his expression remained stony. Detective Myers stared back at him and swallowed, before addressing the policeman. "You heard me. Cuff him and book him on first-degree murder."

The uniformed man grasped Mr. Kemp's arm and hauled him out of his chair. "Come along."

Mr. Kemp dragged his feet. "I'm telling you, I didn't kill anyone. I was never on that veranda, and I've never shot an arrow in my life."

Detective Myers waved him off, and we could hear Mr.

Kemp's protests fading down the corridor. The detective didn't follow; he hadn't finished with us yet. "I warned you before not to interfere with police business, Miss Cross."

Jesse started to defend me, but I spoke up for myself. "I am here only as a witness to Mr. Kemp wearing the stolen clothes. That is all."

He shook his head at me. "Why am I having the utmost trouble believing you?" He shifted his gaze to Derrick, looked about to speak, but apparently changed his mind. He addressed Jesse instead. "Chief Rogers is going to hear about this. And I don't think he'll take it lightly."

"As you will" was all Jesse had to say before gesturing to Derrick and me and leading us out of the room.

Chapter 17

The house known as Castle Hill sat at the base of a high, broad peninsula overlooking the Atlantic Ocean and the mouth of Narragansett Bay. Its Queen Anne design featured a peaked and latticed portico, a turret with a bell-shaped roof to the left, and, to the right of the front door, a wing that bowed gently out from the front of the house. Like Kingscote and Chateau-sur-Mer, Castle Hill was no imposing stone palace, but a graceful home designed with warmth and coziness in mind, a haven where one felt sheltered from the vagaries of the nearby sea.

Having learned never to compete with the ladies of the Four Hundred, I had dressed simply, but not inelegantly, in a day dress of slate blue muslin, and I wore my armband to signify my mourning. Grace wore no sign of mourning at all, but I could not find it within me to judge her for the omission. She, as always, looked a vision in layers of crisp off-white organdy detailed in exquisite lacework. With her coral sash and matching hat, shoes, and handbag, she very nearly vanquished all notion of summer's official end being

but days away. The weather had cooperated as well, bestow-
ing on us a June-like day, neither too hot nor too cool, with
a calm ocean undulating below the peninsula and lazily drifting clouds occasionally bringing relief from a brilliant sun.

Grace and I entered through the double front doors, which
had been thrown wide for the occasion. We were directed
through a bright vestibule and into the coolness of a wide
central hall, my impressions being of hardwood floors, paneling, and beams stained in a lovely golden brown, while
crisp white ceilings brought a sense of airiness. The butler
ushered us past a fireplace and seating area decorated with
art from the Orient, and to the conservatory. A semi-oval
room, with solid banks of windows all the way around, the
conservatory embraced dazzling views of lawn, sea, and sky.

Most of the furniture had been removed. Guests mingled
as they drifted through the room, some of them spilling out
through another set of doors onto a flagstone terrace. I noticed many of the usual faces, both men and women; many
of them had been at Wakehurst a week ago. There were un-
familiar faces as well, who, I assumed, were Dr. Agassiz's fellow academics. Tables lined the room beneath the windows,
and the guests proceeded from one to the next, bending slightly
and holding up monocles and lorgnettes to view a variety of
scientific displays. I spotted Alexander Agassiz, Castle Hill's
owner, standing proudly at the center of the space. Though
in his midsixties, the balding, grizzled Swiss native seemed in
no shortage of energy or enthusiasm as he greeted his guests
and answered their questions.

"Mrs. Vanderbilt," he boomed as Grace and I approached
him. His plain American accent revealed no trace of a child-
hood spent in Europe.

"Dr. Agassiz, how lovely to see you." Grace held out her
hand; he grasped it and raised it to his lips. "May I introduce
Miss Emmaline Cross."

"Ah, yes, I know you by reputation, Miss Cross." He shook my hand politely. "I fear I spend so much time traveling the world, and so little time attending Newport's social functions, that we have never crossed paths before this."

"Dr. Agassiz only just returned from several months at sea on the Pacific," Grace told me, her admiration evident, "exploring the formation of coral reefs."

"It must have been fascinating," I said in earnest, thinking about the difficulties and deprivations of being so long at sea. "And quite an adventure."

"Indeed it was, and if you'd like to hear about some of those adventures for your newspaper, I'd be happy to oblige you. I do hope you'll write about today's gathering. The Harvard Museum could use all the publicity, and donations, it can garner."

I promised him I would. But then another thought struck me and I almost blurted out that it would behoove Dr. Agassiz to exercise the utmost caution until Judge Schuyler's murder had been solved. For I had suddenly remembered that, before dedicating his life to science full-time, Alexander Agassiz had made a fortune in mining, first coal and then copper. Technically, he still served as president of the copper mines, though he had long since sold his controlling shares of coal stock. But did our killer know that?

Realizing this was no time to issue such warnings, Grace and I moved off to explore the exhibition. At the sight of so many specimens from Dr. Agassiz's world travels, I drew an excited breath. Cases filled with preserved insects, arthropods, exotic birds, small mammals, and sea creatures drew murmurs of appreciation and, in some cases, astonishment. There were also glittering geodes, amber, and other semiprecious gemstones, as well as the bones and imprinted fossils of creatures that lived eons ago. Photographs and placards revealed the sites where many of the specimens had been found, explaining that Dr. Agassiz himself had held the camera. It seemed our host could add photographer to his list of accomplishments.

My fascination aroused, I wished to fully explore these displays, yet my purpose in having come to Castle Hill held only one objective. "Grace, do you see Miss Denholm?"

Grace's lovely long neck craned as she searched the conservatory. An array of colorful hats made identification difficult, until one moved into closer range. We did just that, greeting others as we passed them. I noticed that, here, I tended to be more accepted than I had been at Wakehurst. Perhaps the spirit of the occasion—that of exploration and education, and the assumption that I'd come as a journalist—prompted them to look more kindly upon me. At any rate, I was asked to give my opinion on several occasions, as well as regaled with a few adventure stories from recent travels.

Suddenly Grace tapped my hand and gestured with her chin. "There," she whispered, indicating a young woman—a girl, really—who couldn't have been out of short skirts more than a couple of years or so. That night at Wakehurst, at the archery run, I hadn't gotten as good a look at her as now, with the sunlight streaming in through the myriad windows.

With plain features many might have considered unfortunate in a wealthy young miss, Eliza Denholm wore spectacles, a sign she gave little thought to her appearance. Her chocolate-brown hair formed a bun at her nape, with no effort to produce curls, and she bore the typical English complexion of pale skin and pink, almost ruddy, cheeks. She looked as though she had just come in from the cold. Apparently, she did not subscribe to the use of powders or lotions to even out those dueling tones.

All of this, coupled with her having renounced her English title upon her arrival in America, persuaded me to like her immediately.

Grace called out, "Eliza, dear. How are you? Is your mother here?"

Miss Denholm turned away from the tray of arachnid species she had been studying. "Good afternoon, Mrs. Vanderbilt. Yes, Mother is here, somewhere." She spoke the Queen's English in a firm, clear voice. Her gaze searched the room, but lit on no one in particular. "Perhaps she's gone outside."

"That's all right, I'm sure I'll find her." Grace gave her head a friendly toss. "Tell me how you are."

"Quite well, thank you, Mrs. Vanderbilt, all things considered."

"Oh yes." Grace flashed her a sympathetic look. "Forgive me, I'd forgotten how close you and Imogene Schuyler are. She must be inconsolable. Her mother, too."

Miss Denholm's hesitation spoke volumes. "Yes. They are. I'd be with Imogene now, except she insisted I come here today. She understands how interested I am in the sciences."

A bluestocking, as Grace had told me. My opinion of her rose yet more.

"That was very brave of her." Grace elegantly turned to draw me into their conversation. "Miss Denholm, do allow me to introduce my very good friend and cousin by marriage, Miss Emmaline Cross. Or have you met?"

"No, we haven't had the pleasure." Miss Denholm extended a lace-gloved hand, and I was taken with her poise, for one so young. And yet, a wariness entered her expression, explained by her next words. "Imogene has mentioned your name to me, Miss Cross. She said it was you who found her father that night."

"Yes, regretably. I feel keenly for your friend, Miss Denholm. To think of the upset to her life. I understand she was to be married soon. The delay must only compound her distress."

Having witnessed firsthand Imogene's sentiments toward her affianced, and understanding Miss Denholm to be Imogene's close friend, I hadn't expected her to agree enthusiastically with my comment. She took me utterly aback, however, when a crimson tide engulfed her face and her eyes glittered with ire.

"If something good has come of all this, it's that Imogene will no longer have to marry that man. Her mother won't force her." Miss Denholm turned on her sensible bootheel and stalked away, exiting through the open doors to the terrace. There she halted and stared out at the water, her back straight and her shoulders rivaling the flagstones in stiffness.

A couple of women, society matrons by the looks of them, promptly attempted to engage her. At first, she seemed oblivious of their efforts. Then she turned to one of them, and I could only guess at the expression on her face, for it prompted the women to laugh awkwardly and ease away from her.

Perhaps someone else would have let matters lie, but I was not *someone else*, and not to be put off. I followed her outside, where the coolness of the ocean breeze mingled with the warm sun and the fragrance of the Bourbon roses climbing up the trellises between the conservatory windows. A refreshment table beneath a gold-fringed mossy-green awning stretched the width of the terrace at the far end.

Coming up beside her, I said, "Miss Denholm, forgive me for upsetting you. It was not my intention. I believed Miss Schuyler to be happy in the match, but I see now that I was wrong. I'm glad for her, then, at least in this one matter."

"I should not have said what I did, Miss Cross. I'm sorry for my lack of control." Miss Denholm kept her profile to me as she replied, and I noticed that while from head on, she appeared rather plain, she did, in fact, possess a high, intelligent forehead, a gently curving nose, and a firm yet pleasantly sculpted chin. With a sudden start, she turned and said, as though accusing me, "You're a reporter, aren't you?"

"Yes, but I promise you won't see your words plastered across any pages in the *Messenger* tomorrow." As I gazed back at her, I became struck with the earnestness I detected in her countenance, the honesty. Sunlight lent brightness to her eyes as she regarded me, bringing out gold specks in the blue. Yes, she should learn to be more circumspect, and not say such things in front of people she had only just met, but I suspected that the older Miss Eliza Denholm got, the more she would speak her mind without fretting about the consequences.

I decided to take a chance with her. "Miss Denholm, perhaps you know that upon occasion, I have aided the police in certain circumstances?"

"I do, indeed, Miss Cross. I have heard your name from more than Imogene mentioning it."

"Then perhaps you've already guessed that I would like to discover who murdered her father."

Miss Denholm nodded, a wary look persisting.

"In the spirit of seeking justice, may I ask you some questions?"

She hesitated only a moment. "If I may answer them without bringing any harm upon my friend."

I marveled that such fervent loyalty should exist between two very different young women. Miss Denholm was not at all what I would have expected of any friend of Miss Schuyler's.

"I have no wish to harm your friend," I said, "or her mother." *Unless one of them a hand in the judge's death,* I added silently. I glanced about the terrace. There were about a dozen people mingling there, some of them hovering near the refreshment table, while several others were strolling on the lawn, ladies with parasols leaning on the arms of men in top hats. The rest were still in the conservatory. "Perhaps we might walk a bit?" I suggested.

She nodded and we set off down onto the lawn at a sedate pace. "Miss Denholm, I have heard . . . whispers . . . that the Schuylers weren't happy in their marriage. Was Mrs. Schuyler planning to leave her husband?"

That hesitation, again, as ponderous as a summer storm cloud. Then she said, "Could you blame her if she had been? Ruling his courtroom had gone to her husband's head. He wished to rule at home in similar manner, and Mrs. Schuyler didn't appreciate it. What woman would?"

I couldn't help a quiet laugh. "Certainly not my aunt Alva. Nor even my aunt Alice. For all they are very different women, each rules over her household in her own style. It seems to me society men are happy to allow their wives full rein when it comes to matters of the home. It's a kind of un-spoken bargain. The men rule business, earning buckets of money, and the women rule the nest, spending those very same buckets of money to show off their husbands' suc-cesses. But I assume something went awry with the Schuy-lers' bargain."

"It did, Miss Cross. But Mrs. Schuyler is no timid mouse, and not one to be cowed. No, it was Imogene I worried about. Her father expected a kind of perfection in her no in-dividual can maintain for long. It was eating away at her spirit."

I thought immediately of her cold, spartan bedroom—spartan, at least, when it came to anything personal. There were no sentimental items crowding the shelves, no books left lying on tables, no framed photographs to remind her of loved ones and happy times. Had this been her response to her father's overbearing insistence on perfection? To strip away anything that reflected her inner self and leave only the outer shell of a debutante—flawlessly beautiful, impeccably dressed, thoroughly poised?

"The engagement," I said, "he insisted upon it, didn't he?"

We had turned away from the water's edge, where a rim of cliff face and strewn boulders marked the boundary between land and sea. Walking closely together, we continued parallel to the shoreline, past the house and the driveway. Miss Denholm nodded, frowning. "How did you know that?"

It was my turn to hesitate, before answering vaguely, "I'd overheard something. Do you know why he wished Imogene to marry Jerome Harrington?"

She stopped walking suddenly, and after taking another step, I halted and turned to regard her.

"He believed she was becoming defiant. Rebellious. He said he feared she would do something to embarrass the family. It was either marry, or he'd keep her under lock and key."

"Rebellious in what way?"

Miss Denholm shook her head disparagingly. "Speaking her mind in mixed company, eluding her chaperone, having friends outside her parents' social circle. Even her friendship with me. Things he never would have minded if Imogene had been a man."

I considered this and wondered if perhaps I had judged Imogene Schuyler unfairly. "But why Jerome Harrington specifically?" I asked. "I realize he is of good family, but why not someone more . . . established in his own right?"

"If you mean, why did he saddle his daughter with a man who possesses no fortune of his own?" She frowned again and tilted her head at me. "How do you know that? No one else does. The Harringtons are well-heeled. It's only Jerome himself with a shortage of ready funds."

"I have my ways, Miss Denholm," I said cryptically, and

started walking again. She caught up and resumed her place at my side. Taking it as a good sign that she hadn't cut our tête-à-tête short and returned to the house, I hurried along with my questions. "I understand why Mr. Harrington would wish to enter into the marriage, but what motivation did Judge Schuyler have?"

"That I cannot tell you, Miss Cross. I didn't understand it, and neither did Imogene."

We entered a tree-lined path that hugged the contours of the steep shoreline. The leaves were trimmed with gold and the beginnings of russet, as if nature couldn't decide to cling to summer or burst into full, glorious autumn. From this vantage point, I could see the very tip of the Castle Hill Lighthouse, short in stature but vital in guiding vessels into the mouth of Newport Harbor. Mr. Agassiz had sold the plot of land it sat upon to the United States government for the specific purpose of building this lighthouse, but with the stipulation that he must not be able to see it from his house or lawns.

As we descended the sloping path, I stepped carefully over the uneven terrain, at the same time ducking beneath low-hanging branches. I had worn my second-best boots today, the tan leather ones with French heels and contrasting toe-caps in a rich, nutty brown. Stylish, but impractical for a stroll along rutted pathways among trees and rocks. "Getting back to Mrs. Schuyler, then you do believe she planned to leave the judge?"

"I don't know for certain, but Imogene believed her mother planned to formally separate from her husband after the wedding. You see, she planned a trip to Europe next month, and Imogene suspected it was her way of putting symbolic, as well as actual, distance between them. The judge knew nothing about it. Mrs. Schuyler swore Imogene to secrecy."

Then I had been correct about that. But did Mrs. Schuyler's planned trip in any way incriminate her in the death of her husband? She considered divorce out of the question, a social humiliation, but that could account for her planned departure to Europe, where she could remain technically married, but beyond her husband's reach.

What about Mr. Gould's "accident"? It was a far stretch to believe Mrs. Schuyler had driven the motorcar that ran him off the road. Or were the murder and the "accident" two separate incidents with no connection? Despite my aversion to coincidences, I had to admit it was possible.

"Miss Cross, all this is rather a moot point, now that the judge is no longer with us. I don't see how any of it could pertain to his murder. Certainly, you aren't implying that either Imogene or her mother had anything to do with it." Miss Denholm stopped and studied me intently. Her earlier anger reemerged as she apparently read the truth in my expression. I tried to deny that truth, or, at least, tried to temper its importance.

"I am only exploring all possibilities, Miss Denholm." Though I hadn't ruled out either woman, I spoke the truth. "Neither Mrs. nor Miss Schuyler have anything to fear if they are innocent."

By the outrage in her eyes, I saw that I had failed to mollify her. "'If'? How dare you invite my confidence, only to use it against my friend?"

"I'm doing no such thing. I'm only trying to paint a clear picture—"

"You reporters are all the same. Shifty, selfish, and ruthless. You don't care whom you injure, so long as you have your story."

Before I could protest to the contrary, she whirled away and stomped down the path toward the lighthouse. I knew better than to follow. I was sorry to have upset her to such an extent, and regretful to have made an enemy of someone who had so quickly gained my admiration.

At least I had confirmed the conclusion I'd reached at the Schuylers' residence concerning Mrs. Schuyler's plans. I only wished I had been able to learn why Judge Schuyler had wanted to marry his daughter to an impoverished gentleman, as well as how that gentleman had become that way.

I started the climb back toward the house, wondering how I might be able to question Jerome Harrington. He had been keeping himself well hidden since the incident at Wakehurst, so the chances of simply running into him were slim. A direct approach might become necessary. Jesse couldn't do it, not unless he could concoct some excuse to link Mr. Harrington to the break-ins at Oberlin's, even if only as a witness. Detective Myers wasn't likely to take the initiative, as he believed he had already found his man—or his man had been found for him—in the person of Ernest Kemp.

A sudden scream brought me up short. It was a woman's voice. She screamed again, and I realized the sound came from the lighthouse. I wheeled around and took the downward slope at a run, risking going over headfirst. Where the trees gave way to stunted ground cover, I broke through the foliage and onto the boulders that tumbled down to the water's edge.

I skidded onto the first boulder, my footing made unsure by tiny pebbles and loose dirt cast there by the tides and weather. My feet flew out from under me and I came down hard on my rump. As the pain reverberated up my spine and down my legs, my eyes teared, stinging yet more from the salty spray hitting the rocks. Even so, I looked all about me, seeing no one. The lighthouse stood nestled between two outcroppings on its stone block foundation. The waves lapped against the rocks in their timeworn pattern, while gulls swooped and dived in their quest for lunch. No lightkeeper's

This took a good deal more effort than when I had turned Judge Schuyler at Wakehurst. He had been lying on his side, but this man lay on his stomach. I heaved, and the body flopped over with the sickening motion of a fish out of water, ending with the hideous thud of a deadweight hitting the ground.

"Dear heavens," Miss Denholm said in a tight, small voice. "I think I'll be ill."

"Then look away," I told her. But I myself had to look. The features were bloated from death, and from lying face-down against the damp earth. Who was he? The clothing—tailored daywear—told me he was a gentleman. My gaze again went to the camera, a handheld box model that had been smashed, perhaps against the tree trunk beside which its pieces lay. "He'd come down to the lighthouse to take pictures," I murmured. "A pleasant morning or afternoon excursion. Or perhaps he came to capture the sunset." Castle Hill was a popular place for photography.

"What's that, Miss Cross?" Miss Denholm's voice shook.

I didn't repeat my comment. What did it matter now?

"Can you tell who it is?"

Every instinct urged me to turn away, to push to my feet and rush off to find help. I looked, nonetheless, and soon those distorted features began to take shape. A name, heard only yesterday at the police station, echoed in my brain. Felix Mathison, whom Ernest Kemp had admitted to threatening that night at Wakehurst, a man he held partly account-able for the deaths of twenty-five miners.

Given when this man must have died, Ernest Kemp had not yet been in jail.

Chapter 18

Detective Gifford Myers agreed with my assessment that, taking into consideration the timing, Ernest Kemp could have committed this latest murder. Not that he asked for my opinion, nor had I given it. He reached his conclusion on his own. Whereas I allowed for the possibility that such circumstantial evidence could be misleading, Detective Myers believed he had his case all sewn up.

I had experienced a moment of fear when, after the detective first arrived at Castle Hill, he had turned his razor-edged gaze on me and murmured, "Well, Miss Cross, it seems you have a knack for finding dead bodies. It makes one wonder if there is a reason for that."

He had then berated me upon learning I had touched the body. I had disturbed evidence, he had said; though, really, I couldn't see what difference I had made. That Felix Mathison had been killed by a blow to the head with a rock was obvious. It was also obvious by the way he lay, head wound facing up, that he had not fallen on that rock accidentally. Other than rolling him over, I had disturbed nothing. I had touched neither the rock nor the camera—nor anything else on Mr. Mathison's person, but the side of his neck and edge of his shoulder.

All this fell on deaf ears. The man sorely tested my patience, and I felt half inclined to give vent to my nausea, which had lodged like a rolling tide in my stomach since I had encountered the body, all over the front of the good detective's coat.

Instead, I irritated him further by asking a question. Mr. Agassiz hadn't known that Felix Mathison had come to take photographs. Because the scientist no longer owned the land immediately around the lighthouse, people could enter the area from several different footpaths without needing his permission or knowledge. But surely, someone had noticed Mr. Mathison's absence over the past day or so.

"Has he been reported missing by friends or family members?" I asked.

Detective Myers gritted his teeth and then replied, "His wife is off island, has been for several days. We're attempting to contact her. Now, if that will be all, my dear Miss Cross, I have work to do."

Once he retired behind the closed doors of the large parlor to conduct his business, I hurried to where Grace and some of the other guests had gathered in the central hall, the large, airy space open to the Stair Hall. I heard others in the adjoining conservatory. Grace came to her feet and met me partway. Before she could utter a word, I said, "Grace, go home, please."

She took my hands and squeezed them, as if loath to let go. "Can you come with me?"

"I wish to stay awhile longer and see if I can learn anything." I spoke quietly, well aware of the curious stares.

"After what that odious man said to you, do you really think he's going to tell you anything he learns?"

"No. But the other officers might." I had been relieved to see Scotty Binsford enter the house on Detective Myers's heels. Scotty had acknowledged me with the slightest of nods and afterward spared me not so much as a glance, which was smart of him. This way, Detective Myers would have no reason to admonish him not to speak to me.

I had another reason for staying. I needed to speak with Dr. Agassiz. Earlier, I'd remembered his connection to the coal-mining business, but I hadn't wished to cast such a shadow on his zoology event. But after finding Felix Mathison, another possibility had occurred to me. The camera. Dr. Agassiz was also a photography buff, as his displays proved. Could the culprit have followed Felix Mathison, believing him to be the scientist?

After a bit more persuasion, Grace took her leave. The results of the spill I'd taken had receded to a dull ache in my right hip, but even so, I couldn't sit. Instead, I paced the room, wearing a path back and forth from the vestibule to the conservatory. Before I found an opportunity to approach Dr. Agassiz, a young woman, halfway between Eliza's age and my own, sidled up to me, where I had paused at the double windows beside the fireplace, and simpered as if she were flirting with a potential beau.

"It's too horrible, Miss Cross, is it not?"

I regarded her flaxen curls and obviously rouged lips. She knew my name and must surely know of my profession. What did she want? "It most certainly is," I replied, at a loss for anything further to say. What more could one add?

"Eliza Denholm was with you, wasn't she?"

"She was."

"I heard you arguing with her earlier." She smiled in a manner that made her unattractive, despite her careful efforts to make herself beautiful. Her name came to me—Penelope Benscoter. Her great-grandfather had made his fortune in shipbuilding. Her family had taken her abroad last spring for her first European Season, and she had returned home still single. For a young woman of her social standing, it had to have stung not to be able to boast of an engagement to an earl or duke or prince.

"Were you following us?" I asked, taken aback, not that she had eavesdropped, but that she had admitted as much to me.

"A little. Are you sweet on her?"

I visibly flinched and my face heated. "What?"

"You heard me. If you are, you'll have a difficult time of it. Miss Denholm's affections are already engaged."

"I don't know what you are talking about, nor is it any of my business." Usually, I avoided being this blunt with members of the Four Hundred, but just then, I didn't care what she thought of me.

"Ever heard of a Boston marriage, Miss Cross?"

My mouth gaped briefly before I pinched my lips shut. Yes, I had heard of such things. I had once heard the term whispered in relation to my cousin Gertrude and her dearest friend, Esther Hunt—daughter of Richard Morris Hunt, who had designed so many of Newport's cottages. Even my aunt Alice had fallen prey to the gossip, fearing the girls' close friendship might lead to a ruination of her daughter's reputation, and she had doubled her efforts to see Gertrude married as soon as possible. Gertrude herself had silenced the rumors with her marriage to Harry Whitney, a love match if ever there had been one. They were wildly happy together and everyone knew it; Gertrude had blossomed into a vibrant and artistic young woman in the few short years of her marriage.

But Imogene? And yet . . . perhaps it explained her vehemence in rejecting Jerome Harrington, not to mention Miss Denholm's keen loyalty and protectiveness toward her friend. But could I trust the word of Penelope Benscoter?

"It isn't nice to spread gossip," I said. It was Miss Benscoter's turn to stand openmouthed as I walked away.

Yet, despite my admonishment, I couldn't completely discount her insinuations. I thought of Eliza Denholm's anger when she thought I suspected Imogene and her mother of ill doing. Eliza had been at Wakehurst that night, too. Modest and quiet, she hadn't attracted the attention of others. Which meant she could have gone up to the veranda at any time. Had Miss Denholm wished to be rid of the judge to prevent her friend from marrying?

"Emma, there you are."

At the familiar baritone, I hurried toward the vestibule. Derrick held his arms out to me, but as it wouldn't do to put on such a display with so many others still present, I slowed to a sedate walk and allowed him to take my hand in both of his and raise it to his lips.

"Jesse called the *Messenger* and told us what happened." He didn't ask me if I was all right. Anyone could plainly see I was not. How could I be? "Are you allowed to leave?"

"I suppose I am. I've already given my statement. Scotty is here, though, and I'm hoping he might be able to tell me something."

"You can catch up with him later, when Detective Myers won't overhear."

Derrick had a point, but I said, "That's not my only reason for lingering."

Taking his arm, I guided us across the house away from the others. We passed the staircase and found the empty study. Here I explained my conversation with Miss Denholm, Miss Benscoter's assertions, and the scenario that had taken shape in my mind.

He scowled. "I know our dear Miss Benscoter. She's a harpy in silk petticoats. I wouldn't put stock in anything that comes out of her mouth."

Chapter 19

Derrick felt less inclined to dismiss out of hand my concerns about Dr. Agassiz, his connection to the mining industry, and the coincidence of him and Mr. Mathison both dabbling in photography.

"Do you think it's possible the killer came here looking for Dr. Agassiz, saw Mr. Mathison strolling down the path with his camera, and mistook him for the former?" I stood facing Derrick, gazing into the steadiness of his dark eyes as he considered.

"They don't look much alike, other than being of a similar age," he said at length, and then added, "and Mathison was in coal as well."

"But that's assuming our culprit is well acquainted with the identity of his victims. In this case, he might have read Alexander Agassiz's name somewhere, knew of his scientific interests and photographic endeavors, learned he would be at Castle Hill, and came here to kill him. When he saw an older man strolling down the path toward the lighthouse with camera in hand, he believed he had his victim."

"Yes, I agree Agassiz needs to be warned, but not alarmed."

I nodded. "I'd bring my concerns to the detective, but it's highly doubtful he'll listen to me. But," I continued with sudden inspiration, "he might listen to you."

"Not if he knows of my affinity for a certain nosy, interfering lady reporter." He showed me a lopsided grin and ducked when my hand came up, threatening a smack. I placed my palm against his cheek, instead, and he turned his head to nuzzle it with his lips. "There's one problem with your plan," he said, sobering. "With Ernest Kemp behind bars, Myers will believe Dr. Agassiz to be out of his reach and therefore safe."

"That's why the good doctor must be warned."

"I just thought of a way we can do so before we leave." Derrick patted the breast of his coat, and the pocket sewn inside. It was a symbolic gesture, as his next words proved. "Agassiz is no doubt shaken by a murder in his own backyard, but I assure you he still has the good of his museum in mind. He'll be more than happy to accept donations, and I intend to give him one. While I make my pledge, he and I will have a blunt discussion."

"Tell him the best thing for him would be to return to Cambridge and his museum, and not to come back to Newport until this business is resolved."

We left Castle Hill a short time later. Despite our resolve not to alarm Dr. Agassiz, Derrick's warning had done just that. But perhaps it was just as well. The man planned to leave Newport the following day.

"I only wish it were as easy to speak with Imogene Schuyler," I mused on the way to Gull Manor in Derrick's carriage. "More and more, I feel her answers to certain questions are vital, but with her in mourning, it's virtually impossible to approach her. Surely, the Schuylers' servants have been given orders not to admit any but their closest acquaintances."

"A pity my mother couldn't be swayed to act on our behalf," Derrick mused aloud. We rounded Brenton Point, turning into the crisp breeze blustering in off the ocean. Though the sun continued to shine, the temperature had dropped in relation to the rising of the wind, and I sensed a coming storm, probably by that evening. We both raised a hand to hold our hat brims, while narrowing our eyes against a wind-borne assault of sand and grit.

I had to laugh at the absurdity of his suggestion, yet a wistfulness tugged at my heartstrings. On rare occasions, I allowed myself to imagine a life where Lavinia Andrews approved of me. She *had* approved, for an all-too-brief time, but my actions—in my efforts to trap a killer—had convinced her I could never be good enough for her son, or the Andrews family.

With a sigh, I released my regrets to a draft of air and remembered that Derrick didn't allow his mother or anyone to dictate his life.

"You could always sneak in dressed as a maid again." He flashed me a grin that told me not to take this suggestion seriously.

I didn't, yet I shook my head and explained why that wouldn't suit my intentions this time. "I had planned to snoop that time, and what better way than disguised as a maid? This time, if the opportunity arises, I intend to be direct. Speak my mind, confront her with what I've learned, and gauge both her answers and her reactions."

"Still believe she could be responsible?"

"No, I don't, actually. For her father alone, perhaps. A woman could have fired that arrow as easily as a man. Miss Schuyler has good aim and a strong arm when it comes to handling a bow. But taking Felix Mathison into account, along with the attempt on George Gould?" I shook my head. "I don't think Miss Schuyler is responsible. At least, not directly."

He turned his head and met my gaze. "Then she is not to be exonerated?"

"Not completely, not yet," I said steadily. "Nor her mother. But then, there's Jerome Harrington. Where has he been hiding?"

"Actually, he's been moving around, from what I've heard, staying at the homes of different friends and avoiding his parents."

"Avoiding his parents, or anyone who would like to ask him questions about that night?"

As we turned onto my drive, the front door opened and Patch came loping out. Katie followed and shut the door behind her. While Patch's yips expressed his happiness to see us, Katie's more urgent expression seized my attention. Derrick brought the carriage to a halt and I jumped down rather than wait for his assistance.

"Something is wrong," I said, stating the obvious.

"No, Miss Emma, everything here is all right. I think." Her cheeks were flushed and her eyes glittered almost feverishly as she glanced over her shoulder at the parlor window. She turned back and spoke in a whisper. "I didn't want you to be taken unawares. You have a visitor. Miss Imogene Schuyler. She's waiting for you in the parlor."

"What?" I tossed a glance at Derrick, who had alit from the carriage. This news clearly puzzled him as much as it did me. "Did she say why she's here? And how she got here?" I saw no other carriage waiting on the drive.

"To answer the second question, she didn't wish her carriage to be seen here, so she had her driver drop her off. As for why she's here, she said only that she wishes to speak with you. When Mrs. O'Neal told her we had no notion when you'd be home, she sat right down on the parlor sofa and announced she'd wait. Mrs. O'Neal has been supplying her with tea and pound cake for the past half hour."

I turned to Derrick and took his hand. "Perhaps you should go. It might be better if I speak with her alone."

He was nodding before I'd finished the suggestion. Leaning, he planted a kiss on my cheek, wished me luck, and said he'd be back later. Katie and I went into the house, with Patch excitedly racing in ahead of us. As if wishing to announce our guest to me, he sauntered into the parlor and sat facing me at Miss Schuyler's feet. To her credit, she placed a hand on his neck and absently stroked his fur. Nanny rose from one of the chairs across from our guest. I wondered if Imogene Schuyler had been taken aback with what she must have perceived as Nanny's presumption in keeping her company until my return.

"Good afternoon, Miss Schuyler. This is a surprise." As I spoke, Nanny gave me a look of relief and slipped from the room.

Miss Schuyler remained seated. Dressed in black, her hair dressed sedately beneath a small matching hat with a veil, an onyx brooch at her throat her only adornment, she had been utterly transformed from the bejeweled, frivolous girl of the Elizabethan Fete. Her blue eyes regarded me somberly. "I'm sorry to intrude, Miss Cross, but it is important."

"It's no intrusion, I assure you." I pondered for a moment whether to sit beside her on the sofa or across the low table from her, in one of the easy chairs. I decided on the familiarity of the sofa. "Tell me what I might do for you."

"First I'd like the truth." Her delicate nose flared, and an ominous sensation came over me, not wrongly, as it turned out. "Did you pose as a maid to enter my home?"

Mrs. Andrews. Having been unable to achieve my arrest, she had obviously gone to her friend Mrs. Schuyler, perhaps to urge her to press charges. With a sigh, I nodded. "Yes, I did."

I expected an angry rebuke, a threat to report me to the

police. Instead, she compressed her lips and continued to study me. "And did you learn anything significant?"

"Not much," I admitted, and then decided I had little to lose in revealing at least part of the truth. "I found your bedroom to be particularly unrevealing. You leave few, or make that no clues lying around as to the kind of individual you are."

"Were you hoping to find evidence of a murderess?"

How calmly she asked that question. I answered her in kind. "No, I was not hoping that at all." I almost added that I understood her lack of personal effects now, but that would have been to reveal my conversation with Eliza Denholm earlier. If Miss Denholm wished to apprise her friend of what we discussed, it was up to her.

Would Miss Schuyler next ask me what I discovered in her mother's room? I readied myself to give a reply, which never came, for Miss Schuyler changed the subject. "I heard of that man's arrest. Kemp, is it?" She waited for my nod. "Well, it's ridiculous. The police should let him go."

This surprised me, to say the least. "Why do you say that?"

"The detective told us the man is a foreman at some mining company back home in Pennsylvania. My father tried to help the miners, not hurt them. What reason would any of them have to murder him?"

"I've been wondering about that myself," I conceded. "And I'm guessing you have another idea."

She turned more toward me, as if preparing to confide. "I've heard about you, Miss Cross. I do understand why you've been making inquiries and sneaking about. That's why I'm here. I want you to catch my father's killer, and I believe I know who it is." Without waiting for me to urge her on, she said, "Clarice O'Shea. She's an actress and was one of the players at Wakehurst. The woman has been having an affair with my erstwhile fiancé, and I fully believe she murdered my father to ensure Jerome and I never married."

She left off and pulled back a few inches, but her gaze never left mine. She was measuring my reaction to this news, a revelation, or so she obviously believed. I hated to disappoint her. "I've already spoken with Miss O'Shea."

"You have? How did you know . . ."

"I have my ways, Miss Schuyler." I certainly didn't feel the need to tell her I'd been eavesdropping on her and Jerome Harrington that night. "According to Clarice O'Shea, her affair with Mr. Harrington lasted only briefly and ended nearly two years ago. She claimed to have had no contact with him until they saw each other at Wakehurst."

"And you believed her?" A bit of the arrogant Imogene emerged as she pursed her lips and narrowed her eyes.

"She also said you would be a fool not to marry him."

A look of mystification came over her, but only for an instant. "Why would she say that?"

I shrugged. "Because she believes it. But she didn't elaborate, so I can't give you specifics."

"Perhaps she enjoys being the mistress, rather than the wife."

"That's very cynical, Miss Schuyler."

"Is it? We're discussing the man who wished to marry me for my money, or have you forgotten?"

"No, I haven't forgotten. But are you sure that's all he wanted?"

"What else could there be?"

I regarded her beautiful face, her golden hair, and considered her obvious intelligence despite her haughtiness. Yes, Imogene Schuyler was a spoiled young woman, but how could she help being otherwise, given her upbringing? How often had I seen it—an indulgent mother, an imperious father. Or sometimes vice versa. Yet the results were usually the same: a sense of entitlement that obscured the individual's better qualities.

"You sell yourself short if you believe that."

She started to rise. "I've said what I came to say. If you won't take me seriously, perhaps I should go to the police with my suspicions."

I had it on my tongue to wish her luck getting Detective Myers to take her—or any woman—seriously. Instead, I blurted out a question before I could think better of it. "Where were you when the joust began?"

She dropped back down onto the sofa cushion. "Why do you ask that?"

Again I tempered my words so as not to reveal my having eavesdropped. "A little before it began, I noticed you heading toward the house. Your father tried to stop you, but you evaded him and kept going."

An eyebrow went up, forming a disdainful little peak above her eye. "Accusing me of murdering my own father, are you?"

"No, I'm asking where you went."

She leaped up from the sofa. I feared I had driven her away and fully expected her to toss the front door open and march directly out. But she only went as far as the front window. Her back to me, she said, "I went upstairs to one of the guest rooms. I wished to be alone."

"I see." Yes, I saw more than she thought I did. Despite her stony exterior that night, the argument with Jerome must have upset her greatly. If I'd had any doubts about that, the tears suspended in her eyes, when she turned back to me, banished them.

"Jerome was a cad to me that night. I caught him flirting with that actress and then he had the gall to tell me I had no choice but to endure it. I threatened to tell my father just what kind of man he was, but he only laughed and told me it was my father, after all, who was insisting on this marriage. So, I . . . I ran inside like a little coward and hid. My mother followed me. You may ask her if you wish." She hung her head. A tear dripped from her cheek and splashed onto her dress.

"Your mother was with you?"

She nodded. "Not that she was able to provide much comfort. She was as powerless to stop the marriage as I was."

"When you learned your father had been murdered, you broke down. Yet, there were no tears, Miss Schuyler, were there?"

"No, there were not. Upon hearing that news," she said with an almost trancelike calm, "I felt as a prisoner does when the door of his cell is suddenly opened after many years, when he doesn't know if he is being set free or walked to the hangman's noose. He knows only that his sentence has come to an end, and in either case, he is free of his constraints. I cried out because only in that moment did I realize how much of my life he had destroyed, including my chance of a happy marriage with J—"

She broke off, but I heard the beginning of a name. My heart went out to her, and I suddenly understood something that had eluded me previously. "Miss Schuyler, please come and sit." She hesitated, but finally returned to the sofa. I waited for her to resettle herself before leaning slightly toward her and saying, "You care for him, don't you? For Jerome."

Her face contorted and I feared a flood of tears. It took her only seconds to recover her composure—shaky, though it remained. Folding her hands on her lap, she gazed down at them. "I did. I would have been very much for this marriage, had it happened for the right reasons. We've known each other for some years, but last spring, in Paris, I came to see him, not as a boy, but as a man, and I admired what I saw. He had . . . principles. He was different from men like our fathers. Forward-thinking, fair-minded. Or so I had believed. I was ultimately proven wrong."

"How so?"

She looked at me incredulously. "By being the same as every other greedy man. Marrying for money. The notion galled me, humiliated me. It reduced me to a means to an end." She shook her head. "I tried to get him to deny it. Tried lashing out, accusing him, hoping he would deny wanting only my money, but he never did. He couldn't, because it was the truth."

Could Jerome Harrington be the very man Reggie had spoken of, the one Imogene had secretly set her cap for back in the spring, in Paris? "Did you ever try letting him know the truth of how you felt?"

"What? And risk the humiliation? No, never. And a good thing, as it turns out. I was terribly wrong about him."

"Perhaps not. Don't you see? Clarice O'Shea told me you'd be a fool not to marry him. Perhaps because he confided in her that he felt the same way about you."

For a moment, she looked stricken. Then she shook her head. "Then why has he not admitted as much to me?"

"For the same reason you didn't. It was too much of a risk."

"I don't know . . ." Again she shook her head, sadly. "It's too late now. Too much has been said."

"I'm sorry, Miss Schuyler."

"Are you? Aren't you the least bit satisfied to see a woman of my social standing brought low by her circumstances?"

"I take no pleasure in that at all," I said earnestly. Those two young people might have found happiness together, if only Imogene's father had left well enough alone.

She searched my face. "No, perhaps you don't." From outside on the drive came the sound of carriage wheels. She looked toward the window. "That will be my driver come to collect me. Please, Miss Cross, don't discount my theory about Clarice O'Shea."

We both came to our feet. She held out her hand to me, and we shook as if we were old acquaintances. I cannot deny that my opinion of her had softened considerably in the past few minutes. "Miss Schuyler, before you go, perhaps you can answer one other question for me." I waited for her nod, then asked, "Did you see anyone hovering on the veranda when you went into the house? Or when you came back outside?"

She immediately shook her head. "No, only the footmen. You don't think one of them murdered my father, do you?"

I assured her I didn't and walked her out. The footman opened the carriage door for her. Taking his hand, she placed her foot on the step, but then hesitated and turned. "There *was* someone else on the veranda when I returned to the garden. I'd almost forgotten. That annoying fellow. The one in bright colors and bells who was always tumbling in people's way. Do you think *he* could have murdered my father?"

Burt Covey had lied.

Or perhaps Imogene did. But if the latter, why would she have chosen the jester, of all people, to place on the veranda that night? If she was protecting someone, herself included, why admit to having seen anyone at all? To create a scapegoat?

I didn't think so. Her revelation might very well explain the thefts Mr. Van Alen had reported following the fete. It might explain more than that.

Derrick returned to Gull Manor as dusk fell, and not a moment too soon. That storm I had sensed earlier broke as he drove his carriage into my barn, and a pelting rain chased him through the kitchen door, sending Katie for the mop. He and I sat together in the parlor, while Nanny put the finishing touches on dinner and Katie set the table in our little-used dining room. I told him what I had learned from Imogene Schuyler.

"She has no reason to wrongly implicate Burt Covey," I said, raising my voice slightly to be heard over the rain striking the windows, "not when she believes Clarice O'Shea shot that arrow. Burt Covey, on the other hand, deliberately implicated Ernest Kemp, never making mention of his own jaunt up to the veranda. That's highly suspicious."

Derrick stood up from the sofa and grabbed the fire poker to enliven the flames in the fireplace. The night had turned chilly. "Why would Burt Covey murder Judge Schuyler?"

I heard by his tone that he wasn't challenging my theory; he was helping me reason it out. "We don't know very much about him," I pointed out. "He could be from Pennsylvania and once stood before the judge in the courtroom. Because of Clayton Schuyler, he might have spent time in prison. He certainly doesn't strike me as the most upstanding citizen I've ever met."

"He did go to great lengths to avoid you." Derrick leaned the poker in its stand and returned to the sofa. As he sat, he wrapped his hand around mine. "And let's face it, theater life is no picnic. The uncertainties, the roving lifestyle, the disappointing performances. Many resort to thieving just to keep food in their mouths."

I thought it over, frowning. "That doesn't seem enough of a motive for murder."

"Being sent to prison?"

"His sentence would have to have been extreme to prompt him to take such measures."

"Not necessarily. Not if he had people depending on him who suffered while he served his sentence."

"That's true. Unless he had some other reason for being on that veranda, one he felt compelled not to reveal when he and I spoke."

Wind spiraled in the chimney, a whistling sound that made me shiver. Derrick reached an arm across my shoulders and pulled me close. "Miss Schuyler came back outside just before the joust began, and that's when she saw Burt Covey on the veranda."

"Yes."

"And you saw the judge alive before she went into the house."

"Right before. And before the altercation between Neily and Mr. Kemp. Burt Covey helped break up the argument, but after that, I didn't see where he went. Nor did I see what became of Mr. Kemp. Or Jerome Harrington."

"Or Imogene or her mother," Derrick reminded me. "You only have Imogene's word for their whereabouts."

"That's true." A dull ache throbbed behind my eyes as I tried to make sense of it all. "The judge died after Imogene went into the house, and before I became aware of the barking dogs. Not a lot of time, a matter of ten minutes or so. To think the judge might still be alive if he hadn't wished to smoke that cigar, or if he had been rude enough to smoke it around the other guests."

"Egads," Derrick said with a mock shudder. "I'm glad I've never taken up smoking."

Chapter 20

Wednesday passed uneventfully, except that upon awakening, I experienced a marked stiffness in my right hip, which had taken the brunt of my fall at Castle Hill. I gritted my teeth and bore it as I prepared for my day, and found that by the time I climbed into my carriage for the drive into town, I was feeling considerably more limber.

That evening, Derrick and I decided to attend the theater. More specifically, we planned to enter the building, but the drama that would unfold would be far different than the musical marriage farce written by John Philip Sousa.

Tonight was to be the dress rehearsal for *The Bride Elect*, so we had little doubt Burt Covey would be there. When we reached the Opera House, a small line extended from the front door along the sidewalk, a drizzle keeping people close to the building front. These would be friends of the crew and actors, invited to give the players a feel for how the audience would react on opening night. We took our places at the end of the line, our heads bowed against the misting rain; we shuffled along with the rest as they filed through the entrance, and we tried to look as though we belonged.

"Name," a doorman with a clipboard asked as we reached him.

Derrick didn't answer, and when the man looked up from his list with a quizzical expression, Derrick held out two folded dollar notes. The man's eyebrows went up, and Derrick said, "We're leaving in the morning, and the missus here had her heart set on seeing the show. Surely, you can see your way to letting us in . . ." He held the money beneath the man's nose.

The doorman looked us up and down. Apparently, we passed muster, for the money disappeared into a pocket in his uniform and he waved us in. We hurried through the lobby, but didn't take our seats among the others. Instead, we slipped through a door and into a corridor that skirted the main part of the theater and brought us backstage.

Here we met with a flurry of activity, the actors and stagehands too busy to pay us much mind. When someone did challenge us, Derrick said in his most authoritative voice, "*Newport Messenger,* here for exclusive interviews with several of the cast."

"Don't get in the way."

A woman stepped into our path and simpered. "I'm Lily Carmichael, and you can interview me as soon as we're done with rehearsal."

Derrick nodded. "Carmichael, Lily. Very good. We'll find you."

I didn't know exactly what part Burt Covey would be playing, but he had told me he was part of the chorus, and what we heard now coming from the stage didn't sound like a rousing vocal number. Those were yet to come. We hurried along to the dressing room, me leading the way, since I had been backstage only days earlier to see Clarice O'Shea. I looked for her, half hoping I wouldn't see her and not have to offer an explanation.

As it turned out, we ran into Burt Covey quite by accident. He came hurrying in through the stage door, out of breath as if he were late and had run all the way here. He saw us and halted, his gazing shifting from me to Derrick and back to me. Actors and stagehands passed between us, but as if no one else existed, Burt Covey's gaze never left us. He was poised on the balls of his feet, making me believe he might do an about-face and bolt.

I shook my head and spoke so as not to be overheard. "Don't, Mr. Covey. We only wish to speak with you."

"I have no wish to speak to *you*." His gaze shifted back and forth again. "Either of you."

"I'm afraid you have no choice." In a swift motion, Derrick moved forward and grasped his arm. "When do you go on?"

He seemed to debate whether or not to reply, but said, "In a little while. After the first act. But I need to change and get on my makeup."

"Not to worry. We should have ample time for what we've come to discuss." Derrick gestured with his chin toward the stage door, which led out behind the theater. "Outside, unless you want witnesses to hear what we have to say."

"Look, I don't even know who you are," the erstwhile jester protested.

"Derrick Andrews, *Newport Messenger.* I believe you're already acquainted with my associate Miss Cross."

His mouth slanted with disdain. "Yeah, I remember her."

"Nice to see you again, Mr. Covey." I smiled my most cordial smile and pointed to the door, where two more cast members had just entered. "Shall we?"

We walked out to a square lot between the theater and the businesses along the south side of Washington Square and those facing Thames Street. Tall trees lining the perimeter provided us with some shelter from the drizzle. Several carriages and a couple of wagons also provided a measure of privacy from anyone going in or out of the stage door. From the streets around us came the sounds of evening traffic: horses, carriages, even a motorcar or two.

Burt Covey shuffled his feet and thrust his hands into his pockets. "What do you want?"

"What we want, Mr. Covey, is for you to come clean about whether or not you truly saw Ernest Kemp on the veranda of Wakehurst the night of Judge Schuyler's murder." Although I matched the quietness of his voice, I spoke forcefully.

"Who?"

Derrick stepped closer to him, effectively pinning him against the side of the wagon at his back. "The man you claimed to have seen climb the steps of the veranda that night. His name is Ernest Kemp. Don't play games. You know very well Miss Cross means the man she described to you when you spoke together at the Topside Tavern."

"All right, yes, I saw him on the veranda."

"Really, Mr. Covey?" Again I smiled. "Because someone else saw *you* on the veranda, right about the time Judge Schuyler was killed."

"What? Who said that?" Fear skittered across Mr. Covey's features. "They're lying."

"I doubt that very much," I said. "This person has absolutely no reason to incriminate you. In fact, it was mentioned only in passing, without any insinuation that you might be guilty. And yet you lied."

"I did not lie. You . . . you never asked if I was on the veranda."

While I clenched my teeth in frustration, Derrick said in a threatening tone, "You lied by omission. Why? What were you hiding?"

Before he could answer, I found my voice. "You must

have seen where the footmen stowed the archery equipment. Is that what sent you up there, an unforeseen opportunity to murder an adversary?"

"'An adversary'? And, no, I had no idea the archery equipment was on the veranda. I told you, I was too busy helping to pack up the stage."

"So, then, if we ask every member of the cast that was there," I pressed, "they'll all corroborate your story?"

Mr. Covey hesitated, panic flickering in his eyes. "All right, I might have walked up there. Just to look out over the garden to where the jousting was. I wanted to see it."

"Are you from Pennsylvania, Mr. Covey?" Derrick stepped closer to the man, prompting him to press tighter to the side of the wagon. "Did you come before the judge in his courtroom?"

"Yes, Mr. Covey," I joined in, "have you harbored a grudge that you decided to satisfy that night?"

"No! Look, everyone was distracted, so I ran up, not to the veranda, to the house. All right? I snuck into the dining room and . . . and I took a few things. Nothing much, trifles. Nothing anyone would miss. Have you ever known hunger, either of you? Ever slept outside for nights on end because you couldn't afford a room? Look, I'm sorry, I'll give it all back. But I didn't murder anyone. I swear. I never even heard of Judge Schuyler until he turned up dead. I had no reason to kill anyone." He left off, close to tears. An act? Possibly, considering we were dealing with an actor.

"What about Mr. Kemp?" I challenged him yet again. "Did you actually see him on the veranda, or were you trying to set someone else up to be blamed for your thievery— and whatever else you may have done?"

"There was nothing else, I swear. And, no, I never saw this Kemp fellow. When you came asking questions, I thought at first it was about what I took. When you made it clear it was about the judge's murder, I thought if someone remembers me up there, they'll think I killed him. But I didn't. I remembered Kemp from when you were trying to break apart those two men. I told you I saw him on the veranda to put suspicion on someone else."

"You were willing to let another man be wrongfully accused of murder in order to protect yourself from a theft charge?" Derrick grabbed a fistful of Burt Covey's coat front. "Why, I should—"

"That's enough, Mr. Andrews." Jesse stepped out from behind the carriage parked to our right. Scotty Binsford followed him. Derrick released Burt Covey and dropped his hand to his side.

The actor took in this latest development with horror dawning on his features. "What is this?" His gaze connected with mine, his expression one of disbelief. "You set me up."

"That's right, we did, Mr. Covey," I said "You see, no one likes a liar. Obviously, you are a thief. For that alone, you must answer to the law. As to the rest, time will tell, won't it?"

"How many times do I have to say it?" He took on a pleading tone, but I detected the anger beneath it. "I didn't murder the judge. I don't know who did."

"As Miss Cross said, 'Time will tell.'" Jesse signaled to Scotty, who came forward with a pair of handcuffs.

"You can't arrest me." Mr. Covey attempted to slip away between Derrick and the wagon. Derrick reached out and gripped the man's arm and helped Scotty wrestle both hands behind his back. The cuffs locked into place. "I have a show to perform in."

"Not tonight, Mr. Covey." Jesse again signaled to Scotty, who walked the actor out to the street. To Derrick and me, Jesse said, "He'll be booked on theft, thanks to you two, and Myers won't be able to accuse me of overstepping my bounds.

That should give us enough time to check into Covey's background and see if he has any connections to the judge, as well as the coal industry. If so, it could go very badly for him."

"And if not," I said, "at least we've brought a petty thief to justice."

"Considering he stole from James Van Alen," Derrick said, "it's probably going to add up to more than mere petty theft, no matter the size of the items he stole. Jimmy only collects the best."

Later that evening, Nanny, Katie, and I sat at the kitchen table, enjoying a pot of tea and the honey oatmeal bread Nanny had made earlier that day. The warm kitchen still held the savory aromas of the simple roast chicken and root vegetables we'd had for dinner before I left for the Opera House. I was still in my evening dress, while they were much more comfortable in their cotton nightdresses and warm flannel robes. Katie's long russet braid draped over her shoulder and caught the light from the overhead fixture.

"I tell you both, all that talk of theft tonight has left me feeling terribly guilty about this fan Mr. Van Alen sent me." I circled the rim of my teacup with my forefinger. The fan sat open beside it, the silvery silk and gold embroidery looking impossibly out of place on our scarred pine table. "I've decided to go by Wakehurst tomorrow and return it."

"I think you're being silly." Nanny bit into her slice of oat bread, enjoyment plain on her face as she chewed. "What's a fan to a man of his means? If he didn't want you to have it, he wouldn't have sent it."

"Mrs. O'Neal is right, Miss Emma. Besides, you did do Mr. Van Alen a service, helping to capture the man who robbed his house." Katie's freckled features took on an indignant look. "You do realize one of the footmen might have been blamed and given the sack."

Dear Katie, always championing others in service. She knew what it was like to be wrongfully accused and dismissed from employment. "I'm very glad that didn't happen," I told her. "But Mr. Van Alen sent that fan under false circumstances. I'd fibbed to him and I certainly don't deserve a reward for that."

"But you fibbed for a good reason, Miss Emma."

Where I half expected Nanny to take up Katie's argument, she smiled benevolently across the table at me. "It's like Mr. Vanderbilt leaving you all that money, isn't it? It simply doesn't sit right with you, and that's that. Return the fan, then, and have done with it."

"I intend to."

"Miss Emma, do you really think this Burt Covey character murdered Judge Schuyler and that other man? And ran that nice Mr. Gould off the road?"

I wondered about Katie's description of Mr. Gould. He wasn't particularly known for fairness toward his workers, or those with whom he did business. It was George Gould's terms, or no terms. But her question had no easy answer.

"No matter how one looks at it," I said, "there are contradictory circumstances with both current suspects. Ernest Kemp says he wants restitution for the families of the miners who died in that cave-in. He might certainly have wished revenge against George Gould and Felix Mathison, who were both investors in the mine. He also entered the fete at Wakehurst under false and incriminating circumstances. Yet, if Judge Schuyler ruled in favor of miners' rights, why would Ernest Kemp have killed him?"

"And this Burt Covey?" Nanny prompted me.

"He might have held a grudge against Clayton Schuyler. He's proven by his actions that he is a criminal type. If he'd been sentenced to prison by the judge, Burt Covey might have wanted revenge. But unless we can find a connection between him and the miners, it makes no sense for him to have gone after the other two men."

Katie, seeing I had emptied my plate, passed the platter of bread to me. "Just because you don't know of any connection now, it doesn't mean there isn't one."

"No, that's true." I took the platter from her. Despite my already having had two slices, I took another and absently broke off a piece of it. Before I popped it in my mouth, I said, "One thing has been bothering me. And that's *why* Judge Schuyler ruled in favor of the miners. After what his daughter and others had to say about him, I'm having trouble reconciling the fair-minded judge with the despotic husband and father."

"Everyone has their redeeming qualities," Nanny suggested with an offhand shrug. She lifted the pot to refill her tea and offered more to Katie and me. Katie accepted. I waved her off, still preoccupied with my quandary.

"By all accounts, Clayton Schuyler was a tyrant to his wife and daughter, unable to maintain his temper or a sense of fairness. How on earth can he have played the champion for complete strangers whose interests conflicted with those of his peers?"

"Familiarity breeds contempt?" Katie offered.

Again, I let the comment pass as I continued reflecting. "I also don't understand why he insisted his daughter marry Jerome Harrington, a man who had everything to gain from the match, but little to offer. His daughter has no idea why."

"It would seem only the judge and Jerome Harrington can answer that question," Nanny said, and Katie nodded her agreement.

"Another question Mr. Harrington can answer is where he's been hiding."

"*Has* he been hiding?" Nanny asked. "Or is he merely staying with different friends to avoid having to return to his parents' home? Not to mention staying out of the public eye. One can hardly blame him for that."

"Yes, that's very true," I said with a sigh. "I suppose if the police wished to find him, they would. Unless he's left the island."

"Do you suspect him, Miss Emma?"

"I suppose there is no reason to. Of anyone, he had the most to gain from Judge Schuyler being alive, whereas now he's no better off than he was before. Whoever killed Judge Schuyler had to have stood to gain something significant."

I was about to bid Katie and Nanny good night, when a thought occurred to me, one that sent the blood draining from my face. "I just remembered something. The Harringtons sold off some mining stock recently. I wonder if Jerome was also threatened that night."

Nanny stood to bring our empty plates to the sink. "By Ernest Kemp?"

"Yes, by him, but if Mr. Kemp isn't the killer, could Jerome and his parents also be targets because of their ties to the coal industry?"

"But you just said they sold off their stock, Miss Emma." Katie came to her feet, too, and reached for my cup and saucer.

I handed it to her and said, "They did, but if they were invested in that mine at the time of the accident and had helped put pressure on the mine owners, they could still be held to blame. Depending on who our killer is, they could be in danger."

Chapter 21

Early the next morning, Mr. Stevenson himself, along with an assistant, delivered my newly repaired carriage to Gull Manor. With all the work he had done, it looked and rode like a new vehicle, and the coat of polish he had applied to the panels made them gleam in the sunlight. He and his assistant switched the horses and left in the small buggy I had borrowed from him.

I had planned to visit the police station—and Jesse—first thing to convey my fears concerning Jerome Harrington and his family. But when I retrieved my handbag from the hall table, the extra weight inside reminded me once again about Mr. Van Alen's fan.

A stop first at Wakehurst, then. Despite the relative earliness of the hour, I hoped to find Mr. Van Alen not at home. Or perhaps still abed. That way, I could entrust the fan to one of his servants and be on my way. To that end, I wrote a note expressing my thanks, but declining the gift. The coward's way out? Indeed.

Would he think I believed his gift to be an attempt at flirtation? I certainly hoped he would give me more credit than that, but as I drove up the long, curving drive, I wished I had had the item sent over. Leftover fog from last night's storm silvered Wakehurst's façade and softened its edges, and left the trees and foliage stooped with the weight of the clinging moisture. My hopes for a speedy departure continued as I raised the knocker on the front door, and even as the butler admitted me. I tried handing him the fan and my note, but he would have none of it.

"If you'll be seated, miss, I'll announce you."

"Really, there is no need—" I said to his back.

He walked away as if I hadn't spoken. With little choice but to wait, I meandered to the seating arrangement beside the fireplace in the Stair Hall. I neither saw nor heard any signs of the mastiffs, and I wondered if their encounter with the judge's body had left its mark on them. Did animals experience trauma the way humans did? Most people wouldn't think so, but I knew Patch had learned valuable lessons from his experiences that he passed on to me in the form of the warnings I'd learned to trust.

Moments later, I heard a brisk stride coming in my direction down the Long Gallery. I stood and smoothed the front of my dress.

"Good morning, Miss Cross. What brings you to Wakehurst at this hour?"

I gaped as a figure came into view, not that of James Van Alen, but the much more youthful Jerome Harrington.

"Mr. Harrington," I mumbled in surprise. A good three or four seconds of silence followed as I regained my bearings. "I hadn't expected to see you here."

"Nor I, you, Miss Cross." He offered me an amused smile that reminded me of my manners.

"I'm sorry. No, of course you didn't. I came to return something to Mr. Van Alen. Is he here? His butler seemed to think he was."

"He left quite early this morning, just as the sun was rising. Something about bird-watching out on Sachuest Point with the Wetmores and the Kings, I believe."

"In this fog?"

"You know how bird-watchers are. Took the dogs with him. Asked me last night if I wished to join him. I told him there was nothing I'd rather *not* do." He laughed, for a moment making him appear like a mischievous little boy. Then he apparently remembered *his* manners. "Is there something I can do for you?"

I was about to hand him the fan and my note and take my leave. But after yesterday's revelations, I realized I had stumbled upon an opportunity. "I don't wish to interrupt your breakfast, but have you a few minutes to speak with me?"

"I'd just finished when Henslow told me you were here. Have you eaten?"

"I have, thank you."

"Then come. I always enjoy a morning stroll after breakfast. Let's go out to the garden and you can tell me what's on your mind." He gestured down the length of the Long Gallery, to where the dining room and library let out onto the veranda. "Funny, but we've both returned to the scene of the crime," he joked, though his choice of words sent a chill through me. He must have noticed the slight stiffening of my posture; for in the next instant, he said, "Forgive me, Miss Cross, a poor attempt to be blithe. You must be wondering what I'm doing here."

"I wouldn't dream of asking."

In fact, I had already guessed. He had been moving from place to place all week, staying with different friends, and, I assumed, did not wish to wear out his welcome at any one home. Smart, especially considering his homelessness could extend well into the future. I hadn't realized he and James Van Alen were so closely acquainted. It seemed an odd pairing, considering the difference in their ages. But then I remembered Mr. Van Alen's sympathetic kindness to Neily. No wonder he had offered Jerome Harrington a place to stay.

"I'll tell you, anyway. My parents have cast me out." He delivered this news almost joyfully. The boyish nonchalance returned. "I am not to darken their doorstep until I've mended my ways."

"I'm sorry to hear that. I'm sure they'll relent sooner rather than later." At least I hoped they would, and that this young man wouldn't find himself in the same position as my cousin.

"No matter." He offered the crook of his arm as we reached the steps down to the garden.

Wisps of fog drifted lazily over the footpaths and flower-beds, enveloping the statues and shrubbery. Purple asters, orange *Helenium,* pink and yellow chrysanthemums, and other autumn flowers blurred one into another like an Impressionist painting. Even in the muting haze, the garden offered a glorious riot of color I hadn't fully appreciated the night of the fete. Now I reveled in the beauty of it, breaking into a smile of admiration. We stepped onto the main path at the garden's center, avoiding walking on the damp grass.

"I'm glad to have run into you, Mr. Harrington," I began. I didn't wish to blurt a warning all at once. And I wished to satisfy my curiosity first. I had, after all, been hoping to speak with this young man for several days now. "There are some questions about the judge that have been puzzling me. Perhaps you can answer them."

"Ah, yes. The reporter has questions." He held out his free hand as an invitation for me to continue.

"I understand Judge Schuyler ruled in a case involving miners who were striking for fair wages and working hours."

He nodded. "Yes, I know about that case."

"He ruled in the miners' favor. That strikes me as unusual, considering the judge's background and social position."

"It does, doesn't it?" He pushed some strands of sun-streaked hair back from his brow. "Perhaps he had an attack of conscience. For once."

"Then you found him difficult, too?"

" 'Too'?" He stole a sideways glance at me, his lips curling in a small smile. "To whom else have you been talking?"

I saw no reason not to tell him. "A few of the Schuylers' servants, and Miss Schuyler as well."

"Imogene?" He sounded startled. His face swiveled toward mine. "She agreed to speak with you?"

"Actually, she came to see me. She has a theory as to who murdered her father."

We reached the statue at the apex of the garden, and as if by unspoken agreement, we turned smoothly to the right, to where the Shakespearean stage had stood the night of the fete.

"Whom does she suspect?"

I watched him carefully as I replied, "Clarice O'Shea."

He stumbled to a halt. "*What? Has Imogene lost her mind?"

"She believes you and Miss O'Shea have been having an affair, and that the actress might have murdered her father to prevent your marriage."

"That's madness. Clarice and I . . ." He trailed off, his jaw working. "She and I had an association at one time, but that was almost two years ago. Clarice has moved on, as have I. Or . . . I *believed* I had." Sadness drenched those last words in such profusion, I couldn't help thinking of Imogene's desperate confession regarding her feelings for him. Could it be . . .

"Mr. Harrington, Imogene believes she has good reason to

suspect Miss O'Shea. If you can convince her otherwise, you should do so without further delay."

We stopped almost directly in front of where the stage had been, and I turned momentarily to gaze back up at the house. How far away and ghostly it seemed from the emptiness of the garden. The night of the fete, when dozens had packed these pathways and decorations festooned the greenery, the property had appeared and felt much smaller. All at once, I realized what a fool I had been to ever entertain as truth Burt Covey's claim of seeing Mr. Kemp on the veranda. At night, from this distance, even with the electric lights on, he could not have identified a man dressed essentially the same as every other man in attendance.

Mr. Harrington stared at the ground and shook his head. "It's too late."

I knew that not to be the case, but I couldn't betray Miss Schuyler's confidence. I could only try to persuade Mr. Harrington to find his courage. "Perhaps not. Perhaps all Miss Schuyler wanted was a reassurance that she needn't fear the competition of another woman. *Had* you reassured her, Mr. Harrington?"

He kicked at the sweet alyssum blossoms bordering a nearby bed. "No, hang it. She and I got off on the wrong foot immediately. From the first, it was a battle of wills, and there seemed nothing I could do to change it. And I refused to be perceived as a mooning puppy trotting after her."

Indeed. Judging by what I had overheard at the fete, he had proven as stubborn and proud as his fiancée.

We started walking again, and he surprised me by offering an explanation. "She believed I was marrying her only for her money."

"Were you?" I asked him gently. "You wouldn't be the first man to enter into marriage negotiations for that reason."

"I admit to needing the money, Miss Cross, but not for myself. That money would have been for Imogene herself, to continue living in the style she grew up with, until such time as I could support her properly." He again turned his face toward mine, and the tears glistening in his eyes astonished me. "I loved her, Miss Cross. I still do, I believe."

"Good heavens, then you must speak to her at once. Please, Mr. Harrington, set aside all other considerations." I meant, of course, his pride and his desire to protect his heart, but I could never utter those words outright to someone I barely knew. "Simply speak to her. You might find that . . . things have changed."

He searched my face, even as Imogene had done. I allowed him to read into my words what he would, but I had said my piece; decency would allow no more. We continued walking, nearing the tall hedge that separated the formal garden from the outer perimeter of the property, that wide swath of lawn where the jousting had occurred. Mr. Harrington's argument with Miss Schuyler had also occurred there, a joust of words, and my face heated at the memory of my eavesdropping as we approached the wall of fading greenery. Droplets of condensation, formed by the mist, clung to the tips of each leaf, quivering when the wind stirred.

"Mr. Harrington, there is something else I must say. Oh, nothing more to do with Miss Schuyler," I quickly assured him when his gaze darted warily to my own. "No, this has to do with the mining incident, and a very real threat that might have been responsible for Judge Schuyler's murder. There was another death—did you hear of it?"

"Felix Mathison?" When I nodded, he nipped at his bottom lip and shook his head sadly. "Poor Mathison. I only heard about it last night when I arrived at Wakehurst. I've been avoiding the newspapers, as you can imagine."

"I can. But you see, Felix Mathison was heavily invested

in coal, as is George Gould. They had shares in the mine in question. Someone tried to run Mr. Gould off the road a couple of nights ago."

"You don't say? Was he hurt?"

"No, he was lucky. But my concern now is for you and your father. I understand he has coal investments as well, as do so many of the Four Hundred." I didn't wish to tip my hand by admitting I knew they had sold their stock. "Please have a care."

"My *father*." He expelled the word from his lips as if he had tasted something sour. We turned at the hedge, walking parallel to its length. Mr. Harrington's arm tensed beneath my hand. "Yes, he was invested, and like Gould and Mathison, he had shares in that particular mine."

"Oh? Did he sell?" I knew perfectly well he had. A detail suddenly became clear to me. "Mr. Harrington, did your father relinquish his shares at your insistence? Is that the reason for your estrangement, at least in part?"

A flush suffused his face. "How astute you are, Miss Cross. Yes, when I discovered what had happened to those miners, I confronted my father. I told him to sell out or suffer the consequences." A cutting edge crept into his voice. "The notion that anyone should profit over the deaths of innocent workers is despicable."

"By 'consequences,' I assume you mean you threatened to go to the press."

"Among other things. You know as well as I that no matter how wealthy or powerful, the Four Hundred avoid scandal at all costs. What my father and the others did was tantamount to manslaughter, at the least."

"I'm glad you hold lives to be more important than money, Mr. Harrington." It must have been ethics such as these on which both Clarice O'Shea and Imogene Schuyler had based their opinions of this young man, at least initially in Imogene's case. Once more, he reminded me of Neily, setting principle ahead of fortune.

"Precious few of the Four Hundred would agree," he commented with a wry smirk.

We passed the first two arches cut into the hedge. "Judge Schuyler put the miners' lives first," I reminded him.

Another smirk. He reached out his free hand, swiping at the hedge and sending a barrage of droplets showering to the ground.

"Why do you think he agreed to let you marry Imogene, knowing you were without fortune?" As with siding with the miners, this seemed out of character for a man like Clayton Schuyler.

He struck the hedge again; the water hit the ground like a volley of pellets. "I gave him little choice."

"I don't understand." I almost asked what sort of leverage Mr. Harrington could have had to force the judge's hand. But I held my tongue, seeing that he was about to continue. That wasn't the only reason I didn't speak. Something in his countenance had changed. I saw no sign of the boy now, only a disillusioned, angry man.

"The good judge certainly had the last word where Imogene was concerned, didn't he?" He spoke with bitterness, as if I weren't there, as if voicing his thoughts aloud in the privacy of his own company. "Still, I thought as long as the marriage went through, and I got Imogene out from under her father's thumb, I would have the rest of my life to prove to her my feelings were genuine."

He still hadn't explained. A destitute gentleman in love with the daughter of a wealthy and powerful man—sincere or not, Mr. Harrington would normally have had no chance of being accepted. Once again, what leverage had been at his disposal?

A feeling of dread swept over me. I stopped walking and slipped my hand from his arm.

"The miners, the ruling . . ." My hand flew to my lips as I gasped. Had Judge Schuyler *not* acted in the miners' best interests? Had he somehow played a double hand—was *that* Jerome Harrington's leverage? The question that had been meandering through my mind suddenly hit its answer squarely. "The ruling," I whispered in growing horror. "It was a ruse to hurry the miners back to work, to distract them from the danger of repairs that had never been done."

He met my gaze, the pupils of his eyes contracting to black pinpoints. "I had every faith you'd get it eventually, Miss Cross. Clayton Schuyler knew what he was doing when he made that ruling. As did his friends, the lot of them. Including my father. The price of those stocks had been plummeting due to the union demands, and they couldn't allow that, could they? Especially Mathison. Seems he'd made an ill-advisedly large investment in that particular mine, and his fortune could not endure having it fail. It was he who engineered the whole disgusting debacle."

"Good heavens." I forced myself not to drag my gaze away from the icy conviction in his countenance, not to look desperately up at the house in hopes a footman—anyone— had come outside. How very far away the house loomed now, a distant fortress that offered me no protection.

Mr. Harrington grasped my wrist. His tone both insisted and pleaded. "Surely, you see they deserve to be punished for their crime, don't you, Miss Cross? The families of those dead miners will never receive compensation—at least, not enough to make a difference. Some of them will starve on the streets. Innocent women and children. They deserve some measure of justice, don't they?"

My heart hammered, and the world around me stood out in stark relief, as if all of the beauty had been squeezed from the garden, leaving a dry husk. "Of course they do, Mr. Harrington. You're quite right."

"As for Judge Schuyler, he compounded his sins by ruining everything for me with Imogene. It was he who constantly drove home the point that I was marrying her only for her inheritance. And once the idea lodged in her mind, she turned against me entirely. He made her loathe me. It was his revenge for being forced to agree to the marriage in the first place."

"Yes, I understand. You can't be blamed for being angry." I tried to start us walking again, tried to turn him toward the house. He didn't budge, nor did he release his hold on my wrist. He stared into my face, searching, studying every line, until I longed to shield myself with my hands.

His jaw firmed and his mouth flattened. "Your family, too, Miss Cross. Those Vanderbilts. Do you think they're any different? If the old man hadn't died when he did—"

"Don't say it, Mr. Harrington. I know you don't mean that."

"Do you?" He fell into motion and tugged me along behind him. I found myself half running to keep up and not be dragged, until we reached the next arch. I let out a cry that was easily swallowed by the foliage and muffled by the fog. A cry that would never reach the house.

Please, please, someone look out a window. Come out onto the veranda. See what is happening.

He dragged me through to the other side, and with a wrench of my arm, he spun me around to face him. "I don't think you *do* understand. Because you're like them, you're one of them."

"I'm not—"

"I saw how you were dressed the night of the fete. Oh, you might not be as rich as your relatives, but I know you hold them in high esteem, and you're not averse to accepting their gifts. You don't care what they do, so long as they keep you in their little circle and supply you with ready cash. You fool. It's a circle of hell, Miss Cross, and you should have realized it a long time ago."

Before I could cry out again, his grip opened and my arm came free. He just as quickly advanced on me, his arms outstretched, hands reaching to encircle my throat. I struggled against him, fighting for a scrap of breath. As my surroundings began to fade, I heard the cawing of crows, the squawking of seagulls, the tittering of sparrows. How odd, I thought, that the birds should be going about their business as I slowly died.

Chapter 22

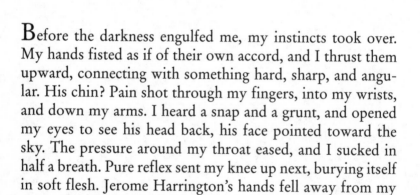

Before the darkness engulfed me, my instincts took over. My hands fisted as if of their own accord, and I thrust them upward, connecting with something hard, sharp, and angular. His chin? Pain shot through my fingers, into my wrists, and down my arms. I heard a snap and a grunt, and opened my eyes to see his head back, his face pointed toward the sky. The pressure around my throat eased, and I sucked in half a breath. Pure reflex sent my knee up next, burying itself in soft flesh. Jerome Harrington's hands fell away from my throat. He doubled over. Without hesitation, I drove the heel of my boot into his kneecap.

After that, I fled, his howls at my back. Under the nearest arch, across the garden, through the flowerbeds, sending droplets and petals scattering. My lungs shrieked for air; I still hadn't filled them completely, but I pushed on, my only conscious goal that of reaching the house.

I heard a shout, then barking, and indistinct smudges of brown streamed down the steps and bounded toward me. The dogs. With their bull-nosed features and their intimidating size, they enveloped me in warm fur and wet noses and streams of saliva. I'd never been so happy to be taken off my feet, but down I went, sinking first to my knees and then toppling sideways, landing on one dog, while the other snuffled my arms and hands and neck. Running footsteps came from the house, and the voice shouted again.

"Who goes there? Name yourself!"

I recognized Mr. Van Alen's voice. Thank goodness, he had returned home from his bird-watching. Relief poured through me. I tried to sit up, and raised myself high enough that the dog that had cushioned my fall wiggled out from under me, sprang up, and trotted back to his master. The other dog continued his nuzzling and snuffling, soaking my cheek and my sleeve. "Mr. Van Alen—" I called to him, and broke off. My voice rasped and I fell to coughing.

Were we still in danger? I realized I had no idea if Jerome Harrington had a weapon on him. Perhaps he had deemed his hands weapon enough and hadn't needn't to extract a pistol or knife from a convenient pocket.

Using an obliging mastiff for leverage, I managed to come to my feet. Once upright, I found my legs could barely hold me, so I placed my hand on the back of the dog's sturdy neck. He reached above my waist while sitting, so I didn't have to lean to find my support.

"Miss Cross? What the devil is going on here? My butler told me you had come. Why are you dashing roughshod through my garden and destroying my flowers? And where is Jerome?"

His words spurred me forward, and I ran to meet him partway. When I reached him, I all but collapsed against him. His arms came up and caught me, and I could feel the astonishment in the tensing of every muscle in his body. "What in the world?"

"He attacked me. Jerome. It was him." The words tumbled from my lips. "He murdered Judge Schuyler and Felix Mathison, and ran George Gould off the road."

"What? My dear girl, surely not. You are mistaken, Miss Cross. Jerome would never—"

I lifted myself from his coat front and raised my face to his. "Listen to me. He confessed it, right before he tried to strangle me." To prove my point, my voice hitched, and coughing once again overcame me. I doubled over, sputtering and gasping.

"Now, Miss Cross, did a little flirtation get carried a bit too far? Is that what this is about?"

I stared up at him, incredulous. "We need to get back to the house."

"Yes, a good idea, that. We'll get a good strong cup of tea in you. Then you'll feel better."

I gave up trying to reason with him and hurried to the house, glancing back over my shoulder every few steps. I didn't see anyone in the archway, but I wondered if Mr. Harrington was watching us, or if he had fled the property.

The moment we stepped into the dining room, I turned to my disbelieving host. "I must use your telephone. Where is it?"

"My butler's pantry. But, really, Miss Cross—"

"Which way?"

"In there." He pointed to a door secreted within the paneling in the corner of the room.

I hurried to it, issuing an order over my shoulder. "Have all the doors and windows on the ground floor locked immediately." Reaching the door, I pushed my way through and saw the wooden telephone box mounted on the wall beside the counter. I snatched the ear trumpet and turned the crank.

"Newport exchange. How may I direct your call?"

"Gayla, it's Emma. Put me through to the police station right away. Please."

"Goodness, you sound out of breath. Is everything all right?"

Had everybody lost their minds this morning? "Gayla, *please.*"

"All righty, hold your horses."

Once connected with the police, I had another few minutes to wait while Jesse was found. "Emma? I'm glad it's you. I've discovered something, or rather Derrick did. He's here now, and he—"

"Jesse, I'm at Wakehurst, and Jerome Harrington just tried to kill me." I heard Jesse's exclamation across the wires, but kept talking. "He admitted to killing the judge and all the rest. Come out here at once, and bring plenty of men with you." I hung up to forestall any further conversation.

Mr. Van Alen continued to believe his version of events: Jerome Harrington and I had engaged in a tryst that went awry. Why else would we have gone behind the hedge? After several tries, I gave up my attempts to dissuade him, repeatedly declined his offers of refreshments, and waited for Jesse's arrival. With the two mastiffs flanking me, apparently having gotten it into their heads I needed their protection, I stood at the library window and kept my eyes peeled on the distance, alert for movement in the garden. My fall had soaked my skirts, anyway, and I didn't wish to ruin one of Mr. Van Alen's costly chairs.

I also checked once again that he had instructed all the doors and windows to be locked. He insisted he had, and I only hoped he was telling the truth. But, surely, Jerome Harrington was no longer on the grounds. Only a fool would linger to be arrested, even if his wish to silence me remained a priority.

Where would he go? His parents' home? Not likely. Long Wharf and the first outgoing steamer? I hoped Jesse had left word to have the wharves and train depot alerted. Mr. Harrington certainly wouldn't appeal to Miss Schuyler to help him—I hoped. The sudden pounding of my pulse points begged to differ. What if, failing to strangle one woman, he tried another? Without stopping to reason whether or not he had enough motive to want Imogene Schuyler dead, I about-faced. Mr. Van Alen sat in an armchair upholstered in gold satin damask, staring into the unlit hearth.

"Sir." He flinched as if I'd startled him awake. "Someone needs to telephone over to the Schuylers' residence and warn them about Mr. Harrington."

Deep ruts formed above his nose. "Are you sure you wish to apprise Miss Schuyler of the activities between you and her fiancé?"

"Good heavens, Mr. Van Alen!" At a loss how else to convince him, I tugged my collar down to reveal the bruises Mr. Harrington's hands had surely left. "Look at my neck. Jerome Harrington did this to me."

Mr. Van Alen's eyes went wide and he jumped to his feet. "Why didn't you show me this sooner? Yes, yes, I'll ask my butler to make the call."

"I'll go. You come here and keep watch out the window."

My telephone call to the Schuyler home proved brief, once the housekeeper agreed to put me through to Imogene. She had seen no sign of Jerome Harrington and doubted she would. She also sounded as dubious about my claims as Mr. Van Alen had been, but she agreed to have the house locked up and ask the footmen to keep watch. I told her I would suggest to the police that they send over an officer, just in case.

Back in the library, I sat tapping my foot against the carpet, while trying to deduce where Mr. Harrington might go from here. Mr. Van Alen, convinced of the danger now, kept darting from window to window, out into the Long Gallery to issue orders, then back in, to start the cycle again. I left him to it and turned inward to my own thoughts.

Escape seemed the most logical course, but I feared Mr. Harrington had lost all hold on logic. He wanted revenge against the men responsible for the deaths of the miners. In his sickened mind, his cause seemed a noble one. But then, Judge Schuyler had "compounded his sins," to quote Jerome Harrington, by turning his daughter against her new fiancé.

Would Jerome have allowed Judge Schuyler to live, if not for that? Was the judge's agreement to the marriage enough to exonerate him in the young man's mind? I thought it might have been. But Clayton Schuyler hadn't realized he had purchased his own life by allowing his daughter to marry Mr. Harrington, a boon he had then squandered with his duplicity. Perhaps the judge simply hadn't been able to help himself. Duplicity seemed to have become a way of life for him, a habit he perhaps had believed gave him the upper hand. How easily Mr. Harrington had dispatched him. It had undoubtedly been Mr. Harrington who had offered the judge the cigar—forbidden fruit—that sent him into the shadows that night.

But what, I wondered, had induced Mr. Harrington to confess his guilt to me? Had he been incapable of schooling his anger? As we had discussed the miners and Imogene earlier, he had grown more and more agitated. I had felt his mounting distress, but I hadn't recognized the danger until it was too late. The truth, I believe, was that Jerome Harrington had lost his grip on sanity. Those twenty-five deaths had left an indelible stain on his family's honor, and had shown Jerome the depth of his father's greed, as well as those of the other men involved. I almost pitied him the burden thrust upon his young shoulders by the heedless acts of his elders. Did he believe himself guilty by association? Were the murders a form of self-hatred, as much as they were a form of vengeance?

He had turned his anger on me. That, too, I had discerned only when it was too late. He saw me as part of the Vanderbilt family, and that, in his eyes, made *me* guilty by association.

That thought sent me to my feet so quickly, I startled Mr. Van Alen on his most recent trek across the room. He stared at me in alarm, prompting me to explain, "I think I may know where he's gone."

A pounding on the front door preempted further clarification. He and I hurried down the Long Gallery as the butler opened the door upon Jesse, Derrick, and several uniformed officers. Derrick wasted no time in lunging across the threshold and gathering me in his arms.

"What happened? What did he do to you? Are you hurt?"

"I'm all right, but never mind that for now." I spoke against his shoulder, barely able to draw a breath because he held me so tight. I began to pull away and he let me, either realizing we had an audience or fearing he was hurting me. I immediately turned to Jesse. "I think he may have gone to The Breakers. To find Alfred. And probably Reggie, too."

Without asking me to explain why I thought so, Jesse signaled to his men. "You heard her."

That sent them scrambling back into the police wagon they'd arrived in. Jesse's carriage sat on the drive, and he, Derrick, and I climbed in. As Jesse set the horse in motion, Mr. Van Alen called from the doorway, "Shall I go with you?"

"No, sir," I called back. "Stay here, and keep the house locked until you hear that it's safe."

The horse broke into a trot, and within minutes, we passed through the front gates of The Breakers.

All lay quiet in front of the house. We parked at the gatehouse beside the police wagon, and before proceeding on foot, Jesse asked Shipley, the gatekeeper, if he had seen anyone enter the property. He hadn't, but that only meant Mr. Harrington hadn't entered by the main drive. The fog lingered over the front lawn, rendering the graveled circular drive nearly invisible. It also masked our arrival, and we walked on the grass to muffle our footsteps. Before us, the house seemed to float, its red tile roof standing out against a brooding sky.

The uniformed officers had gathered beneath the shelter of a stand of elm trees inside the perimeter wall, quietly awaiting their orders. "We don't wish to go storming into the house," Jesse told them. "We'll assess the area first. Spread out around the house, see what you can. Keep close to the walls and glance into each window before you move on. Be stealthy about it."

The police team scattered in different directions. It was a sound plan, but I had another in mind. "Jesse, I think I should go inside. I know the house. I can make my way through without being obvious."

"No." Jesse and Derrick spoke at once. Jesse scowled at me. "He tried to kill you. Do you want to give him another chance?"

"They could be anywhere." I scanned the front of the house. I saw no one at any of the windows, nor any flicks of the curtains or other indications we were being observed. "If he's here, he might already know *we're* here. He might be watching your men surround the house. That should keep him busy. I can, at least, go in and locate him."

"And then what?" Derrick leaned to bring his face close to mine, a face shuttered with the kind of conviction no argument could penetrate. "Do you think you'll find him and simply walk back out to tell Jesse where he is? No, Emma. If you go in, you might never come out alive."

He spoke bluntly, with no attempt to soften the words. I understood. But it was my cousins in there, and I couldn't help but feel responsible for the danger they might be facing. "Come with me, then," I said. "We'll go together."

"Wonderful. That's all I need." Jesse groaned and let his eyes fall closed.

Derrick studied me a good long moment. Without a word, he took my hand and started for the front door.

"No, not that way," I said. "Through the kitchen."

We about-faced and stole along the front of the house to the north side, where a staircase led down to the service entrance. As I had expected for this time of day, the door wasn't locked. We entered through a large storeroom and passed through two more storage rooms into a hallway. There were workers about, and when one approached us, obviously about to question us, recognition brought a smile to his face.

"Miss Cross. What are you doing coming in this way?"

"I've got my reasons, Zachery, but I can't share them right now." I didn't bother to warn him to stay downstairs; there was no reason these estate workers would ever ascend to the main part of the house.

Another stairway brought us up to the kitchen, scullery, and butler's pantry. We were on the main floor now, but in a separate wing from the rest of the house. We were stopped again, this time by the housekeeper. I cautioned her to keep everyone within the service wing.

Wariness shone in her eyes, but she nodded and asked no questions.

Derrick and I continued into the dining room. As in the other rooms I'd visited only days earlier, the furnishings and light fixtures were swathed in fabric, as phantomlike as the patches of fog outside. There was no one else in the room, and the silence fell heavily around us. At a second doorway that led back out into the Great Hall, we paused to listen. The nearby fountain beneath the Grand Staircase had been turned off, a sure sign the family would not be inhabiting the house again until next summer, at the earliest. The notion filled me with sadness. We heard no sounds from the billiard room, either.

We hurried beneath the staircase to the front of the Great Hall, and then along the perimeter, staying well beneath the overhanging gallery in hopes of preventing anyone upstairs from noticing us. Outside the library, we once again listened for voices. Nothing. The packing must have been completed. Was Alfred even here? What about Reggie? Had I brought everyone here on a fool's errand?

At the bottom of the smaller, secondary staircase the family used on an everyday basis, I pointed upward, and Derrick and I started the climb. Perhaps both of my cousins were still abed. After all, by the standards of the Four Hundred, it was early, still an uncivilized hour. If so, they would be tucked safely in their bedrooms on the third floor. Unless Alfred had decided to take the master bedroom, which I highly doubted this soon after his father's death.

At the top of the stairs, I spotted them directly across the open expanse of the upper portion of the Great Hall. My heart stopped, then catapulted into my throat. They were outside on the second-story loggia. Alfred had his back to one of the pillars that support the arches. I could see his face—though from this distance, not his expression. Jerome Harrington's back was to me. His hand was raised. He held an object in it.

"What is it?" Derrick murmured. He craned his neck and strained to see. "A pistol? It's too dim out there to see."

"I don't think so. Look at how he's holding it, the angle of his arm, the bend in his elbow." I studied Mr. Harrington's position another few seconds. "It looks like he's threatening to strike Alfred with whatever it is."

Derrick nodded. He glanced up and down the gallery and along the two sides that ran perpendicular to us, overlooking the Great Hall and ending at bedrooms. Again I didn't hear any voices. The Breakers, this great house that had known the echoes of happy occasions for far too short a time, felt like a forgotten tomb.

Derrick caught my gaze. "What now?"

What, indeed! "Do you think Jesse and his men have spotted them?"

"They might hear their voices, but unless they're backed up halfway across the lawn, perhaps not. Alfred is behind the pillar, and Jerome is standing in the shadow of the roof. We'd better go back outside and let them know."

I shook my head.

"Emma, we have to go." He took my hand and gave a tug.

"There might not be time. Jerome could decide to attack Alfred at any moment."

Derrick blew out a breath. "You're right." He turned to me, taking both of my hands. "Emma. Go down. Tell Jesse to send his officers up. I'll try to distract Jerome."

I shook my head again. "No, Derrick—"

"What did *you* have in mind? That you'll distract him? That isn't going to happen." His chin came up, and he sent a fiery look at me, a glare that forestalled any argument I might have offered. "Go," he ordered in a way that, in any other circumstance, would have filled me with indignant fury.

But there was no time for pride or anger or arguments. A life was at stake. "You'll need a weapon," I said.

"I'll look for one on my way." He kissed my hands and quietly hurried away, down the gallery past Uncle Cornelius's and Aunt Alice's bedrooms, to the short corridor that led either into Gertrude's bedroom or out onto the upper loggia. He reached the outer door and turned back to gaze at me across the distance. I saw no improvised weapon in his hand and yearned to call him back. I didn't dare alert Jerome to our presence. Derrick nodded once and clutched the door latch. With a heart filled with misgivings, I turned and raced down the stairs.

* * *

Downstairs, I let myself out the front door. There were two policemen on either side of the porte cochere, keeping watch. I approached one of them.

"Where is Detective Whyte?"

"Around back still, I think, miss."

I started on my way and he darted a whisper at me. "Miss! You don't want to be seen through the windows."

"It's all right, I know where they are," I whispered back, and kept going.

I found Jesse on the terrace just beyond the ground-floor loggia, along with several officers. Their weapons were in their hands, and they were all gazing upward, yet staying close enough to the house that Jerome wouldn't be able to see them unless he stood at the railing and looked directly down. I climbed the steps and tiptoed to Jesse to prevent my boots from making any sound on the pavement. When I reached him, he pointed to the second-floor loggia. I nodded.

"Derrick is just inside the door, on this side," I whispered, and pointed up at Gertrude's window.

"What in the blazes is he planning to do?" At the same time he shot his question at me, Jesse made a hand gesture, beckoning three of the uniformed men over to him. When they came within whispering range, he gave them their orders.

From above us came a shout. I recognized Derrick's voice calling out Jerome's name. Footsteps pounded on the loggia tiling, and then Alfred moved away from the pillar, into view beneath one of the arches. Jesse and the remaining officers moved to the far edge of the terrace, where they had a better view. Jesse frantically waved up at Alfred.

"Mr. Vanderbilt, move out of the way."

Alfred scrambled to the far side of the loggia. Now Derrick and Jerome Harrington came into view. They were struggling, each with a hold on the other. Jerome was swinging his weapon, trying to strike Derrick. My breath froze as the two men stumbled closer to the stone balustrade, first one seeming to have the upper hand, then the other. The object swung back and forth.

The pounding of my heart made me dizzy and weak. Suddenly Jerome shoved at Derrick, who staggered and bent backward over the balustrade. I watched helplessly while the terror of his imminent fall spiraled through me. Alfred darted back into view. He came up behind Jerome and attempted to grab his arms. Jerome must have felt his presence. He swung out behind him, striking my cousin with the object gripped in his hand.

Derrick aimed a kick into Jerome's midsection, forceful enough to send him scrambling backward. Derrick then launched himself off the balustrade and into Jerome. I could no longer see them clearly, could see little more than their shadows, but seconds later, Jerome's weapon came flying over the balustrade and landed on the terrace with a crash that sent stone chips flying.

Their struggle continued. Jesse, at the center of the terrace, raised his arms and pointed his gun, clutched in both hands, at the loggia. I very nearly screamed that he mustn't take the chance, for he could too easily miss and hit Derrick or Alfred. Jesse shouted Jerome's name and fired the pistol. At the last moment, he had jerked his arms higher and aimed over the roof.

The report sent me to my knees on the pavement, my hands over my ears. The echo ricocheted out over the water and seemed to double back against the house. It seemed the world stopped, and then rushed headlong at frightening speed. I lifted my face to find Jesse standing over me, reaching down to help me up. Shouts once again poured from the loggia, several at once.

"It's all right, my men have him."

"Derrick?"

"I'm all right, Emma." Derrick leaned over the balustrade above me. Though he panted to regain his breath, a grin spread across his face. Tears streamed down mine. I took Jesse's offered hand and came to my feet.

My boots crunched on chipped stone, and I bent to retrieve the object that had fallen from the upper loggia. A iron doorstop in the shape of a locomotive engine weighed heavily in my hands and would surely have proven deadly had Alfred—or Derrick—been struck on the head with it.

But Alfred *had* been hit. I shouted his name. An instant later, he appeared beside Derrick, massaging his own shoulder, but otherwise appearing unharmed.

Jerome Harrington shouted his objections to being restrained by the three officers who had charged him and were now cuffing his hands behind his back. Moments later, Reggie, in his house robe and looking sleep-tousled, shuffled out onto the loggia. He took in the scene around him, glanced down at me and the others, and appealed to his older brother.

"What the devil is going on, Alfred? I could hear you all the way upstairs. You woke me from a sound sleep, and I don't particularly appreciate it."

"Once again, you put yourselves in harm's way and were both nearly killed." Nanny clucked her tongue at Derrick and me even as she set tea and sandwiches on the table before us. We had gathered in the morning room, its large window looking out on the still-foggy landscape and a choppy ocean.

To my eyes, though, it had turned into a beautiful day. Alfred was safe; his shoulder sore, but neither fractured nor dislocated. Reggie, too, for that matter, not that he'd had an inkling of the danger that had arrived at The Breakers until it was over.

After leaving The Breakers, Jesse had brought us back to Wakehurst, where I finally returned Mr. Van Alen's fan—with a humble apology—and retrieved my carriage. Derrick's and my ride here had been a quietly emotional one, the two of us pressed up against each other's sides, he driving one-handed and holding my hand with the other.

"'All's well that ends well,' Nanny," I said, considerably calmer for tea and home and the warm, cheery fire in the fireplace. The remark earned me a stern look of admonishment, but Nanny's expression cleared quickly enough. "Let's not forget," I continued after a bite of my chopped chicken and walnut sandwich, "that Jesse will receive the credit for Jerome Harrington's arrest, not Gifford Myers. I only hope it's enough to earn Jesse back his position as chief homicide detective."

"Hear, hear." Derrick clinked his teacup against mine.

"Truly, Miss Emma, I think it's you and Mr. Andrews who deserve the credit." Katie blushed at having spoken in front of Derrick, but I was glad to see her learning to overcome her timidity. "But why were you at the police station at the time, sir?"

"My goodness, yes." I had forgotten all about it. "Why *were* you there?"

"A telegram came from Providence," he explained, "from one of the *Sun's* reporters doing a little snooping for me. He came across a tiny article buried in an obscure Scranton newspaper that suggested Judge Schuyler had ruled, not in favor of the miners, but the investors. Later, there had been a retraction and an apology. And it appears no one else made similar insinuations. But it was enough to send me to Jesse about it. At that point, we still hadn't guessed at Jerome's guilt, but I suggested we talk to him to see what he might know." He put his teacup on its saucer and bit into his own sandwich, then conveyed his appreciation to Nanny in the form of a long, satisfied *mmm*.

* * *

No one considered it a good idea when I announced my intention of going into town to the *Messenger*. As I could have predicted, Nanny insisted I needed rest and the news could wait until tomorrow. Katie asked if I didn't think I'd done enough for one day. Only Derrick shook his head in disapproval, but forewent arguing with me. I accommodated Derrick's wishes far enough to allow him to take Maestro's reins while I relaxed against the leather seat.

Just as I had done days ago, when we arrived at the *Messenger*, we walked straight into a confrontation—with Derrick's mother. Lavinia Andrews was dressed for travel in a dark suit, with fitted sleeves and a waistline that hugged her trim figure to perfection. The addition of a small feathered hat, which fit close to her coiffed hair, lent a prim dignity that suggested she had come prepared for a fight. So did her expression.

Her mouth a tight pucker, her chin squared, and her nostrils slightly flared, she ignored me and spoke to Derrick. "I'm returning to Providence. I'd like you to escort me, please."

"Good morning, Mother." Derrick removed his hat and set it on the unoccupied desk. Our editor-in-chief's desk sat unoccupied as well. I could only imagine the sight of Mrs. Andrews had sent Mr. Sheppard scurrying for cover at the rear of the building, perhaps behind the printing press. One finger at a time, Derrick removed his driving gloves and calmly set them beside his hat. "You're looking well today."

"Did you hear me? I'm returning to Providence, and I'd like you to come with me."

"I'm terribly sorry, but I can't simply drop everything at a moment's notice and run up to Providence. Surely, you're not traveling alone. Isn't your maid accompanying you?"

"That's beside the point."

"Mother, you haven't said good morning to Emma."

Just as I was beginning to think I should slip into the back rooms, Derrick came to my side. Though he didn't take my hand or otherwise make physical contact with me, I felt his presence, like a gentle bulwark, shielding me from his mother's scorn, even as he challenged her to be civil.

Her gaze darted to meet mine. "Good morning, Miss Cross."

"Mrs. Andrews." I didn't extend my hand. Her greeting would suffice and I saw no reason to vex her further.

She dismissed me with a flick of her head, which set the black feathers on her cap quivering. "Derrick, is it really too much to ask you to spend a day or two at home? Your father could use your help at the *Sun*."

"Are you forgetting I was there only two weeks ago?"

"Yes, but—"

"I'm sorry you wasted your time coming here, Mother, although I am glad to see you before you leave. You must realize my life is here now. I have a newspaper to run."

"This little . . ." She trailed off without the criticism she had surely been about to utter, but the disdain showed clearly on her face.

"Yes, this little rag is fast becoming a respected local establishment, and I'm proud of the work we have done with it." He applied emphasis to the word *we*, and then his hand did curl around mine.

His mother saw it, pinched her lips, and shook her head. "I don't understand you."

"Perhaps not, but you'll always know where I am, should you wish to be part of my life. But that life includes Emma, and until you accept that, I'm afraid we'll remain at odds."

She left without good-byes, and despite his firm words, I knew her departure left Derrick hurting. He watched her retreating back until she stepped up into her carriage and the vehicle pulled away.

"I'm sorry," I said. "I wish . . ." It didn't help to make wishes, I knew, but I couldn't quash a lingering optimism despite Lavinia Andrews making her position plain.

He remained staring out the window a moment longer, making me wonder if he regretted the entire matter. Regretted me. But then he turned to me so suddenly, I started. He raised my hand in his. "Was I correct in what I said? Does my life include you?"

Good heavens, he looked worried. I didn't keep him in suspense. "Of course it does. Why would you even need to ask?"

Countless emotions flitted across his face, until I, too, began to worry. Just as I was about to ask what was wrong, he reached into his inner coat pocket and drew out a velvet pouch. He brought my hand to his lips and then released me. With a little tug, he loosened the strings and opened the pouch, upended it, and caught the shiny object that tumbled out in his palm.

He took it between two fingers and held it up to me. It was a filigreed band of yellow gold, set with a round diamond, surrounded by smaller stones. "Emma . . . my *darling* Emma . . . would you—*will* you—make me the happiest man alive by agreeing to be my wife?"

Of the many replies I might have given, the overwhelming joy I might have expressed, the first words that staggered from my dumbfounded brain were: "Where on earth did you get that?"

A frown creased his brow. "In Providence, before I knew your uncle Cornelius had died."

"You mean, you planned this all those days ago?"

"I'm not sure you could call it a plan. I'd hoped. Yes."

I grinned like an idiot. He grinned back and opened his arms. The next moments were a blur of impropriety before the plate glass window that overlooked Spring Street. Did people stare in at us, shocked and dismayed by our behavior? Perhaps, but if they did, I didn't notice, and I'm quite sure Derrick didn't, either.

"I certainly didn't mean to ask you here," he said, breaking a kiss with a breathy laugh. "I wanted someplace much more romantic. What an oaf I am."

"No. Here is the *perfect* place. At the business we've built up together. *Ours.*" Like the life we would build together.

But then something he had said moments ago came hurtling back at me, along with the reality of my situation. I eased out of his arms and turned away.

"Emma, what's wrong?"

"I can't accept that ring. Not now."

"Why can't you? Emma, are you still not sure?"

"Of course I'm sure." I turned back to him, hoping he could see the truth of my feelings in my eyes. "But . . . Uncle Cornelius. Derrick, the entire family is in mourning. I can't think about a wedding, couldn't even begin to plan for one. Or flaunt this ring and our engagement. It would be too disrespectful, too hurtful."

"Is that all?" His grin returned. When I nodded, he grinned all the more. "It's but a small obstacle, and time will erase it. For now"—he drew me back to him, took my hand, and slipped the ring on my finger—"it'll be our secret. Ours, Emma."

"Yes," I agreed, and right before his lips touched mine again, I repeated, "ours."

Author's Note

James J. Van Alen was the son of James Henry and Mary Van Alen, who made their full-time home at an estate called The Grange on Ochre Point Avenue in Newport. The Van Alens' comparatively modest fortune had been made in real estate. When James Van Alen proposed to Emily Astor, the eldest daughter of William Backhouse and Caroline Astor, the bride's father objected and challenged Van Alen to duel. James Van Alen accepted, but, luckily, both backed down and the marriage took place without further ado.

James and Emily had three children, but shortly after the birth of the third, and after only five years of marriage, Mary died. It's said James was so inconsolable his father gifted him with a parcel of land from The Grange on which to build a new house. This house was Wakehurst, located between Leroy and Shepard Avenues. When James H. died a few years later, son James had The Grange pulled down in order to extend his gardens off the south side of the house.

James Van Alen certainly was an eccentric who loved all things English and Elizabethan. As in the story, he enjoyed sprinkling his conversation with Elizabethan jargon. Wakehurst is almost an exact replica of Wakehurst Place in England, and many of its furnishings—entire rooms' worth—were brought over from great estates in Europe. While I was able to find ample pictures of the interior, I did use my imagination to expand upon the details of his Elizabethan gardens, as well as inventing the Elizabethan Fete. Although, it was no stretch of the imagination to envision James Van

Alen hosting just such an occasion. My description of the smaller garden behind the house, which is bordered by Lawrence Avenue, is also my invention. Like Ochre Court, Wakehurst is now part of Salve Regina University and is not open for tours.

Cornelius Vanderbilt II, grandson of the first Cornelius, who had been known as The Commodore, died on September 12, 1899, from a cerebral hemorrhage. He had suffered multiple strokes since 1896, the same year his son and namesake, nicknamed Neily, married Grace Wilson, of whom his parents did not approve. Although I set the reading of the will in New York the morning after the funeral, the actual reading took place at The Breakers a month later. The family had waited for Alfred to return from a world tour to celebrate his graduation from Yale University. For all practical purposes, Cornelius disinherited Neily, except for half-a-million dollars and the income from a 1-million-dollar trust fund. However, as in the story, Alfred, the brother who took over as the primary heir, reinstated approximately 6 million dollars of Neily's inheritance. Alice Vanderbilt blamed her son for her husband's untimely death, and they would not truly reconcile for nearly three decades.

Grace Vanderbilt was pregnant in September 1899, but gave birth that month, rather than being at the beginning of her pregnancy, as I have it in the story.

Being an old Dutch family who made a fortune in New York real estate, Schuyler is a prominent name in New York's history. However, the branch of the family in the story is fictional. Felix Mathison is a fictional character as well.

The incident in Carterville, Illinois, culminating in several deaths at the terminal of the Illinois Central Railroad, took place on September 17, 1899. It involved union and nonunion miners, divided by race, with Black nonunion workers

fired upon while waiting to board their trains to exit the
town at the end of the workday. Was this an act spurred by
racial tensions, or one of union rights over nonunion rights?
Given the circumstances, it was probably indicative of both.
The incident was decried in the newspapers as "prearranged,
preconcerted, premeditated murder," with local officials
calling in troops to restore peace and bring the culprits to
justice. The reaction in the story of Stuyvesant Fish, who
was the president of the Illinois Central Railroad at the time,
is my own invention.

This story marks Emma's first trip to Castle Hill, the estate owned by Dr. Alexander Agassiz, scientist, engineer,
surveyor, and director of the Museum of Comparative Zoology at Harvard University. I have not been inside Castle Hill
in a good number of years, and the floor plan proved to be
an elusive subject, with very few pictures available in either
books or on the internet. With the COVID-19 pandemic
prohibiting travel, there was no trip to Newport in the summer of 2020. Many thanks to Lisa Stuart, friend and member
of the Newport Point Society, who came to my rescue with
photos of every room and a hand-drawn diagram of the lay-
out. Castle Hill is now an inn and restaurant.